# BITTERSWEET
# DREAMS

# Virginia Andrews® Books

**The Dollanganger Family Series**
Flowers in the Attic
Petals on the Wind
If There Be Thorns
Seeds of Yesterday
Garden of Shadows
Christopher's Diary: Secrets of
    Foxworth
Christopher's Diary: Echoes of
    Dollanganger
Secret Brother

**The Casteel Family Series**
Heaven
Dark Angel
Fallen Hearts
Gates of Paradise
Web of Dreams

**The Cutler Family Series**
Dawn
Secrets of the Morning
Twilight's Child
Midnight Whispers
Darkest Hour

**The Landry Family Series**
Ruby
Pearl in the Mist
All That Glitters
Hidden Jewel
Tarnished Gold

**The Logan Family Series**
Melody
Heart Song
Unfinished Symphony
Music in the Night
Olivia

**The Orphans Miniseries**
Butterfly
Crystal
Brooke
Raven
Runaways

**The Wildflowers Miniseries**
Misty
Star
Jade
Cat
Into the Garden

**The Hudson Family Series**
Rain
Lightning Strikes
Eye of the Storm
The End of the Rainbow

**The Shooting Stars Series**
Cinnamon
Ice
Rose
Honey
Falling Stars

# Virginia ANDREWS

# BITTERSWEET DREAMS

**SIMON &
SCHUSTER**

London · New York · Sydney · Toronto · New Delhi

A CBS COMPANY

First published in Great Britain by Simon & Schuster UK Ltd, 2015
A CBS COMPANY

1 3 5 7 9 10 8 6 4 2

Simon & Schuster UK Ltd
1st Floor
222 Gray's Inn Road
London WC1X 8HB

www.simonandschuster.co.uk

Simon & Schuster Australia, Sydney
Simon & Schuster India, New Delhi

A CIP catalogue record for this book is available from the British Library

Hardback ISBN: 978-1-47113-381-7
eBook ISBN: 978-1-47113-383-1

Printed and bound by CPI Group (UK) Ltd, Croydon, CR0 4YY

MIX
Paper from
responsible sources
FSC
www.fsc.org    FSC® C020471

Simon & Schuster UK Ltd are committed to sourcing paper that is
made from wood grown in sustainable forests and supports the Forest
Stewardship Council, the leading international forest certification organisation.
Our books displaying the FSC logo are printed on FSC certified paper.

*For Gene Andrews,*
*who so wanted to keep his sister's work alive*

# BITTERSWEET DREAMS

# Prologue

Beverly Royal School System
18 Crown Jewel Road
Beverly Hills, California

*Dear Mr. and Mrs. Cummings:*

*As you know, the school has been conducting IQ tests to better address the needs and placement of our students. We always suspected that we were going to get extraordinary results when Mayfair was tested, but no one fully understood or anticipated just how extraordinary these results would be.*

*To put it into perspective, this is a generally considered scale by which most educational institutions judge these results.*

*IQ scores of 115 to 129 indicate a bright student who should do well with his or her educational pursuits.*

*We consider those with scores of 130 to 144 moderately gifted and those with 145 to 159 highly gifted. Anyone with scores between 160 and 179 is recognized as exceptionally gifted.*

*Rare are those whose scores reach 180. We consider such an individual profoundly gifted. To put it into even better perspective for you, statistically, these students are one in three million; so, for example, in the state of California, with a population of approximately 36 million, there are only eleven others who belong in this classification with Mayfair.*

*Needless to say, we're all very excited about this, and I would like to invite you in to discuss Mayfair's future, what to anticipate, and what to do to ensure that her needs are fully addressed.*

*Sincerely yours,*
*Gloria Fishman, Psychologist*

# 1

"For what you did, you belong in a juvenile home, maybe a mental clinic, but certainly not a new school where you'll undoubtedly be coddled and further spoiled, an even more expensive private high school than Beverly Royal," my father's new wife, Julie, muttered bitterly.

Even though they had been married for years, I didn't want to use the word *stepmother*, because it implied that she filled some motherly role in my life.

Her lips trembled as anger radiated through her face, tightening her cheeks. If she knew how much older it made her look, she would contain her rage. I did scare her once by telling her that grimacing too much hastened the coming of wrinkles.

It was the morning of what I thought would be my banishment from whatever family life I once could have claimed, something that had become a distant memory even before all this. I knew that few, least of all Julie, would think that mattered much to me. They saw me as someone who lived entirely within herself, like some creature who moved about in an impenetrable bubble, emerging only when it was absolutely necessary to say anything to anyone or do anything with anyone. But family did matter to me. It always had, and it always would.

I didn't have to go on the internet and look it up to know that a family wasn't just something that brought you comfort and security. It provided some warmth in an otherwise cold and often harsh and cruel world. It gave you hope, especially when events or actions of others weighed you down with depression and defeat. All the rainbows in our lives originated with something from our families.

In fact, all I was thinking about this morning was my mother, the softness in her face, the love in her eyes, and the gentleness in her touch whenever she had wanted to soothe me, comfort me, or encourage me, and how my father glowed whenever we were with him. How I longed for that warmth to be in my life again. Yes, family mattered.

True friends mattered, too, even though I had few, if any, up to now. Just because I was good at making it seem like I was indifferent and uncaring about relationships, that didn't mean I actually was. Students in the schools I had attended thought I was weird because of what I could do and what I had done, most of it so far above and beyond them that they didn't even want to think about it. I didn't need to give them any more reasons to avoid me, especially adding something like being a social misfit, which in the minds of most teenagers was akin to a fatal infectious disease.

I knew most avoided me because they believed I was too arrogant to care about anyone but myself. I mean, who could warm up to someone who seemed to need no one else? From what they saw or thought, I didn't even require teachers when it came to learning and passing exams. I was a phenomenon, an educational force unto myself.

Maybe I didn't need a doctor or a dentist or a parent, either. I already knew as much as, if not more than, all of them put together. It wasn't much of a leap to think I didn't need friends. I'm sure most wondered what they could possibly offer someone like me anyway. Besides, being around me surely made them feel somewhat inferior. They were afraid they would say something incorrect, and who likes to worry about that, especially when you're with friends? I would have to confess that I didn't do all that much to get them to think otherwise. Perhaps it really was arrogance, or maybe I simply didn't know how to do it. I didn't know how to smile and be warm just for the sake of a friendship. One thing I couldn't get myself to do was be a phony. I was too bogged down in truth and reality.

Julie moved farther into my room, inching forward carefully, poised to retreat instantly, like someone approaching a wild animal, even though the wild animal was in a cage. Thinking that was where I was made sense. If anyone should feel trapped and in a cage right now, it was I.

In fact, the more I thought about it, the more I

realized that wasn't much of an exaggeration. That was what I felt I was, and not just because of what I had done and what was happening today. I'd always felt this way. Deep down inside, despite my superior intellect, I sensed that people, especially educators and parents of other students, believed I was like some new kind of beast that needed to be kept apart from the rest of humanity, a mistake in evolution or the final result of it, and because of that, I was chained to something I'd rather not be, especially at this moment: myself.

As she drew closer, the sunshine streaming through my bedroom windows highlighted every feature of her face. I wished it hadn't. I was sorry I had opened the fuchsia curtains, but I had needed to bring some light in to wash away the shadows gripping my heart. I had no desire to look into Julie's hateful, jealous, dull hazel eyes. Sometimes they followed me into dreams, those envious, vicious orbs floating on a black cloud, invading my sleep like two big insects that had found an opening in my ordinarily well-locked and guarded brain.

I hoisted my shoulders and stiffened my neck as if in anticipation of being struck. My abrupt action stopped her, and she retreated a few steps. She fumbled with her cowardice. She never, ever wanted to look like she didn't have the upper hand in this house, especially when it came to confronting me. However, she never seemed to get the satisfaction she sought—at least, not until now, when I was most vulnerable, practically defenseless, but with no one to blame for that but myself.

"I don't care how smart people say you are. You never fooled me with your complicated excuses and fabrications concerning things you have done and said. Right from the beginning, I could see right through you as if you were made of clear glass," she said, more like bragging, to give the impression that she had some special insight that neither my teachers, my counselors, nor even my father had. She was always trying to get my father to believe that, to believe he couldn't be as objective about me as she could and thus was blind to my serious faults.

To emphasize the point, she narrowed her eyes to make herself look more intelligent, inquisitive, and perceptive. I nearly laughed at her effort, because she was so obvious whenever she did that and whenever she spoke with a little nasality and used multisyllabic words like *fabrications* instead of *lies*. She was the queen of euphemisms anyway, always trying to impress my father with what a lady she was, never without a perfumed handkerchief, the scent of her cologne whirling about her, her head held high and her posture regal. She loved giving off that aristocratic air, practically tiptoeing over the floors and carpets as if she floated on a private cloud.

I think Julie had long ago convinced herself that somewhere in her background and lineage there really was royal blood. She believed she was born with class and had inherited elegance and stature. Heaven forbid she heard any profanity out of my mouth or her daughter's. Didn't we know it was unladylike, made us look cheap and unsophisticated? She would go into hyperventilation and have to sit quickly, especially if it happened in front of my father, who would rush to her side to apologize for me, because he knew I wouldn't. He couldn't see that small smile of satisfaction sitting on her lips, but I could.

Why were men so easy to fool or so willing to tolerate phoniness just to sail on smooth water? What wouldn't they compromise to keep the pathways to their beds unobstructed? Were women really the superior sex? Was sex, in fact, a big disadvantage for men? Ironically, I had been thinking about writing a paper on that topic. Women seemed more able to avoid sex, hold off longer than men, and certainly use it as a weapon when necessary or a device to get what they wanted. I had read a theory that developed the idea that women craved sex with nearly the same intensity as men only when they were ovulating, while men craved it continually.

"I always knew you were very capable of being mean, evil, and selfish," Julie ranted. "Your intelligence doesn't make you any sort of angel. In fact, in your case especially, it's just the opposite. You're sly and conniving. We already know how effective you are at manipulating people, especially someone younger than you. You're just better at these evil ways than most people."

She waited for my reaction, but I just continued to stare at her as if she was some sort of curious form of life. It was getting to her, despite her claims of invulnerability.

"You don't intimidate me with that 'I'm better

than you' look. It hasn't happened to you yet, in my opinion, despite what others might think, but someday you'll get your just *desserts*," she concluded.

I finally had something to say. "From the way you're saying it, I have a feeling that you would spell that expression wrong," I said.

"What? What on earth are you talking about now? What expression?"

"'Just *desserts.' Deserts* in the sense you mean is actually spelled with one *s*, not two. You're using that expression to mean I'll get my proper punishment."

She continued to glare at me but now with her mouth fallen slightly open, her salmon-pink tongue looking like a dead fish.

I straightened up, and I'm sure it looked to her like I was in front of a classroom, my classroom. I was a good inch and a half taller than she was, a little broader in the shoulders, but with just as small a waist, long legs, and just as ample and firm a bosom. Despite the fact that we had no facial resemblances or similar hair color, I was always afraid that someone who didn't know us might make the wrong assumption that we were actually related.

"*Dessert* with two *s*'s is the course in the meal that gets people excited and happy. And getting what you deserve might also mean you're finally receiving the accolades and rewards you've earned. That's certainly nothing to fear. But the expression does come from a playbook called *A Warning for Fair Women*. The exact quote in question is 'Upon a pillory—that the world may see, a just desert for such impiety.' It's spelled with one *s*, coming from *deserts* in the sense of things deserved. Understand?"

"Understand? That's how you treat what I say even after all you've done? Do you think I'm one of your dumb high-school classmates? Why, you pedantic little bitch," she said, spitting the words out through clenched teeth. "I bet you think you're so superior to the rest of us because of that computer you have for a brain and those bureaucratic school administrators who fawn over you as if you were the next Albert Einstein or something. They're just as much a cause of all this as you are, by encouraging you to think of yourself as . . . as someone who doesn't need to go to the bathroom or something."

I didn't change expression, even though I was laughing at her on the inside. My father wasn't home. He had an errand to do before we left, so he didn't hear her say all this, not that I thought he would have done much to reprimand her for saying any of it anyway at this point. I recalled the expression on his face yesterday when he didn't think I saw him looking at me. It was soaked in disappointment. Vividly recalling that look, I thought he might even agree with her now, every nasty and mean word. I imagined him nodding and putting his hand on her shoulder, not mine, to bring her comfort and whisper something to make her feel better and show her how concerned he was for her welfare. "Don't get yourself too upset," he might tell her. "It doesn't do anyone any good for you to get sick, especially now, in the middle of all this."

"I don't mean to be condescending," I said, with

just the quiet, matter-of-fact tone that irritated her heart. "You use the expression so often, Julie, that I thought you might want to know about it. I know how important it is for you not to look like a fool in front of your friends. Not that any of your so-called friends would know the difference anyway. If you surround yourself with mediocrity, you become mediocre," I added. "You probably think you stand out, but believe me, they pull you down, not that you had all that far to fall."

Her eyes widened, and her face reddened, with cheeks that looked like fully ripe red apples. She balled her fists and readied her vocal cords for screaming. I loved the way I was getting inside her and tying her already twisted little heart into tighter knots. For me, it was sweet revenge, and for the moment, it took my mind off the pool of trouble in which I was swimming, maybe drowning.

"It's not unlike another favorite expression of yours," I continued. I felt like I was on a roll, like a contestant on *Jeopardy*. "'The icing on the cake.' I notice you're always using it for negative remarks, like 'His wife's suing him for divorce is the icing on the cake.' It really is used more for positive comments. Think about it. Who doesn't like licking the icing on a cake?"

She continued to glare at me, as if hoping her fiery eyes would make me explode and drop into a pool of dust at her feet. She could do that so easily to her daughter.

"Is that what you do? You analyze all my

expressions?" she asked, amazed. "You judge my every word and do a critique behind my back?"

I shrugged and turned away. "Believe me, it's not brain surgery," I said, hiding my smile.

"What else have you criticized about me? Well? Let me have the whole bag of ugliness you're so capable of filling and flinging in my direction before you leave us. We already know some of the distortions and lies about me that you spread, and don't think I was ever unaware of what you told your father about me. You never understood how important I've become to him and how much we trust each other now. Well? Go on. What else? What other things have you told my daughter? You might as well get it all out before you leave."

I acted as if I didn't hear her anymore. I knew that was one of the things she hated the most. A woman like Julie couldn't tolerate being made to feel as if nothing she said or did mattered. She couldn't stand being ignored. Her ego would stamp its feet, pull its hair, and scream.

The truth was that most of the time, I didn't really listen to the things she said, even if I gave her the satisfaction of pretending I was listening. I didn't only do it to her. I could shut people out as quickly as I could shut off a light, especially someone like her. I didn't go into a trance. There was no faraway look in my eyes that would reveal that I was gone. It was almost impossible to know when I was listening and when I wasn't. Sometimes I imagined that I had two sets of ears and two brains. You know, like an extra hard drive in the computer that she thought was my brain?

My mind had a zoom lens. I could just focus on some interesting thing and cut out the distraction.

But this morning, unfortunately, I did hear her every mean-spirited word. To be truthful, I welcomed her verbal whipping, even though she was certainly no one to accuse anyone else of being mean and selfish and had no right to assume the role of judge and jury. If there ever was someone who should be restrained by being without sin before casting the first stone, it was my father's wife, Julie. It was lucky she didn't have a twin. She would have smothered him or her in her mother's womb just to be sure she would get all of her parents' attention.

But despite what she thought, I wasn't feeling particularly superior this morning. She was at me like this because she knew I was down and incapable of defending myself very much. That was usually when someone like her would pounce. I call them coyote cowards. They're parasites who will only swoop down on the small, wounded, or handicapped. Otherwise, they hover in the shadows, feeding their green faces on envy with hopes for your failures, waiting for you to become crippled and weaker but too frightened to challenge or compete when you weren't.

"I don't know how you will live with yourself," she continued. "If I were inside you, I'd scratch and kick my way out."

I turned and glared at her. Despite what she claimed, I knew I could frighten her with a look like the one I had now. I had practiced it in the mirror. It was a look I often employed at school. My eyes were like darts. I had the face of someone capable of sending out curses like emails.

Fear began to overtake her in small ways. She embraced herself quickly, swallowed hard, and took another step back.

"At last, we agree about something," I said. "If *you* were inside *me*, I'd rip you out. You know, like a bloody cesarean section." I held up my hands as though they had just been in a mother's womb and were dripping with blood down my arms.

She gasped, turned quickly, and marched out, holding her head high. She was always worried about what she looked like, even when she was alone and wouldn't see anyone else. However, frustrating and defeating her didn't give me as much satisfaction as she thought it had. I had long ago given up on baiting her and making her look foolish in front of my father, hoping it would open his eyes. I certainly had nothing to gain from it today. It was far too late, too late for many things. I was soaked in regrets.

I stood by the window in my bedroom, looked out toward the Pacific Ocean, and thought it should be gray and rainy today, at least. That would fit my mood, everyone's mood. I didn't pay much attention to the weather. Maybe that was because we lived in Southern California and took beautiful days for granted, or maybe it was because I spent most of my time inside, my face in a book or at a computer screen. I wasn't one of those people who stopped to smell the roses. We actually had beds of them out front, along with other flowers. If I stopped, it wouldn't be to enjoy the scent and beauty of anything but instead to examine the flowers, looking for some microscopic genetic change. I couldn't help it. As my teachers were fond of saying, and which was probably true, it was part of my DNA.

Moments after Julie had stopped bitching and left, I heard someone behind me and thought she might have returned to say something else that was even nastier that had crawled into her clogged brain, a brain I imagined infested with little spiders weaving selfish, hateful webs of thought. This time, I would face her down more vehemently, not with calm sarcasm but with what she hated: cold, dirty language. When I spit back at her, she would rush to cover her ears, as if my words would stain her very soul.

However, when I turned, I saw it was my thirteen-year-old stepsister, Allison. That surprised me. I was sure her mother had told her to stay away from me, especially this morning. She probably told her I had done her enough damage, and maybe, like Typhoid Mary, I would contaminate her further. "Stay in your room, and keep the door locked until she's gone," she surely had said. She was unaware of the short but honest and sweet conversation Allison and I had had the night before. Her mother was on her this morning, however. She wanted nothing to happen to change anything now.

Allison did look very nervous sneaking in here, but, like last night, she looked very sad, too, sad for both of us. She stood there staring at me.

"What is it, Allison? I thought we said our good-byes last night."

"I know, but I remembered something. My father gave me this pen the last time I saw him," she said, holding up a silver pen. "He said it was a special pen, one of the ones the astronauts used in space. You could write upside down or sideways with it, everything. I wanted to give it to you to use." She stepped forward to hand it to me.

"You want to give it to me? Why? Do you think I'll be upside down or sideways?"

"No," she said, smiling. "It's just a very special pen."

I looked at it. On the surface, it didn't look like anything terribly unusual, but I did make out the word *NASA*.

"Please take it," she said, waving it. She looked like she would cry if I didn't.

"Your father gave it to you? Are you sure you want to give it to me?"

"Yes."

"Why?"

"The words you'll write with it will be better than the words I'll write."

The way she said the obvious truth, with no self-deprecation or self-pity, made me laugh. In some ways, Allison was already head and shoulders above her mother.

I took the pen.

"Okay. Thanks. Who knows, maybe I will hang from my feet in my closet when I do my homework up there. Some people think I'm a vampire."

She smiled. "No, you're not. No one thinks that. You're too pretty to be a vampire."

"Pretty?" I glanced at myself in the mirror. I didn't feel especially pretty today. I thought my face was pale, my eyes dull and dim, and my hair unkempt. If anything, I looked more like some homeless girl wondering what in the world had happened that she should find herself so lost and alone.

"That's a nice color on you, too, turquoise. Remember? I made my mother buy me the same blouse, but it didn't look as good on me as it does on you."

"It will," I said. "You're going to have a nice figure, Allison." As hard as it was for me to say it, I added, "As nice as your mother's." What was true was true. Julie was physically attractive. If only she could be kept under glass like a wax figure, I thought, and not bother or hurt anyone else.

Allison smiled again. "Okay, see you when you come home for the holidays." She started to turn to leave.

"We don't get holidays," I said.

"Really?"

"I don't know. Things are very different there. I'll let you know."

"Will you? Really? I mean, let me know and not my mother first?"

"She'll know, even though the moment I leave, she'll have a moat built."

"A what?"

"Forget it. Okay. Like I said last night, I'll send you an email or text you."

"I know you said it, but will you really?"

"You sure you want me to do it, Allison? You

know you'll have to keep it secret from you-know-whom."

"I'm sure. Please, send me emails. My mother doesn't know how to use a computer."

I stared at her with a hard look. She knew why.

"I'll keep this secret. I swear," she said in a deep whisper, with her hand over her heart, and then turned and went to the door, checking first to be sure her mother didn't know she had come in to see me. She looked back, smiled, and then hurried away.

I put the pen into my bag.

My father's wife was in her glory, my father was in a deep depression, and my stepsister was terrified of breathing the same air I breathed.

How would I go about explaining all of this to anyone if I had trouble explaining it to myself? I thought I should write it down so I could study it all exactly the way I would study a math problem or a science theory, pause, step back, and analyze. Maybe if I did a full, intelligent, and objective review, I would have an easier time living with myself, not that it was ever easy to be who I was or who I was going to be.

Was I cursed at birth or blessed?

I suppose the best way to answer such a question is to ask yourself how many people you know your age or a little younger or older who would want to trade places with you, would want to have your talents and intelligence, or envied you for your good looks enough to accept all the baggage that came along with it.

Right now, in my case, despite my accolades and

awards, people like that would be harder to find than the famous needle in a haystack.

But the thing was that despite it all, I didn't even want to look. I didn't want to be validated, complimented, or even respected in any way.

I looked in the mirror again. Allison was right. This was a nice color for me.

I wondered, would anyone where I was going notice, and if they did, would they care?

I must have wanted someone to care. I did want to have friends, and I did hope that there was some boy out there about my age who would find me attractive.

Otherwise, why would I have taken so long to choose my clothes, the way a prisoner on death row might contemplate his last meal?

# 2

When the phone rang in my room, I thought it was probably my father giving me an update on the time we would be leaving, but it was Joy Hensley, my new and only best friend ever since I'd made an effort to help her with her anorexia, something her own mother hadn't been addressing properly. The school nurse wasn't effective, probably worrying about a lawsuit or something, and there certainly weren't any other girls at the school who would give her a second look or show any concern. I would have to admit that when I first considered helping her, it wasn't out of any particular affection for her. She interested me the way anything abnormal might. There aren't too many species that deliberately do something harmful to themselves.

Joy fit so many descriptions of potential anorexia sufferers. She was heavy when she was younger and thought being thin would win her more friends and admirers. I suspected that she was afraid of growing up; she wanted to be a preadolescent forever. In short, she was afraid of sex. Eventually, I was fascinated with what I could do to change or heal her.

"I really didn't say good-bye to you properly," she began.

"Is there a proper way to say good-bye, Joy?"

"You know what I mean," she said, and followed that with the jingle of a giggle she usually used when she was nervous or frightened.

"I'm beginning to wonder if I know what anything means, Joy."

"Oh, no. If anyone does, you do."

For months, I had tolerated Joy's exuberant compliments, knowing she was desperate to keep me as a close friend, but I had gotten so used to over-the-top compliments that I almost didn't react to them anymore.

For most of my life, people, especially teachers and other adults, were more interested in what I thought than in what I felt. It was as though being given almost supernatural intelligence deadened my feelings or diminished them to the point where they weren't necessary or important. If I was sad, I could think my way out of it, you see, and the only way I could be happy was to discover a new fact or add something to my encyclopedia of knowledge. That's what they believed about me. No wonder they saw me as some kind of monster, a brain creature who had microscopes for eyes. Despite how ingratiating and fawning Joy could be, I had no doubt she harbored some of the same feelings about me. Ironically, she was very fond of me, respected me, but was also at least a little afraid of me. Can you have a close friend with that combination of feelings about you?

"Is your new school more expensive than ours?"

"Yes, very," I said. "Julie was just complaining about that, as a matter of fact."

"I guess you'll meet more very rich kids, then," she said sadly.

"There are only fifteen students, if that many."

"Fifteen? It sounds more like just one class. How can that be a school?"

"I'll let you know," I said dryly.

I hadn't told Joy much about where I was going. She was one of those who were under the impression that I was leaving our school to enjoy better opportunities, and while that was probably going to be true, it wasn't what had motivated my father and Julie to agree to it.

It was true that Beverly Royal was a ritzy private school in Beverly Hills, which I had attended along with the sons and daughters of famous Hollywood actors, producers, and directors, not to mention wealthy business executives. Everything was new and clean, with the finest equipment and the latest technology. The over-the-top security, with metal detectors, surveillance cameras, and half a dozen security personnel, gave the students' parents a sense of comfort that was rare in, if not totally absent from, public schools. The teachers were among the highest paid and most likely the best qualified. Administrators at Beverly Royal liked to brag that while the lowest five percent of college graduates went into teaching, Beverly Royal hired only from the top five percent. Who would want to leave such a school voluntarily?

My father and Julie would deny that I was being sent to this new school as a kind of punishment. My father would deny it because he really believed it wasn't. Despite what my stepmother had just told me, she couldn't have me sent to some penitentiary or mental clinic. She was trapped. She had to put on an act and claim that I was being offered a unique opportunity, because she didn't want the scandal to grow. She was always very protective of her lily-white reputation. She was terrified that her friends would gossip about her the way she and they gossiped about other people.

Of course, in your heart, if you were me, you would know it was at least partly a punishment, and no form of sugarcoating would change that.

"So I guess someone like me couldn't get into your new school even if my parents wanted to spend the money, huh?" Joy asked. If I were going to just another private school, I had no doubt Joy would pressure her mother to put out the extra money and send her there, too.

"No, Joy. Despite what most of the others at our school believe, money can't buy you everything. You have to qualify, and the standards are very, very high, so high you need oxygen."

"Huh?"

"You know what I mean."

I was never falsely modest about myself. If

anything, I thought that would be futile. It would be like a blind person pretending he could see. I was what I was, and being modest and humble didn't change anything. I was profoundly gifted. The whole faculty and all of my father's and Julie's friends knew it.

Whenever anyone heard me called that, he or she would look at me and surely wonder, *What's so special about her? What's her gift?* On the surface, I supposed I didn't look different from any other girl my age, although I'd been accused of being very pretty. I say *accused* because for most of my teenage life, I had done relatively little to make myself look beautiful. Until recently, I had rarely dwelled on my hair, clothes, makeup, or jewelry. There had never been an actress or singer I wished I resembled. Unlike the other attractive girls in my classes, I never flaunted my good looks and figure, and I never flirted with or teased any boy.

But I did recognize that real beauty, natural beauty, didn't need to be emphasized or exaggerated. It couldn't be hidden, and perhaps that was the sort of beauty I possessed. I supposed I should be more grateful, feel more blessed, but the truth was, I hadn't yet gotten control of it the way I controlled most things in my life, and that made me nervous and insecure. A girl my age who was beautiful but didn't dwell on it or even realize it was always surprised at how others, especially men, treated her. She was always at some disadvantage, and I hated being at any disadvantage when it came to relationships with others my age, or actually, with anyone regardless of age, especially men.

People who heard I was gifted didn't fully

understand what that meant. They might expect me to get up and play Beethoven when I was only five or create a magnificent work of art. Those are truly gifted people, but they are gifted with a quickly and easily displayed talent. I'm different.

"I know, Mayfair," Joy said, with some discouragement in her voice. "You're a genius, and the school probably takes only geniuses."

"You know I hate that word, Joy."

"I know you do, but you are."

"A genius is someone who supposedly doesn't make mistakes. They are expected to be right always."

"You always are."

"Believe me, Joy, I'm not. Besides, people anticipate that great things will come from geniuses, and I'm not sure anything of great value will ever come from me."

"It will," she insisted.

My faithful friend, Joy Hensley, I thought. She was practically the only person I might miss, besides my father, of course.

"You're lucky," she added.

"Lucky?" Now I was the one to follow what I said with a jingle of a giggle.

"Of course. Look how much you know and how fast you can learn anything."

Joy didn't understand and probably never would, but when you're young and brilliant, especially if you're female, people think you don't want the same things so-called normal or average young girls want, like love and romance or even sex. From where do they get these ideas? Don't eggheads have hormones?

And why is falling in love unusual for someone who can solve the most complicated algebraic equations?

Maybe that's what made most boys hesitant about approaching me even though I was quite attractive, even having been called voluptuous. They thought that if they did get to make love to me, I would be analyzing them and then might reveal that they had premature ejaculation or something. What hurt a boy's feelings more than a girl thinking and saying he was poor in the sack? Why risk it?

"Yes," Joy insisted. "You are. Will you write to me as soon as you can?"

"As soon as I can," I said with a very noncommittal tone.

"I'll miss you, Mayfair. It's not going to be fun going to school anymore."

"I hope you have more self-confidence now, Joy. You're doing so much better. Don't let any of those bitches push you around."

"It wasn't hard when you were there to help."

"You've got to be on your own sometime, Joy. Just think about what I would do, what I might say, okay?"

"Yes, thanks," she said in a small voice.

Here I was giving someone else advice when I was the one who needed it the most. My self-confidence surprised even me now. What right did I have to do it?

"I've got to go, Joy. Still packing."

"Well, have a good trip," she said. "I guess you'll email me sometime."

"I said I would. I want to hear good things about

you. You know I don't like failure, and I've invested time and energy in you."

She laughed. "I'll try."

"Don't try. Do. Remember what I told you. What doesn't destroy you makes you stronger."

"I'll remember," she said.

After I hung up, I realized I'd been giving myself that advice, not her.

If my grandmother Lizzy, my mother's mother, was still alive, she'd be chiding me for showing even the slightest evidence of self-pity. I knew I took after Grandmother Lizzy more than any other relative, including my own parents. She had a way of saying things that not many wanted to hear. She would often say that something was "plain and simple." I appreciated her more than anyone else did, and when we looked at each other, we knew we were special. She wasn't gifted, of course, unless you would consider being bold and coldly truthful a gift. With all the phoniness raining down around us these days, maybe that could be a very special gift after all. She didn't understand my superior intelligence or what it would come to mean, but she tried to treat me as if I were no different from any other little girl my age. She didn't want to bring any unusual attention to me. Now that I think back to that, I realize how impossible a task that was for her.

There was no way I wouldn't attract unusual attention. I wasn't looking for it, but I couldn't help it. At three years old, I was reading on an eighth-grade level. When I entered grade school at five years old, I was already reading books meant for at least college sophomores.

I can still hear Grandmother Lizzy's rippling laughter when I astounded relatives with my recitations of famous speeches, world capitals, scientific facts, or math equations and then offered quotes from Shakespeare, not only reciting them from memory but also explaining them.

"The kid's a walking computer," my uncle Justin, my father's older brother, would say. He was the comedian in the family. He'd spin me around, claiming he was looking for the plug and wires. No one in my family loved me any less because I was so smart, especially not Grandmother Lizzy. I don't think anyone hugged me more or made me feel as precious, but grandmothers can be like that.

After I said something brilliant and Grandmother Lizzy would clap and then hug and kiss me, I'd look at my mother and see the love and pride in her face. There was nothing more protective than a real family, even for someone like me, despite what people like Julie thought. People like her thought that because you were very smart, you didn't need support, but I thought it was just the opposite. You needed your family around you, caring about you, even more. They cherished my being gifted. Maybe it made them feel that their family lineage was special. I didn't know, but I enjoyed their affection and soaked in their pride.

It wasn't that way when I was with strangers. Once you were labeled profoundly gifted in the educational system, you might as well have *weird* tattooed on your forehead. No one really wanted to be friends with you. Some were even afraid of you. Many thought I was like Spock from *Star Trek*, the one who knew everything but had no feelings. I thought they even expected me to have pointed ears or something frightening about my eyes, especially when I looked at them.

Often, especially when I was younger, I would hear things like "Stop looking at me, you freak."

How this made me feel would be no surprise. When I was younger, it was always harder, of course. Despite my brilliance, I still had to develop defenses, especially social defenses. I could think of clever comeback lines, but they wouldn't win me acceptance or sympathy. Maybe I would be feared and avoided, but was that something a young girl wanted?

Regardless, I had to develop a harder shell. Young kids especially enjoy seeing how they can get to other students, bring tears to their eyes. I don't know why it's truer for young kids, but the rage in bullying today clearly demonstrates it. They tried to bully me from the get-go, maybe because of all the attention I was receiving, but I frustrated them. It got so they believed I had no tears and couldn't cry, so they finally gave up.

Even though I had attended a fairly big school, as far as I knew, I was the only one at my grade school who had ever been formally labeled profoundly gifted after all sorts of testing. In fact, I had the impression that there had never been any student like me in the history of the entire school district, which included four other schools, as well as in the entire county. I used to wonder if one of the eleven others estimated in the state at the time were in Los Angeles, too, and what it would be like to meet one of them.

Would we both just know? Could we look into each other's eyes and see some rich pool of brilliance that only we and others like us could see? Were we truly like alien creatures that had been smuggled into the human population? I dreamed that someday we would all meet or maybe would deliberately be brought together by the government or some corporation. Everyone else would expect us to take over the world or do something significant.

According to what I had been told and what I had read, I would meet some others who were somewhat, if not exactly, like me very soon at this new expensive private school that Julie thought was much more of a reward than a punishment. But this wasn't exactly how I had imagined I would meet them. It felt like we were being herded together, corralled and contained.

Anyway, I didn't want to rule the world, especially this world. In my mind, despite how we could impress teachers and others and despite what they imagined we would invent or create or discover, we weren't really welcomed. People could tolerate us for a short period, the way they might enjoy a magician, but who wanted someone pulling rabbits out of hats all the time?

Maybe Julie would get her wish. Maybe my new school would turn out to be more of a prison, because in the end, what all these educators and other young people, even some parents, really wanted was to keep us apart, keep us away from their precious children, as if we could somehow ruin them with our intelligence. Maybe they thought we would teach them things that would make them more rebellious.

I had started to get these ideas from the moment the grade-school psychologist, Mrs. Fishman (I called her Fish Face because of her Botox lips), started treating me like a rare diamond and took credit for the discovery. Like that was hard to do. Whenever she could, she had me perform for teachers and administrators, defining words, reading high-school textbooks aloud, solving difficult math problems in minutes, or simply reciting some fact that others would need to discover on an internet site. Sometimes I felt like I was doing a little ballet but with facts instead of ballet slippers. I felt like a monkey performing when a bell was rung.

After I was diagnosed as being profoundly gifted, Mrs. Fishman brought my parents in to discuss what it meant. I remember overhearing my mother tell my father, "She's so excited about Mayfair, I thought she was having an orgasm."

For quite a while, I struggled with the comparison. I didn't have to ask my mother what *orgasm* meant. In fact, since I had become a good reader and an expert on my computer, I rarely asked her or my father questions or definitions of words. I've heard people say that computers and smartphones are running our lives now. For kids like me, unless your parents put some sort of lock on what you could see and read, nothing in the world was out-of-bounds or prohibited. I knew so many girls and boys who had gone to their computers to learn about sex. I bet you did. I bet you're doing it now.

Few did it when they were as young as I was at the time, of course.

But remember, I was profoundly gifted. I was one in three million. Can you even picture three million other people? Can you imagine looking at sixty thousand or seventy thousand people in a stadium and thinking, *There is no one here remotely as brilliant as I am*? And even if you did think that, can you imagine thinking of it not arrogantly but just as a simple fact? That might make me seem very cold, I know, but it wasn't something I chose to be.

Anyway, I learned that both men and women have orgasms and that it was an autonomic physiological response, which are big words for *you can't stop it if you've gone too far*. Parents were always warning their kids not to go too far, and this was the reason. When you were very little, they warned you not to go too far from the house. Well, this meant not to go too far from your self-control.

After I read about the word and understood the physiological activity, which is a fancy way of saying what goes on in the body, whenever I was with Fish Face, I would look for symptoms, especially something in her face to tell me it was happening, symptoms like her being flushed or breathing too hard. I even wanted to take her pulse and tried to figure out how I could get my fingers on her wrist. My intense concentration rattled her, and one day she finally asked me why I was looking at her with such an engrossed expression.

"When you glare at people like that, Mayfair, you make them feel quite uncomfortable. What is it about me that makes me so fascinating to you right now?" She sat back, waiting for something intriguing to come out of my mouth, something she could blabber about in the faculty lounge. Her face looked like a big saucer ready to catch all my gems.

"I'm studying you to see if you're having an orgasm," I said, as casually as anyone would say "to see if you are feeling okay."

Remember, this is coming out of the mouth of a five-year-old.

She turned a dark shade of red and looked like she would choke on her own saliva. Then she sat forward, entwining her chubby fingers, which made each arm look like it was holding on to a shoulder for dear life. Her lips were so tight that little white spots popped out in the corners, and her shoulders looked like they would rise higher and higher until her head sank down between them completely. I was quite fascinated with her reaction.

"We all know you're very intelligent, Mayfair, but you have to learn what is proper and not proper for a little girl to say," she told me.

"Who decides what is and is not proper?" I fired back.

She narrowed her eyes and nodded as if she was confirming a suspicion about me.

She had given my parents some booklets about profoundly gifted children, and one described them as "often argumentative, more like lawyers challenging words and comments." That definitely sounded like me, but it wasn't something I was conscious of doing. It was just natural to me to question and challenge anything and everything I heard or saw.

"Never mind that. Just think before you speak," she told me.

"I always do. I have to think before I speak. Don't you? Maybe you don't. Maybe that's why you say silly things sometimes." She had a habit of saying something she didn't mean to say and then pressing the back of her hand against her mouth as if she were trying to stop a leak.

At this moment, she looked like she was going to explode. Her cheeks ballooned, and her face went from red to white very quickly. "You can go now," she said.

After that little exchange between us, she didn't parade me about as much or ask to see me as much, and when she did, she was very formal and always on her guard, trembling in anticipation of something I might say that would embarrass her. I enjoyed her discomfort. Was I already showing some signs of meanness or disrespect?

Anyway, she had called my parents in again, this time to warn them about me. Suddenly, it was both a curse and a blessing to have a profoundly gifted child. That excitement she had first evinced was gone. She was full of new warnings, pointing out red flags like someone from homeland security.

"If you're not careful," she told them, "you'll lose control of her. Like conniving, manipulative little lawyers, profoundly gifted children find loopholes in all the rules you lay down. If you tell her it's time to turn off her lamp and you don't add 'and go to sleep,' she might turn off the lamp but switch on a flashlight and continue doing what she was doing."

"What are you saying? You're making her sound dangerous or at least like a burden," my mother countered. "Why this sudden change?"

For some reason, she didn't mention my reference to her possibly having an orgasm. Maybe she really was and was ashamed or shocked that I had discovered it.

"I'm just telling you what I know," Fish Face responded, a bit sullenly.

Both my parents were quite upset with Fish Face after that, and neither of them really heeded her words when it came to how they treated me or evaluated anything I did or said.

All of it was quite a learning experience for me, but then again, just about everything in my life was.

"The world is my classroom," I often said. Some people would smile, but most would look at me as if I had just stepped off a spaceship. "She really is Mr. Spock!"

I knew that calling the world a classroom sounded boring, but if there was one thing I never was, it was bored.

Maybe if I were once in a while, I'd have been happier or, as my stepmother said, normal, because I'd look for amusement instead of information.

"It's normal to want to have fun once in a while more than you want to have facts," Julie said one time.

She laughed and added, "That's been my life's motto, Mayfair. When in doubt, have fun, and you can't be any more normal than I am."

I wanted to reply, "If you're what is considered normal, I'm signing up for Abnormals R Us." But I wasn't quite at the stage where I would confront her head-on instead of subtly or with words and analogies she would never understand.

I did think, however, that something was missing inside me, something that might be necessary in order for someone to be happy with herself. It was true that I was not happy most of the time, and I was envious of girls my age who had far lower IQ scores but who looked like life was just one exciting roller-coaster ride full of screams and laughter, all happening while someone warm and handsome was holding on to you. I would think about that image very often.

I would think about it, but I wouldn't confess to anyone else that I lacked anything that important. I would come to realize that I was very attractive, and that bothered some girls because it seemed to them that I had everything: good looks, a great figure, a rich complexion, soft healthy hair, and brains. I was always so self-confident that I never dreamed a time would come when I would admit that anything was wrong with me, that something important was missing, especially to myself.

I guess I didn't know everything after all.

Even though I was profoundly gifted.

# 3

We were on our way to my special new school, Spindrift. Somebody very creative, of course, came up with that name. Students there were supposedly the crème de la crème, the best of the best, and the purpose of the school was to get them to live up to their enormous potential so that everyone would benefit from their achievements.

Just in case someone considering the school for his or her child didn't understand the name, the booklet explained it: "Spray blown up from an ocean wave is called spindrift. It is expected that our graduates will spray the world with their brilliance." Can't you just see the faces of our proud parents? Who wouldn't want their child to spray the world with brilliance? Every word from their mouths would be dazzling.

From the booklet, I also knew that the motto above the main entrance read: "A brilliant mind wasted is a sin beyond redemption." The quote belonged to Dr. Norman Lazarus, a biochemistry research scientist whose discoveries included a drug to treat bone cancer. As our school psychologist and guidance counselor had explained to me, Dr. Lazarus had donated most of his profits to educational institutions. He established this special school for gifted students, which was his favorite project. I supposed the motto was intended to make us all feel guilty if we didn't live up to our potential. If you were brilliant and lazy, you were like a person who had a talent to play the piano beautifully but wouldn't take a lesson or touch a key. People who lacked any talent could really despise you for that and hate the fates that wasted their powers on giving you the talent.

I wasn't afraid that I would enter Spindrift and fail to meet anyone's expectations for me. I was afraid that I would enter the special school and fail to meet my own expectations. The implication was very obvious. I could almost hear my own father saying it again: "If you can't be happy here among your own kind, Mayfair, you'll never be happy."

My own kind? Even my father thought I belonged to a different species now.

I wasn't too happy and didn't expect that I would be the most pleasant new student. I was never good at hiding my displeasure, which goes back to my taking after my grandmother Lizzy. I should have taken lessons from Julie while I had the chance, I thought. Maybe that was really how you got along in this world.

I gazed out of the car window and saw that the few clouds streaming across the sky looked like white ribbons floating over a sea of Wedgwood blue. Whenever my real mother saw a sky like this, she would say something descriptive like that. She would often speak in beautiful metaphors, which were sometimes quite spiritual, even though she wasn't very religious. We would go to church only on holidays or for special occasions like weddings and funerals, but she believed in a holy spirit in us and around us.

She'd say, "Look, Mayfair, God is tying ribbons in earth's hair. Isn't she beautiful?"

"Why do you say 'she'? How do we know the earth is female, Mother?" I would ask.

My father would laugh and say, "What a kid. Look at what she thinks of at this age."

But my mother would stay serious and kiss my cheek or my forehead before running her fingers through my wheat-colored hair. She wanted me to wear it long then, and she enjoyed brushing it for me. I would look at her in the mirror while she sat or stood behind me, and I would study her face and wonder, *Do all mothers look at their daughters like this, with such pure love?*

I thought that as long as I had my long hair, I would have my mother's deep love. It had grown to reach halfway down my back before she died. After that, I chopped it down to just at the nape of my neck and did such a bad job that I usually wore a hat, even when my father took me by the hand to a beauty salon for repairs.

"We know the earth is female because of all that's born from her," she told me. "And you know mothers are the ones who give birth."

That was logical, so I accepted it. I always appreciated that my mother would try to be logical when she answered my questions, even when I was only three. She never ascribed anything to fantasy. Just as there was no bogeyman, there were no good fairies. Mothers do seem to know their children better than fathers do. She knew early on that make-believe wouldn't work with me.

When my father wanted me to believe in Santa Claus, I simply told him that it was physically impossible for one man to deliver gifts to all the children in the world on one night, much less keep a record of who was naughty and who was nice.

"Not even FedEx can do that," I said, and he roared with laughter.

"This kid's better than television," he told my mother.

"Don't you want there to be a Santa Claus, Mayfair?" my mother asked.

Of course, I did, but I just couldn't believe in him.

"You can't believe in something unless it's true," I said, and my father laughed again. He had such a wonderful laugh then, an infectious laugh that made anyone near him laugh along, including me.

"You poor dear," my mother would say, embracing me. "I hope you can find something wonderful to believe in someday without worrying about whether it's true or not."

"She will," my father promised her. "This kid will do it all."

He was so proud of me back then. If there was any possibility of taking me along with him when he visited someone involved with his public relations business or simply went shopping for something, he would. I knew even at age three that he was eager to show me off, almost the way Fish Face did, but I was eager to please him. And after my mother died, it was even more important to please him. In my mind, I was still pleasing her, too. It was as if part of her floated into him after her death. They were that close when she was alive, and that was as far as I would go in believing anything supernatural.

I was just as eager to please him now, but it had become more difficult, maybe even impossible, because once he married Julie Dunbar, I felt that the part of my mother that was in him had left. She'd have been the first to tell him, "There's not enough room in one heart for two lovers in your life, Roger."

She wouldn't sound angry or upset. She would be smiling softly, her voice gentle and kind. I missed that voice and that smile. All the mirrors in our ten-room Bel Air hacienda-style home surely missed that smile as well. Everything lost its glitter and gleam when my mother died. This was so much her home, down to her choice of every color, every floor tile, every cabinet handle, and every light fixture. Almost without comment, my father had nodded and approved everything she planned or wanted. He had that much faith and trust in her judgment, but more important, he had that much of a desire to see her happy. She was as important to him as she was to me.

Whenever I thought of myself becoming romantically involved with someone someday, I'd think of what my parents were to each other. The parents of so many girls I knew just seemed to be sharing a place to live. I'd overhear their daughters complaining about how much their parents argued. Doors were always slamming in their homes. Parents were often sulking, sometimes for days and even weeks. These girls hated to be home and looked for every opportunity to keep themselves away.

I never felt this way about my home when my mother was alive, and I couldn't remember any doors slamming, nor could I recall my parents being so angry at each other that one would sulk. If either upset the other, he or she became almost desperate to make it better. Love in our house wasn't a goal; it was a reality, the status quo. I could feel it, and that feeling gave me a sense of security. I loved being with them. It was because of them that I was less skeptical about people actually loving each other, caring more for each other than they cared for themselves.

I was always skeptical about almost everything in my life, from when I was an infant until now, but one thing I always trusted was my mother's hand holding mine. I knew she would rather have her arm separate from her shoulder than let go if I needed her. After she died, life without her was like a bird without a voice, just something that glided silently along, jealous even of the screech of a cat.

There were no birds singing now, and I knew a good part of the reason was my own fault. Julie wasn't all wrong. Just because you were brilliant, that didn't mean you couldn't do something terribly wrong, something that would hurt the one person you loved the most in the world. I liked to think that I had more control of my emotions than most people because I was so intelligent, but emotions really did come from another place. Anger and jealousy could be more like viruses eating away at you until you did something you regretted.

And I did.

All the way up to Spindrift, Daddy watched me in the rearview mirror. I saw the sadness in his eyes, but I also saw him anticipating my doing or saying something to show my resistance and maybe cause another serious blowup between my stepmother and me. I knew he was tired of being a referee, and frankly, I was tired of it, too. I wanted out of this game as much as he did.

I caught the hesitation and sadness in his eyes. At times along the way, I thought he was going to stop and turn around, even though I knew that if he didn't go through with this, he'd surely end up in a divorce. Julie had been through a nasty divorce, so she was a veteran of the marital wars and might be quicker to pull the trigger. It was always easier to do something the second time, although even for Julie, it had to be terrible to face the fact that it was difficult for her to hold on to a relationship. I had yet to hold on to any, even a silly little high-school romance, but I knew what disappointment a failure like that could be. No matter what, deep inside, you'd always blame yourself. Surely there was one more thing you could have done, could have said, one more thing that would have saved the relationship.

Although my father didn't say it in so many words, it was obvious to me soon after he married Julie that he was sensitive to the possibility of her eventually wanting a divorce solely because of me. That would be so unfair to him. He was as good a father to her daughter, Allison, as he could be, maybe too good. The blame for any problem between my stepsister and me would always be on me, "because you know better." Most of the time, he would say something like that to please Julie. I realized that was his sole reason and he didn't always believe it. My father had a good poker face, except with me. He knew I could see through any mask he put on.

He would be the first to admit that most things were not what they seemed to be. That was his business, after all, often putting lipstick on a pig. He had no false illusions about it. It was still a pig. Both of us pretended and put on an act for each other when he finally agreed with Julie that I should be sent somewhere far away.

The night before we left for the school, he had come into my room while I was packing and stood silently for a few moments watching me. I knew he was there, but I ignored him. Finally, I paused, and we looked at each other. I saw how difficult this was for him.

"What?" I asked softly.

"This is a really good idea, Mayfair. You need the challenge this school will give you," he said. "You need the personal attention and the chance to go at your own pace."

"Right," I said, even though both of us knew nothing had ever stopped me from going at my own pace and I always enjoyed personal attention when I needed it.

"And as your guidance counselor, Mr. Martin, says, it will be good for you to be with students with abilities like yours. You'll feel more comfortable, and you'll have some competition. You're the one who told me runners go faster when they have someone right on their heels."

"Fine," I said. "You're right. I'm wasting my time here with these Yahoos."

"Yahoos?" he said, smiling.

"In *Gulliver's Travels*, remember? They were disgusting, stupid creatures that resembled human beings."

He stopped smiling. "I don't like it when you're so condescending, Mayfair. Don't look down on people who aren't as brilliant as you are. A little humility is important, especially now," he said. "You should know why better than I do."

Even though he was right, I hated it when he saw something wrong with me. My fear was that perhaps he would love me less, although I would never admit to that fear. I believed that admitting to any fear gives that fear more power over you. "Stuff it" was my motto. I would never show that I was afraid of the dark or of being alone when I was little. And there wasn't another girl or even a boy who could make me cower and retreat. They could see the resistance in my eyes, and they'd usually be the ones who backed off.

But it was always different when it came to my father. I could defeat him in an argument, frustrate him with my logic, but it never made me feel any better. The truth was, it always made me feel worse.

I turned away so he wouldn't see my eyes burn with tears. I took a deep breath and nodded. "Yes, Daddy. I'm sorry. You're right."

"Okay," he said, and came up behind me to kiss me softly and pat my hair. I watched him walk away, slouching like someone in defeat. What had happened to all those wonderful predictions for me, for our family, when I was younger and something of a star not only at school but at home and everywhere we went as a family? I was sure he was wondering where he had failed and that he was troubled with the thought that my mother would be very disappointed.

I packed faster. I owed it to my mother to make it easier for him, I thought. I could just imagine her watching the two of us and looking disappointed in my behavior. That was all she ever had to do, look disappointed. I could practically feel her thoughts. *Don't hurt him, Mayfair. Please*, she would think. *It's not easy for him, either. Help him get through it.*

I was still trying to do that now in the car as we drew closer to Spindrift. I hid any displeasure or regret and acted quite indifferent about it all. I wasn't going to give Julie any satisfaction by pleading for mercy or promising to improve my behavior toward her. To me, promises were like colorful bubbles, pretty but quick to pop and disappear, especially if they came from someone like her. If she had half a brain, which I didn't think she had, she would be able to see through my false face, which I couldn't help but have. After all, as Shakespeare wrote in *Macbeth*, *False face must hide what the false heart doth know*. And when it came to agreeing to all of this with any resemblance of enthusiasm, I had a false heart.

She should have been able to see that easily. Didn't it take one to know one, and who better to see a phony than a phony? That was why my father couldn't see through her. He was too trusting and honest, despite the work he had to do. He was desperate for happiness since my mother's death. I didn't like it, but I had to forgive him. I had to make myself understand and accept.

My stepmother sat with her shoulders hunched up, which made the skin at the back of her neck crinkle like cellophane. She would lower her chin and cramp up tightly when she was nervous. I could imagine all the organs inside her crowding together like frightened mice. And when she was very, very nervous, she would hold her breath until her face turned red. Right now, it was as if she felt that if she made a sound or moved a muscle, it would all go bad, and my father would take my side, turn the car around, and blame it all on her. All the way home, she would think, *So close. There I was, so close to getting rid of her, and I screwed up.*

I knew the silence in the car was driving her bonkers, however. My father wasn't his talkative self. Julie didn't want the radio on, because the chatter made her even more nervous, and I certainly had nothing to say to her. I hadn't said anything to either of them after we had left Los Angeles. I was sure she thought I was just being spiteful, my old spoiled self. I wasn't, but I couldn't help my silence. Maybe I was sadder than I would admit, and I wasn't sulking as much as I was crying inside. But that was something I would never reveal to her.

Everyone talked to himself or herself. Perhaps I did it more than most people, because I had running conversations going as if my brain was on Facebook or something. It was probably another reason so many other students kept their distance at my old school. To them, I always looked as if I were on another planet, in another dimension, listening to some other voices. It bugged some of my teachers, because they thought I wasn't paying attention to their important comments, but when they questioned me to catch me so they could bawl me out, I always had the answer.

Was I very sad about leaving my home? I knew that any other girl would have looked back at the house and gotten all choked up inside. It wasn't only because of what the house was, an eight-thousand-square-foot, two-story Spanish-style hacienda in Bel Air, complete with a beautiful oval pool, a cabana with a built-in barbecue grill, and a clay tennis court. I'd heard my father say the house and the grounds were estimated to be worth upward of twelve million dollars. He bought it when he was promoted to CEO of Pacifica Advertising, which had contracts with major pharmaceutical companies and some entertainment firms. He was now a major stock-holder in the company, a fact I was sure was not lost on Julie.

I had mixed feelings about leaving, because I grew up in this house. My best memories of my mother took place in this house, and now I was being deported from it. *Deported* was the right word. How often I had felt like a foreigner now in my own home. But when I looked back and thought about it more, it was like cutting the umbilical cord again. I wasn't just separating from my father and my mother's memory. I was losing them. They were drifting off like smoke in the wind, falling behind as we drove on. I was never so afraid of being alone.

Nevertheless, I refused to let myself get emotional. I had talents and skills few people had, number one of which was harvesting the most value from any experience. What I had in that house I was taking with me. I was able to internalize all of it. I treasured all the memories, no matter how small or insignificant someone else might think they were. Not Julie, not the school administrators who had come down on me, no one could take any of it from me.

"How much longer?" Julie asked, as if she were being waterboarded.

"Not far now," Daddy said. He turned and flashed one of his rah-rah, sis-boom-bah, high-octane, successful-advertising-executive smiles at her.

"You sure you know where you're going, Roger?"

"He has it on the GPS," I muttered. "If he makes a wrong turn or something, it will let him know."

She ignored me, but my father said, "Mayfair's right. We can't get lost."

"I don't trust those things," Julie said, and I laughed a little too loudly for her. She didn't trust the GPS because she couldn't grasp how to use it. The one in her car was never turned on. She had trouble with a television remote. It was a wonder she could work her blow-dryer, and if it did get too hot and shut off, she'd scream, "Roger, the electricity in the house is off!"

"Try to figure it out yourself, Julie," I would tell her. "How can the electricity be off if the lights are on?"

Just like back then, she glared at me angrily now in the car and then turned quickly away. I didn't have to wonder what she was thinking. She had made that perfectly clear many times. Almost from the day she and my father had married, she'd always accused me of ridiculing her in one way or another. Why should it be any different even after what I had done? I was irretrievable, unrepentant, and impossible to change or improve. You didn't just give up on someone like me, she might say. You shook her completely out of your memory. I was sure she was chafing at the bit just thinking of the free rein she would have in our house now, never worrying about any comment I might make about something she had done or wanted to do.

The midafternoon Southern California freeway traffic suddenly began to swell. Somewhere along the highway artery, there was a blood clot, I thought. We slowed to a crawl. It didn't bother me. Whenever we were on the freeways and traffic slowed to a crawl or came to a standstill, I would continue reading or researching something on the internet. My father had bought me my first laptop when I was just a little more than three, and later he made sure I was always hooked into a satellite or had a PDA so I could get onto the internet. Whenever we had company and someone asked a question no one could answer, he would turn to me and say, "Mayfair, why don't you look that up for us?"

Like a father watching his son in a Little League game, he'd sit back with pride and watch me, at three or four years old, get the right website and come up with the answer, usually in less than a minute.

I was on the internet now, researching the community where Spindrift was located. It was in the Coachella Valley, just outside the small city of Piñon Pine Grove, named for the piñon pine trees that populated its borders. There were some small factories providing building materials and one that made store racks, plus some industrial farms. Not exactly an exciting new community, I thought, but I didn't exactly enjoy Los Angeles, either. I rarely visited the museums or the parks.

Researching the community and the school, I was quite content with the delay, but I knew the traffic jam put butterflies and worms in Julie's stomach. If anyone wanted to get this over with as quickly as possible, it was she. I imagined the only reason she'd come along was to make sure my father didn't change his mind. Of course, she acted as if she was concerned and cared about me, at least for his sake. She was concerned, all right, concerned that I would somehow be rejected at the door and end up back at home with Allison, who had been left behind with the maid. After what I had done, the faster and the farther we were separated, the better it would be in Julie's eyes.

"How do people do this every day?" Julie asked, nodding at the traffic.

"Is that a hypothetical question?"

"What?" she said, turning around to me again. She had to struggle to make it look like a painful effort. She was that tightly wrapped.

"*Hypothetical* means you really don't expect a specific answer. You ask it to begin a conversation, a larger discussion. Do you want an answer?"

She stared a moment. "You have an answer?"

"People do this every day because they have little choice, Julie. Their jobs are far away from their homes. They want their kids to go to better schools. They want to live in safer neighborhoods. The commute and all this traffic on weekends to get to malls or stores," I said, waving at the cars in front of us, "are the trade-off. It's probably far worse on weekday mornings and late afternoons."

She dropped the corners of her mouth and pressed her lower lip under her upper one. "Well, I couldn't do it," she said.

"You don't have to do it. You don't even have to shop for food."

"Mayfair," Daddy said, with that little upturn in his voice to indicate that I should go into retreat.

I knew that the whole episode at school, including

what had recently occurred between me and the girls I called the "bitches from *Macbeth*," had exhausted him. He looked like he had aged years. He was afraid of any conversation between Julie and me continuing for more than a few seconds. He was quite aware of how easily I could belittle her in any argument. I was always good at winning arguments, whether it be with her or with my teachers.

My father had said that ever since I could talk, I had questions and, soon after, good answers, even before I began to read. When he was first dating Julie, he told her quite a bit about me. He wanted to prepare her. In fact, she'd said that some nights, I was the sole topic.

"He's so proud of you," she had told me the first time we met at our house. They were on their way to a charity event, and he had brought her to the house first, explicitly to meet me. He'd asked me to put on something nice and brush my hair.

Anyway, from her tone of voice, I had understood that she wasn't terribly happy about my being so much the center of my father's life. I didn't mind that I was the big topic of discussion when he was courting her, but he had built me up so high in her eyes that she was quite nervous about meeting me the first time. I enjoyed her being so tense. It was like shooting fish in a barrel.

"How pretty you look," she began. "Did your daddy pick out that dress for you?"

"No. I pick out my own clothes," I said.

"Really?" She smiled. I could see it was quite

forced. She really didn't like the dress I had chosen. She glanced at my father, who shrugged. "Well, maybe you'll let me help you choose a dress next time you need one," she said.

"Why would I do that?"

"Mayfair!" my father said.

I gave him one of my innocent looks, and he shook his head in frustration. I really was innocent back then. I was looking for some reasonable response. Was she a clothing expert? What was her justification for the offer? Why would she care so much about how I looked? These all seemed to be logical questions, and my comment hadn't been meant to show disrespect or hurt her feelings. It was meant simply to get an answer that made sense.

However, I could see in her eyes that I had hurt her feelings. I didn't care, and I could admit that I was actually a little pleased. Of course, I would soon realize that my reaction had been natural. Any child, even one who was unafraid of showing her feelings about something, as I was, would naturally make it evident that she resented another woman replacing her mother, not that she ever could. It was merely a pathetic attempt at it.

"Your father's told me so much about you," Julie continued. "I feel as if I've known you for years."

"Does anyone really get to know anyone, even after years?" I asked.

"Pardon?"

"People change so much," I said, eyeing my father. "You never know when they'll do something completely out of character, or the character you thought they were."

His eyes were full of warnings. He knew how sharp and biting I could be, even at that age.

"Oh, well, I suppose. I mean, I don't really mean I know you yet, but I hope in time we'll get to know each other and be more comfortable with each other," Julie said, fumbling for the right words.

"I know a little about you. I know you have a ten-year-old daughter and you were in a bad divorce," I said.

She looked at my father as if he had betrayed a confidence they held dearly between them. "Yes," she admitted, "it was unpleasant."

"Well, there you are," I said. "My point."

"Pardon? Your point?"

"You obviously never really knew your husband if you ended up in a divorce. Either you or he changed so much you had to get a divorce."

She stared for a moment as if she were looking at someone who spoke a foreign language and then looked to my father for a rescue. It was clear she had never had someone as young as me say such things to her. He shook his head at me, smiled slightly, and then declared that they had to get going.

"I look forward to seeing you again, Mayfair," Julie said before she left, holding out her hand.

"Why?" I asked.

She held her breath, puffing out her cheeks and then pulling her hand back, saying, "To get to know you better, of course. I also would like you to meet Allison."

"Okay," I said, with about as much enthusiasm as someone going to the dentist.

She turned to leave, and my father leaned toward me to whisper, "We'll talk later."

Afterward, when we did talk, he made it clear to me that he really liked Julie and thought she would be good for both of us.

"I'd really appreciate it if you would make an effort to get along with her. Any relationship requires some compromise, Mayfair. Besides," he said, "we always wanted you to have a younger brother or sister."

"Don't you know which it is? Allison sounds like a girl."

"Mayfair, stop it," he said. Whenever he gave me his warning to behave, he lifted his eyebrows and pressed his lips together so hard that the blood would leave them.

When he started to spend nights at her house, I knew the marriage was inevitable. I tried to accept it, running through reasons and motivations, but I knew I never would.

The night he'd come into my room to tell me he had proposed to her, I was in the middle of researching the various theories about Hamlet and why he took so long to avenge the murder of his father. It was almost as if something powerful had arranged for me to be reading *Hamlet* coincidentally at that time. I had just read the lines, "A second time I kill my husband dead, When second husband kisses me in bed."

I didn't look up from the paper I was writing.

"Did you hear me, Mayfair?"

"Yes, Daddy. You're standing only a few feet away."

"Well, can you at least acknowledge it, please?"

I turned around and looked at him. "Are you sure you want to marry her? Marriage is a very serious commitment."

He nearly laughed. "I think I know what I'm doing, Mayfair, yes. Don't tell me you didn't think this day would come."

I nodded. "Are you drawing up a prenuptial?"

He shook his head. "What?"

"It's just sensible nowadays, Daddy, especially with your net worth and the fact that you're going to marry someone who has been through a divorce. She might have trouble with long-term relationships."

"Don't worry about it. I'll take care of it," he said. "Why am I talking about this?" He shook his head as if he could restart our conversation. "Can you please make an effort to get along?"

"I can," I said. He was asking only for an effort.

"Thanks." He turned to start out and then stopped. "This doesn't mean I don't miss and love your mother, Mayfair."

"That's not something you should tell me, Daddy. It's something you should tell Julie."

I didn't think I would ever forget the hard, cold look on his face. "She knows," he said before leaving.

For a moment, it was as if he had taken all the air out of the room with him.

But I didn't cry.

I returned to *Hamlet*.

*We're all in a play*, I thought. We all seemed to have roles assigned to us even before we were born. I knew I did. Whether I liked it or not, I was on a stage. The curtain was open, and the lights were on.

Who knew how the play would look when the final curtain was drawn?

# 4

I had met Allison a few times before my father married her mother, of course. I thought she was a mousy, frightened little girl, but that was just a first impression. In the back of my mind, I stored the thought that she was Julie's daughter. She had to have inherited some of her conniving, a little of her phoniness. The innocent, meek look could very well be a deception. Besides, my father was now going to absorb a great deal of her mother's attention and love. She was probably as unhappy about it as I was, and maybe she would do more to sabotage the relationship than I would. I hoped so.

Julie must have prepared her for meeting me. She was polite but very cautious.

"My mother told me you were very smart," she had said, sounding like it was a criminal offense. "I get mostly Bs."

"Bs sting," I said. "Go for As."

"What?"

*Figure it out yourself*, I wanted to say, but I just laughed.

She looked at me suspiciously. "None of my friends get all As, and the girls I know who get all As don't have many friends," she said.

*This is going to be really something*, I told myself. *I'll be living with a Barbie doll for a stepmother and a ditzy tween who thinks she might catch intelligence from me and lose her friends.* Later, because of who and what she was, it would be easy to use her as a way to get back at both the man who abused me and my stepmother, with whom I eventually shared a mutual dislike.

Fortunately, my father and Julie decided not to have a big wedding, so I didn't have to go through all that business with dresses, flowers, pictures, guest lists, invitations, and menus. They were married by a judge and took a week in London as a honeymoon. Allison stayed with an aunt. I was fine by myself with our maid looking after the house and keeping an eye on me, although I could tell that I intimidated her as much as I did anyone else. She spent most of her time avoiding me. She wasn't afraid of me. I was just too different from the teenage girls she knew, her two nieces and their friends. She was always promising to have them come around to meet me. Maybe my father had put her up to it, but she never did, and although I think I would have liked it, I didn't encourage her.

My father called from London during their honeymoon only once. Whenever he was away on business trips that took a week or more, he always called me two or three times, at least. Anyone would tell me that a man on his honeymoon shouldn't be calling home much. Maybe he knew my mind was already cemented when it came to my opinion of Julie back then. I imagined she would make a face or a comment if he mentioned he was thinking of calling me.

I could just hear her. "Why? She's no child, Roger, and she's more intelligent than the two of us together. Don't baby her. She might even be insulted."

Insulted? It wasn't a thought he would have had, but perhaps she put it into his head and that was why I didn't hear from him again until he returned.

I would never have been insulted by his showing me concern. I never was when he went on other trips. I knew he had confidence and faith in me taking good care of myself and the house. He wasn't calling because of that. He was calling because he loved me. I was good at reading people right from the first time I met them. Daddy used to say half-jokingly that I would be an incredible detective. For a few weeks, he was on a real streak when it came to that, talking about forensic law enforcement, CSI stuff, and even international law enforcement. Like all parents, he probably needed the comfort of knowing there was an endgame here, some target or goal for me to achieve, a goal he could understand, that anyone could. Otherwise, what was the point of all this intelligence?

To me, Julie was a simple read. She was one of those insecure people who needed to be constantly reassured of her importance and was threatened by anyone sharing her stage. From what I already knew about her before she had even moved in to live with us, I thought she would even be jealous of the attention my father paid to *her* daughter.

After spending more time with Allison, I came to the conclusion that she was merely shy and battle-fatigued from what must have been a nasty home life and living in the shadow of a self-centered mother. Julie was surely the kind of mother who flaunted her good looks and made her daughter feel she would never be as beautiful. Maybe that was part of what had destroyed her first marriage. I listened between the lines whenever I heard her describing it, and I felt confident that her ex-husband had grown tired of being married to someone who was more in love with herself than with him. I wondered when my father would grow tired of that, too.

From the details I learned from Allison when I was able to get her to talk about it, the fights between Julie and her ex-husband had bordered on physical. I easily imagined Allison behind a closed door with her hands over her ears and her teeth clenched, half expecting the ceiling to come falling onto her head. I had read sociological and psychological studies on domestic turmoil to do a paper for my history teacher, so I knew that when parents went at each other like that, their children feel they're also being pulled apart. If the children are very young at the time, they actually can develop medical problems, such as trouble with digestion, and learning disabilities.

While reading about all of this domestic turmoil

and its effect on children, I felt like screaming. Could parents be so blind that they couldn't see what they were doing to those they supposedly loved? The truth seemed to be that people hurt those they claimed to love more than they hurt those they didn't. I listened and overheard stories other students told about their home lives. To me, it was very clear what was happening and what the results would be. When I mentioned some of this to my father once, he brightened and said, "Maybe you should be a psychiatrist, Mayfair, a child psychiatrist. You'd be great."

I'd be great at anything I did, I thought. That wasn't the point. What was obvious was that my father needed me to be aiming at something tangible, something he could cite. He couldn't explain that his daughter was going to be a student for most of her life, maybe a philosopher. Everyone else's daughter was going to be a teacher, a lawyer, something in the fashion industry, perhaps a doctor. Something.

All of this, my life at home, my father's expectations, my teachers, and the pressures other students subtly put on me, made me want to scream. Often, I was in the school library when this urge came over me. Imagine what that would have done, what it would have added to the image I had at school. The librarian, Mr. Monk, already thought I was something created in a laboratory. The speed with which I went through books seemed to frighten him. He was a tall, thin man with glassy gray-blue eyes and very thin light brown hair. Whether I imagined it or not, he seemed to step back whenever I approached the desk, as if he expected I might throw a book I was returning at him because I found it poorly written or something.

After having done the paper on domestic crisis, I was sure I could diagnose Allison's problems. She seemed to be a classic example of what could result, which was why I wasn't sympathetic as much as I was curious about her. It was as if a good case study had been delivered to my doorstep. My father wasn't too far off with his latest suggestion for my career. Anything to do with psychology was intriguing, so I was happy to have the opportunity to study something firsthand.

In the beginning, I approached her the way a good therapist might. I wanted to know how much her parents' nasty divorce had destroyed her emotionally. I formed my questions carefully. I wanted to see if she had any talents, abilities that her mother had stifled. What would her feelings be about my father and her relationship with him? Would she see him as an interloper, someone who didn't have any business being in their lives, or would she see him as a wonderful change, a hope?

My father mistook my interest and my talks with Allison for a desire to make her feel like my sister. Maybe that was really a part of it. Maybe he was right that I had always wanted a younger brother or sister, but as he and I already knew, forming relationships, any relationships, didn't come easily for me. I had little faith that they ever would. So, in the beginning, at least, Allison was simply another specimen under my microscopic gaze. I admit I had a tendency to treat most of the girls I met the same way, and consequently, building friendships was very difficult, if not impossible. I had always been like this, but it was even worse after my mother's death. It wasn't entirely my fault.

When I entered junior high school, my teachers often separated me from my classmates every chance they had, putting me in small rooms or in the library to read and work on my own, so even then, I never had much of a chance to have a best friend or, for that matter, any real friends. Maybe the real reason I had so much trouble making friends, trusting people, or committing to a relationship was the pain I had suffered when I lost my mother. I was afraid of losing someone else, wasting my affections. Because I was so intelligent, most people misread my reactions to my mother's untimely death.

My mother had died instantly one morning in our kitchen. The autopsy later showed that she had suffered a cerebral aneurism. I was nine and sitting at the kitchen table at the time. I didn't freeze and start to cry when she collapsed. I called 911, and as calmly as I could, I told the operator that my mother had fallen over her bowl of cereal and was unconscious with her eyes wide open.

"I got her down on the floor and gave her CPR," I said, "but I can't revive her. I think she has had a stroke."

I knew exactly what a stroke was. One of the first books I asked my father to buy for me was a medical book. I loved diagnosing illnesses. My father was always amused at how I interpreted symptoms whenever he or my mother had an ache or pain, but I was not yet set on being a doctor and already, even at only nine years old, wondered if I would be good with patients. I could see them complaining about me for not having a good bedside manner. "She treats me like I'm a specimen and not a person," they would say.

See? I could admit to my problems. Right from the days when I could first read and write, I knew that if you weren't honest about yourself, you would never improve or grow.

After I had called 911, I kept myself from crying, because I knew I had to get the correct information out quickly. Then I called my father and basically told him the same thing, but this time, I did begin to cry. Until the paramedics and my father arrived, I sat on the floor beside her, holding my mother's hand, struggling to think of something else I might do to help her. I could almost hear her telling me to stop pretending, because she was already dead and gone.

"You know better, Mayfair. Concentrate now on helping your father get through this," she would certainly say. "He'll be leaning on you, even at your young age. And he'll be worrying so much about you now. Comfort him. Be warm and loving, Mayfair. I'm depending on you."

My father was there minutes after the paramedics had arrived. He stood off to the side, holding me, as we both watched them work desperately. I knew she was gone, but my father clung to hope. He was surely thinking, *This can't be happening*, while I was thinking of how it had happened, what had gone wrong in her body. When the paramedics shook their heads, my father pressed me tighter to him. I put my arms around him, and we walked out behind the stretcher to watch them put my mother in the ambulance.

My father always claimed that I was holding him up. The strength in my arms was what kept him standing, and the look in my eyes kept him breathing.

All through the funeral, my father never stopped telling people how I'd had the foresight to call 911 before calling him and how I had performed CPR. He assured them that I knew exactly what to do. He was probably still in shock himself and kept himself from breaking down by bragging about me. I found it interesting how people wanted me to describe what had happened in as much detail as I could. It was as if that made them feel better or they thought it would help me get through it. I knew almost all of them were surprised at the cool explanation of the physical details from someone my age, but I would have had to confess something. Ever since I was a little girl, ever since Fish Face, I enjoyed shocking people and seeing the expressions of amazement on their faces.

At least I had a sense of humor about something, right?

Anyway, later on, when my teachers informed Daddy and Julie that I had to be separated from the others more often because I was disruptive, challenging things they said or asking questions that were beyond the subject at hand (at first, they thought I had ADD and was unable to concentrate; later they realized I was merely bored), Julie was embarrassed. She surprised me. She wanted my father to persuade them not to do such a thing. They had the discussion right at the dinner table in front of me, as if I weren't there.

For a moment, a small, slight moment, I thought she really cared about how this would affect me. Was she capable of being concerned for me? Then she continued to talk, and that thought died a swift death.

"Separate her? It sounds like they're afraid she'll contaminate the other students. I have many friends with children in this school, Roger. There'll be talk. It doesn't make us look too good, and it makes me wonder about her relationship with Allison, whether I should be worried or what?"

My father didn't see it that way, but Julie pointed out that Allison was going to grade school at the same school and would eventually have the same teachers I was having.

"You know how teachers are when they have the younger sisters or brothers of students who gave them trouble. They think it's a family trait or something."

"She's not really giving them trouble, not in the sense you mean, Julie," he said patiently.

"It's the same result. Your name gets soiled."

"Soiled?" I said, looking up. "You mean made dirty or disgraced?"

"What?"

"Okay, Mayfair," my father said quickly.

"But this is a stupid discussion, Daddy. Allison and I don't share any genetics. Why would my teachers transfer their feelings about me to her?"

"You can still have an influence on her," Julie said quickly.

"The teachers won't make that connection so quickly. Allison doesn't have the same last name. My father hasn't legally adopted her."

"He will someday," Julie said confidently. "Her father will not oppose it, believe me."

I looked at him. *Give her our name?* It simply hadn't occurred to me. As long as she had her father's name, she was still a stranger, sort of a guest, but that would certainly change if she had my last name, too. And what a mean thing to do to her father, I thought.

"Yes," Julie went on. "You think of everything, but you didn't think of that. You shouldn't have been so annoying in class. Teachers don't forget."

"It's not the reason they gave for moving me out of the classroom," I said. "They know I'm beyond what the class could achieve already. It wasn't fair to me, and it wasn't fair to them."

She simply smirked. The principal might have done better if he had told her I had bad body odor. Despite what my father said, she took it hard. She made him feel guilty, too. She kept harping on what their friends would say. She had married into this family. Her favorite expression about me at home whenever she and my father discussed my school situation and the special way I was being treated by my teachers and the school administration was, "She won't grow up normal."

I couldn't help but correct her. "You mean, I won't grow up to *be* normal, Julie. Or you could say I won't grow up *normally*. Adverbs and nouns," I added, "have different destinies in sentences."

"What? What did she say? And when are you going to make her call me Mother? I'm so embarrassed when she calls me Julie in front of other women, and it's a very bad influence on Allison. She's starting to call me Julie, too. I had to slap her this morning."

Allison was nearly eleven at that time, and I was almost fourteen. I wasn't just reading Jean-Paul Sartre and Albert Camus, which was Greek to my class-mates, but I also read science books like *Lives of a Cell* or *The Evolution of Amphibians* and graduate-level sociological and psychological essays and discussions. I was fascinated by everything in my textbooks and never at a loss for a new question, even if it was about something my teachers would not be presenting for months, maybe years. I was that far ahead in my read-ing and my thinking.

Despite what I had told Julie, I knew in my heart that the real truth was that my teachers shoved me out of the classroom to escape from me, not to make things better for me or the rest of the class. They weren't programmed to work as hard as they would have to work if I remained in the room. Calling what I was doing independent study was just a fancy way of saying, "Get her out of my hair."

They were all probably happy that I had been taken completely out of their school, I thought now as we drove on to Spindrift. There was no longer a pos-sibility of having me as a student, of being challenged and made to look inadequate in front of the other students. Some of them were probably saying they had suspected that someday I might do something as outrageous as what I had done. They might even cite some notorious people who were highly intelligent but had done bad things, just so they could justify their antagonism for someone they had to admit was mentally advanced, someone they should normally cherish and nurture.

"She'll probably end up working for some clandestine organization like an even more secret branch of the CIA," one of them would say, and most of the them would nod.

As we drew closer to Piñon Pine Grove, Julie primped her hair and checked her makeup. She never could understand why I didn't care more about my appearance. She actually encouraged me to wear lipstick and paint my toenails and fingernails when I was eleven. Many of the girls in my class were doing just that.

One of the happiest but soon to be frustrating days she spent with me was instructing me in how to put on makeup at her vanity table. I was there because I didn't want to disappoint my father. Allison stood off to the side, watching jealously. I would have gladly given her my seat and let her take my place. My mind kept drifting back to the calculus problem I was attacking in the twelfth-grade math book I was using, so I was inattentive. I was sloppy about putting on fingernail polish.

"Whenever you have no interest in something, you rush it and mess it up," Julie complained, moaning as if I were ruining one of her precious works of art or something. "Maybe some of your grade-school teachers were right. You have ADD."

"No. They were wrong. They've admitted that. They're not the best judges of the problem, despite being teachers."

"How could you say that? They were your teachers."

"You need to be a doctor to diagnose it properly, and many teachers use it as a convenient excuse for why students don't pay attention to their boring presentations of material. Don't you recall having teachers like that? My father does."

She stared at me a moment, at a loss for any way to argue, which was something she desperately needed to do. "I don't care. That's not the point I'm making," she said. When she became frustrated, she always wagged her head, which made her upper torso wag, too. Sometimes she did it so hard I thought she might fall off her chair.

I sighed deeply. "Okay, Julie. What is the point you're making?" I asked.

"Don't you want to look pretty? You have a very pretty face, your mother's eyes, and if you brushed your hair properly, it wouldn't look like a rat's nest."

"Have you ever seen one?" I asked her.

"One what?"

"Rat's nest."

"Oh, Mayfair. It's just an expression."

"Yes, but do you know why people use it? You should know what you're saying when you say something, Julie."

She shook her head and muttered to herself, "Why am I even trying?"

"We compare messy things to a rat's nest because rats build their nests from an assortment of items, including anything that attracts their interest. Their young defecate in them before they're old enough to leave the nests and sleep in their own mess."

"Oh, my God, that's disgusting."

"Maybe then you don't mean to compare my hair to a rat's nest," I said.

She lowered her chin to her chest and stared down sadly at her makeup, all her wonderful new powders and creams, the special scissors, and the variety of brushes, all that beautification magic. She looked like she was about to burst into tears. I must say, from the time my father married her until that moment, I had always found her as curious as I would a new insect. She rarely read a book. She collected fashion and celebrity gossip magazines like a squirrel storing acorns and spent half her day getting ready to go to lunch with other women like herself and the rest of the day talking about what they had talked about at lunch.

Was she a product of evolution going in a different direction?

"I remember when my mother first permitted me to wear makeup and instructed me in how to do it," she said softly, sucking back her tears. "I was very excited, and when I went downstairs to show my father, he looked like he was going to cry. 'My little girl is becoming a young woman,' he said. I was sad and happy at the same time."

She turned to me, narrowing her eyes as if she were the one looking at a specimen under a microscope, and not vice versa.

"Doesn't any of this excite you or interest you at all? You must have some reaction to it, right?"

"It's curious," I admitted.

She looked at Allison to see if she understood anything I was saying, but Allison stood there with that habitual smirk of hers. Unfortunately, she had her mother's ugly habit of dropping the corners of her mouth.

"Curious? What do you mean, curious?" Julie asked.

"We make fun of primitive people for coloring their faces, but here we turn it into a high domestic art form."

"What? You're saying putting on makeup makes us primitive?"

"Consider the whole picture, Julie. Television commercials imply that if you use their products, you'll be as beautiful as the models. They airbrush them and touch up their faces in magazine advertisements and photographs. It's dishonest and makes every girl, every woman, frustrated and unhappy with herself. Look at Allison. She's dying to get to this vanity table, and she's only in the fifth grade. You should take that television set out of her room. It's a carnival."

"No!" Allison cried.

"Don't change the subject, Mayfair. Don't you want to use makeup, wear lipstick, and have your hair look nicer?"

"Not particularly," I said. "At least, not now. I'm not in any mating season."

"Mating season?" She looked like she would cry again.

"I want to use makeup," Allison said. "I want to look nicer now. Let me."

Julie shook her body as if she were throwing off water like a drenched dog. "This is giving me a headache," she said. "I wanted to do something nice for you, and you're giving me a headache. Curious, primitive . . . I've never heard any young girl talk like you do."

"It's interesting, that's all I'm saying, Julie. You know, it wasn't that long ago that girls were forbidden to wear lipstick until they were at least eighteen," I told her. "Think about the changes in social mores that have occurred not only over the past century but over the past decade. There are girls in high school now with tattoos on their necks, breasts, and rear ends, and their parents didn't stop them. Girls wear rings in their noses, their navels, and their lips. They punch holes in their cheeks. Now, there is a tribe in Central Africa—"

"Stop!" she cried, and popped out of her seat with her hands over her ears. Both Allison and I were a little shocked at her burst of frustration. She relaxed and regained her composure, because Allison was looking at her wide-eyed. I might have been smiling. "I need to see about dinner," Julie said. "Either finish putting on your nail polish or wash off what you've done." She scrunched up her shoulders and left her bedroom.

I looked at myself in the mirror. I did have my mother's green eyes, slightly almond-shaped. I had naturally long eyelashes but still didn't understand why Julie coveted them so. My nose was slightly longer than I would have liked, but it was straight, and I had full grapefruit-pink lips that I knew Julie also coveted. Whenever she complimented me on my rich, smooth complexion, she sounded like she was complaining. I knew she thought my beauty was wasted. She wasn't alone. I had heard that sort of comment bitterly made by other girls in school from time to time. I wasn't unappreciative of my good looks. I just wasn't as absorbed with them as she and the other girls were. Maybe that was a fault. I was thinking more about it lately.

My menarche came later than for most girls, but once it had, my body began a determined march to maturity, led by full, perky breasts. I read everything I could get my hands on in articles or books that discussed the subject of female development, and then I analyzed my own reactions to my budding sexual desires. I even thought about keeping a journal about my own development, but I decided there was really nothing unusual enough about me to warrant the effort.

That was the way I was.

I analyzed everything I did or started to do and determined how much time and energy I should spend on it.

Like this makeup thing.

It was easier to wash off the three nails I had painted, give my hair four or five quick brushes so it wouldn't fall over my eyes, and then get back to my calculus.

"You're being ungrateful to my mother," Allison said. The word *ungrateful* was in practically every other sentence her mother tossed in my direction.

"Do you know the meaning of gratitude, or are you just parroting your mother?"

"Don't call me a parrot!" she screamed, and walked out when I began to laugh.

However, there was no question that Julie saw all that as another example of my deliberate failure rather than appreciating what she was trying to do for me. She complained to my father at dinner.

"After all," she said, "I'm making the best effort I can, Roger. I offer to take her to get new clothes, new shoes, anything, but she shows no interest. She has to meet me at least halfway."

He nodded and told me I should be more appreciative. He tried to sound stern, but I knew he hadn't reprimanded me enough to please her. She sulked her way to bedtime.

I suppose what I eventually did to Allison and her English teacher, Mr. Taylor, in a way pleased her, despite how she reacted. It finally turned my father against me and justified her constant complaining about me.

Right now, it was the only reason for any regret, the only reason for my telling my father I was sorry.

But let me explain how I happened now to be in my father's car, with my bags in the trunk and my stepmother, at the prospect of getting me out of the house and out of her hair, practically panting like a dog about to be untied and let free to run.

# 5

I have this tendency to compare Julie to animals often. I remember thinking she must have charged like an elephant in heat at my bedroom door one Sunday afternoon a few months ago. First, I heard her footsteps pounding on the hallway floor. Most of the time, she wore sharp-heeled shoes that clicked over the Spanish tiles, but this particular day, they sounded more like the rat-a-tat of a machine gun. She was moving that quickly and determinedly. Then I heard the rattling of the doorknob, and when I didn't respond instantly, I actually saw the hinges strain. Adrenaline must have been pouring out of her ears.

I had looked up reluctantly from *The History of Western Civilization* to pay attention. I was nearly finished with the book and hated the interruption, especially if it was Julie doing the interrupting. Most of the time, it was about something so minor or insignificant that I could barely listen.

"Why is this door locked?" she screamed. I

envisioned her putting her lips to the hinges to be sure
her voice carried through. "Mayfair! I know you hear
me. Don't pretend you're asleep!" She slapped the
door with the palm of her hand so hard I was sure it
turned bloodred.

"Coming!" I shouted back, but I took my time. I
took so long, in fact, that she rattled the handle again,
this time so hard I thought surely she would break it,
which only made me take longer. I stood there and let
her shout my name one more time and slap the door
again before I unlocked it.

When I opened it, she was standing there breathing hard, her shoulders rising and falling with every
deep, quick breath, her face looking like she had been
in direct sunlight too long. She was so upset she'd
permitted strands of her dark brown pampered hair to
pop up like broken guitar strings and her mascara to
run. Her lips trembled as the rage washed over her face
in small tremors. I was waiting for her to explode and
shatter herself all over the walls and the floor.

In her hands was a book I had lent to Allison. She
opened it and held it up with two hands in front of
herself like a shield so that the cover was facing me.

"What's wrong, Julie?" I asked in a calm, almost
sweet-sounding voice.

"What's wrong? What's wrong? How dare you
give this book to Allison!"

"I didn't give it to her. I lent it to her."

"You know what I mean. Why would you give her
this book?"

"She's more than thirteen years old now, Julie.

Four girls in her class are pregnant. They all probably have mothers like you, terrified to mention S-E-X. You should be thanking me. That happens to be a well-written book on the subject by a renowned expert in the field, presented in a clear, simple manner so someone her age can understand it all easily."

"Thanking you?" She swallowed hard. "Thanking you? A clear, simple manner? You call this simple?"

She turned the book around, flipped some pages, and held up a drawing of a naked man and a naked woman in the missionary position. She turned it back to herself and read, " 'The missionary position is a male-superior sex position in which the woman lies on her back and—"

"I know what it is, Julie. The problem is that Allison doesn't, or she didn't. I hope she got through most of it before you confiscated it, which I think was a mistake."

"Of course I confiscated it. I'm her mother!"

"I know you're her mother, but what world do you live in? Do you think Allison hasn't watched soft porn with her friends, French-kissed at parties, had a boy's hand in her blouse and in her pants?"

She recoiled and then shot back like a rattlesnake. "That's absolutely disgusting. Of course she hasn't. I'd know if anything of that sort happened."

"How would you know?" I asked. "You treat her like she's never menstruated."

She opened and closed her mouth without making a sound.

"If you're not going to permit her to read it, may I

have my book back, please? I'm doing some research on the fruit fly and want to make some comparisons." I wasn't, but I thought that was a funny thing to say.

She didn't. She thrust the book at me. "You can be sure that your father is going to hear about this," she said.

"Hear about it? Sex? I think he knows about it."

"You know exactly what I mean. Don't be . . . be . . ."

"*Facetious*? I think that's the word you're searching for," I said. "It means joking inappropriately, perhaps to satirize or show contempt."

She did what she usually did when she couldn't get the best of me. She nodded repeatedly and looked like one of those toy dogs people placed in the rear windows of their cars. I felt like reaching out and putting my hand under her chin to stop her before her head rolled off.

"I don't understand you," I said in an even calmer voice. "Didn't you want to know these things when you were your daughter's age? Aren't you happy that there are better ways to learn this stuff than listening to misinformation other girls spout in bathrooms or sneaking terrible sex books into your room and reading them under the covers?"

"Allison is . . . is . . ."

"What? She's probably masturbated. Are you saying she is a virgin? Are you absolutely sure? And what if she loses her virginity inappropriately? Wouldn't that upset you more? When you calm down and think about it later, you will definitely thank me," I said with that stone-cold confidence that assured most people that I was right.

Her eyes looked like two balls lit up in a slot machine. I felt like reaching out for an invisible lever on the side of her head and pulling it down. If I got two bloodred pupils, her mouth would open and spill out silver dollars. She opened and closed that mouth, and then she spun on her heels and walked away with her back hoisted like a flag on her iron-pole spine. I envisioned smoke streaming out of her ears.

I closed my door quietly and returned to my book. Usually, I could turn Julie on and off like a light switch, but for some reason, this latest confrontation between us annoyed me more than usual. I had trouble shutting it out of my mind, and it wasn't because I felt any sense of guilt about it or was worried about how my father would react.

My stepsister, Allison, was, in my view, very immature for a girl her age living in California in the twenty-first century. I really did believe I was doing her a favor. It was one of those rare times when I did something in this house without the initial purpose of annoying Julie.

Like most mothers, Julie wasn't even measuring her daughter in terms of herself at this age, recalling the questions and concerns she'd had. Worse, it was as if these mothers believed nothing had changed since they were teenagers. Information for those who sought it was accessible much more quickly and easily. They either were ignorant of or ignored what their daughters could learn on the internet, what sorts of materials they passed around and discussed, and what their personal experiences with boys already were. Had she even ever heard of friends with benefits? Didn't she know the birth rate among teenagers? Didn't she go to the movies or know about sexually explicit films deliberately targeting girls her daughter's age? I could rattle off statistics that would make her head spin. I could have wiped the floor with her if she hadn't run away.

Although I tried, I was unable to shut it out of my mind. Maybe it was because I wasn't happy about my own romantic life, which was a zero. Even though I was good at pretending that it didn't bother me, acting convincingly as if I wasn't interested, it did bother me. It bothered me a lot, and I was very interested. If my mother were alive, I'd have someone to talk to about it. I certainly couldn't talk to Julie or my father, and at this time, I hadn't connected with Joy and still had no girlfriend with whom I could spend hours on the phone, not that Joy was ever a great source of comfort or information for me. I didn't even have anyone to email frequently. There was just no one yet whom I trusted enough to reveal anything more than the weather report.

I couldn't remember when I was last invited to a party or when other girls in my class asked me to do something with them. It was probably a few years, and back then, I was only invited because of my father and his business relationship with the parents of the girl. When I arrived, I could see that no one cared to talk to me. The parents of the girl whose house it was most likely pushed her to be civil to me, and she was barely that. It wasn't difficult for me to see the lack of sincerity.

The girls who finally did talk to me did so on their own initiative, speaking to me as if they were with some foreigner who had just barely learned English. The questions they asked gradually got more and more annoying as their confidence grew. I'm sure they saw how uncomfortable I was getting. Perhaps I wasn't so hard to beat after all. Maybe if they were good enough, they could bring me to tears or send me running from the room. Then they could gather in a clump and giggle as they congratulated one another.

"How come you don't ever have a party at your house or hang with anyone at the mall?"

"Don't you think any of the boys are good-looking at our school?"

"Are you afraid of boys? Is that what happens when a girl is so smart?"

"Who do you dream of being with, at least? What actor?"

"What sorts of fantasies does someone like you have?"

They fired the questions at me so quickly I couldn't answer one. Finally, they stopped and waited.

"There are some good-looking boys at our school," I said. "But when they open their mouths to speak, their faces fall off for me."

"Huh? Fall off? How can someone's face fall off?" Willa Marley asked me. I remembered her question because I could see that she wasn't quite sure whether I was speaking literally or figuratively. Perhaps I did know something about some sort of disease that caused a person's face to fall off.

"It just slides off his skull," I said casually. "Like hot melting butter sliding off a pan."

"Ugh."

"That's not true. That never happens. You're just afraid of boys, aren't you?" Victoria Walters asked. I remember how small her eyes were, beady, how they seemed to retract while her nose grew pointier, and how her mouth twisted, with her lips becoming pale.

"I'm certainly not afraid of boys. Why should I be? Do you think they have some magical powers they hold over us? I'm not afraid of sex, certainly. It's not a disease, and it doesn't require a great deal of intelligence to perform it."

"Perform it?" Victoria said, and laughed with the others as her chorus. "Do you do it on a stage?"

"You're defining *perform* too narrowly."

"Huh? Just answer the question."

"Yes, I'm just as interested in boys and sex as any of you are. I'm just not as obvious about it. I don't walk around with my tongue hanging out like some of you."

"Maybe you should," Victoria flung back at me. "Maybe then you'd attract someone."

They all laughed and shook their heads but still peeled away like frightened birds. I watched them go off into corners to tell the boys about me and laugh. I told myself it didn't bother me. After all, I had gotten the best of them, hadn't I? Who cared what they thought?

But sometimes I did feel like a potted plant, bored and unhappy, just waiting for someone to care enough to water me.

Lately, I felt invisible in my school when it came to boys anyway, even though I had been returned to regular classes. That came as a surprise. I didn't know it at the time, but both my father and Julie had gone to the administration and requested that I not be separated from the rest of the students when I was in high school. The guidance counselor, Mr. Martin, agreed. He said it was damaging to me socially.

"She has to grow as a person and as a student," he said. "I hope she considers joining one of the clubs or going out for drama, something that will help her have social intercourse."

"That would be wonderful," Julie said. "We worry a great deal about her."

I had heard all about it afterward. My father told me about some of the things they'd said when he came into my room to explain why he wanted me returned to classes so I could be more of a regular student. How would I explain to him now that everyone, including some of my teachers, looked right through me most of the time, whether or not I was in a regular classroom? Actually, it was more difficult than ever for me to function within the normal classroom structure. I was happier working on my own. Being in regular classes held me back.

As far as socializing went, I couldn't force myself on the rest of the students, either, by joining a club or a sport, even if it was something like chess club. No one would want to play against me, and all of them would resent how I left them in the dust. The envy and resentment would only be compounded. How could I describe the situation without sounding like I was whining?

Despite how much he loved me, my father would have to face facts, and some of those facts were that other students either were disinterested in putting in the extra effort to make friends with me or simply afraid of me or badly put off by me. We couldn't depend on my teachers doing anything to help, especially those who knew they were incapable of motivating me very much and saw me as evidence of some failure on their part. It was very clear to all that I could do very well without them. Why should they have any concern for me?

I couldn't blame them entirely. The school day was already overwhelming them, with growing class sizes even in our expensive private school and the disciplining they had to do, without adding special attention to someone like me, perhaps special lesson plans or one-on-one sessions. They were struggling to keep up with their normal responsibilities. Watching them and how they were weighted down soured me on ever pursuing a teaching career of any kind.

Yet I wasn't going to disagree with my guidance counselor about all that he was trying to do. It wasn't difficult to see what a miserable school life I was having, if it could even be called a school life. I might as well be attending school on a deserted island or maybe in a monastery where everyone had taken a vow not only of silence but of lack of sight. Never look at each other, and, especially, never look at me.

After I was forced to return, it got so that in class, no matter what subject it was and what we were doing at the time, I could read whatever I wanted even while the teachers were talking. None of my teachers ever bothered me or reprimanded me for it. I had yet to get a grade lower than 100 in any of my subjects. If I ever did pay attention or raise my hand, it was because my teacher had done or said something incorrect. It got so that they looked frightened if I showed any interest in what they were saying. They tried to ignore me, and if they did so long enough, they knew I would put my hand down and go back to what I'd been doing.

There was nothing a teacher hated more than being corrected by a student, especially one like me. Some reluctantly said thank you, but most brushed over it as if it were just a small glitch, not worth more attention. Lately, it had gotten so that even the other students resented me for doing it, as if I had no right to ruin their image of their brilliant teachers.

I had met few teachers so far who would put their egos behind their interest in truly educating someone. Those who did were more secure about themselves and didn't mind a student teaching them, too.

One of them, my tenth-grade English teacher, Mr. Madeo, said, "You're always a student, even when you become a teacher. Once you think you know it all, you're a puppet, with ignorance pulling the strings. Don't stop asking questions, Mayfair."

The point is that the attitudes of most of my

teachers toward me spilled over onto my classmates. They, too, avoided talking to me, even nodding at me in the hallway. I usually sat alone in the cafeteria. Others could accidentally bump into me in the hallways and act as if they had bumped into the wall itself. No one apologized. Sometimes my father brought Allison and me to school on his way to work. Other times, Julie had to do it, and she usually picked us up. If I wanted to go somewhere else, I called a taxi. None of the students who drove ever asked me to go somewhere with them. This was supposed to be the year that I got my driver's license, and my father was getting me my own car. No one even mentioned it now. Like most teenagers, I thought that once I had my license and a car, I'd gain in popularity. I didn't want to admit to myself that it was a motive for getting my license and my own car, but it was.

Of course, I told myself that those kinds of friends wouldn't be sincere. They would use me and make me feel foolish for trying to win their friendship that way. I wondered why other girls and boys my age didn't see all the phoniness hovering around them. Maybe they didn't want to see it. Maybe that was the solution: ignore the truth so that you could feel happy. Perhaps, deep down, that was what my father was doing when it came to Julie. No one who fools himself wants to be reminded of it.

I looked at the book I had given Allison and reread some passages describing foreplay and orgasm. Even though the other girls in my class never spoke to me about anything social, I couldn't help overhearing them talking in the locker room before and after PE or in the cafeteria when they sat at a table close to mine. Most of them struck me as airheads, but I was still somewhat fascinated by the discussions. It surprised me just how much intimate stuff they would reveal.

"He got behind me, put his hand under my blouse, and said I should let him pretend to be my bra," Joyce Brooker told the others one afternoon. "While he kissed me on my neck."

"And?" Cora Addison asked when there was too long of a pause.

"My father came home early."

She was doing this in her own house? Maybe that made it more exciting. Would I want to be alone with any of the boys in this school at my home, in my room? How would I feel if Julie or my father burst in on us? Embarrassed, titillated, or just annoyed at the interruption?

"He got his hands out just in time, but . . ."

"But what?" Denise Hartman asked.

"My father looked at my face and knew something. He didn't say anything, but he told my mother, and she gave me a lecture. I don't know what would have happened if my father hadn't come home early," Joyce admitted. "And I still don't know what will happen next time, despite my mother's lecture."

I thought it was a stunning confession. The others looked mesmerized, lost in their own fantasies, wondering if they would surrender completely, even if it wasn't safe sex. It was written on their faces. They were excited just by the possibility.

As was I.

A similar thing happened whenever I read information about sex and then thought of myself, just as I was doing after my confrontation with Julie about Allison. I'd see myself with a boy, even with a teacher. It wasn't that I grew frightened as much as I grew nervous and unsure of what I would do. The only time I felt as if I were skating on thin ice at school was when it came to boys, talking to them, reacting to their rare flirtations or approaches. Being scientific about it or pointing out that I knew what they were up to was the only way I could be comfortable, but what boy liked that? It was like tearing off their masks or telling the emperor he was naked, that he wore no clothes.

It was clear to me that boys were more comfortable with girls who were either really dumb about it all or good at pretending to be. Boys needed their egos pumped up more than girls did, I concluded. But what other girl would even care to think about it as much? Many times, I was tempted to say something to one of the girls after I overheard a conversation she had been having with a boy she apparently liked. I felt the need to warn her, to guide her, as if she and I were on the same team, but one look at her face told me that I would have my advice or concerns for her thrown back into my face.

"What do you know about it?" she would surely snap at me. "You have the love life of a mannequin." It would bring a crowd of gawking onlookers, who would surely enjoy my being taken down. I wasn't going to put myself in that sort of jeopardy. It wasn't worth it.

However, I was as guilty as Julie when it came to imposing how I felt on Allison. I knew she was thinking about boys constantly now, and I had offered her the book thinking that knowledge would make her feel as comfortable and as safe as it made me feel. Of course, I knew that she would be titillated by it, especially the graphics, just like I was, even though I knew in my heart that it wouldn't be enough. She wanted her romance novels and enjoyed toying with her own emotions. She didn't want to explore in a classroom with a health teacher. She wanted to explore in the rear seat of a car or in a bedroom when no one was home. What I had to offer her would educate her, but it wouldn't satisfy her. I knew that. I knew because it wasn't satisfying me.

Once, when my father was trying to step into my mother's empty shoes and give me some advice about boys and dating, he told me I shouldn't depend on my superior intelligence when it came to physical relationships.

"Just because you're miles above the guy you're with, that doesn't mean you won't lose control, Mayfair. Lots of smart people get into trouble. It happens so quickly sometimes that you don't even know it. You know the drill."

I was acting as if I were listening with half an ear, but I was totally absorbed by what he was telling me. "Drill?"

"Sure. You're at a party. You want to be one of the girls, so you drink or do whatever, too, and then you go off with someone, and you go too far."

"Oh, Daddy, please," I said. "I'm not Suzie Bubble Brain."

"Don't be arrogant when it comes to your emotions, Mayfair," he warned. "Aside from those who were forced into it, I bet there's not one pregnant teenager who didn't know the consequences but did it anyway. Regrets come too easy."

"Okay," I said. "I get the point." I just wanted him to stop, not because I didn't appreciate his concern for me but because he was nudging places in my brain and stimulating thoughts and feelings that frankly frightened me.

All my life, I felt I had complete control of everything and everyone around me.

Sex was an area where I knew I might not.

He shrugged and smiled, holding up his hands. "I've done my duty," he said.

I thought of all that as I thumbed dreamily through the sex manual I had given Allison. I found the graphic drawings and some of the photographs with detailed explanations more than just interesting. They were fascinating, because I was able to see myself in the drawings and some of the photographs. It was like getting on a roller coaster. I was sure that Allison, even though she was much older than I had been when I learned all this, had similar reactions and feelings.

Actually, despite how Julie had reacted, I still was hoping that Allison would come to me and we could talk about it, the way two real sisters might, but Julie wasn't going to let that happen if she had any say about it, especially now. It had gotten to where she was frightened of me herself, not just for Allison. It had been gnawing away at her for some time now. I could feel it. This was why she was at my father so much, demanding that he rein me in as if I were a wild horse, complaining about the influence I could have on Allison. She was champing at the bit to complain every chance she got now, and I was sure she believed she had finally found the in-house scandal big enough to get me severely reprimanded, maybe turn me into a meek and obedient stepdaughter. I braced myself for the inevitable confrontation.

An hour after he had come home from work, my father was knocking on my door. When I opened it, he just stood there shaking his head, a look of great disappointment on his face.

"Okay, Mayfair, exactly what did you do now? Julie is fit to be tied."

"Now, there's a good idea."

"Stop it."

"She's being ridiculous, Daddy," I said. "I didn't give Allison a porn magazine, you know."

"What did you give her?"

"I gave her a scientific, informative manual written by a college professor."

I went to my bed and got the book. I handed it to him, and he opened it and thumbed through some of it. "Kind of graphic stuff," he said. "Where did you get it?"

"I bought it over the internet."

"Didn't they ask your age?"

"That's not a work of pornography, Daddy. It's

a scientific discussion about sex. Besides, what is my age?"

"I'm not talking about your mental age, Mayfair."

"What's more important? Days? Months? An accumulation of years? There are twenty-year-olds who shouldn't be driving or drinking and certainly not having unprotected sex and becoming parents."

"Okay, okay," he said, handing the book back to me. "I'm not going to debate you about that. However, you have to remember that Julie is Allison's mother. She should be the one who decides what she reads, not you. You want to give her something, you ask her mother first. Do you understand? Do you?" he followed when I didn't respond.

"It's not brain surgery."

"Don't be smart, Mayfair."

"You know, there's an interesting word, Daddy, *smart*. If someone just overheard you saying that, they'd think you were a bad father. Don't you want your daughter to be intelligent?"

"Stop it, Mayfair."

I would have, but I couldn't stand him always taking Julie's side, so I continued lecturing him, instead of crying or screaming. "*Smart* also means witty but often in an insolent way, and that's what you mean, I believe. *Smart* can also mean fashionable, as in 'That's a smart-looking suit.' We also hear it used to mean accomplished, talented, as in 'He's a right smart ballplayer.'"

We stared at each other.

Then he shook his head and walked out, closing

my door softly. I had frustrated and defeated him again, but I didn't feel good about it. I flopped onto my bed and looked up at the ceiling. Sometimes, maybe more often than I'd care to admit, I hated myself. It was as if I couldn't stop myself from being who I didn't want to be, who they expected me to be.

I should have known then. If I couldn't stop myself, how could I really do anything about the future I really wanted?

No wonder I was in a car being taken away like someone who was going to a mental clinic.

# 6

Before all this, there were many people, even many other students, who thought I was a lucky girl. I had a wealthy father, I lived in a beautiful house, I was attractive enough to draw the envy of other girls and the interest of men who didn't know me yet, and I was a super-brilliant student, a rock star in the educational system. Because I would never let them, no one ever saw the other side of me, what I might admit now was the tragic side. I didn't want to give anyone the satisfaction of knowing that I wasn't as perfect as I was thought to be. I had come to rely on that image, depend on it to get me through any crisis, whether it was of my own making or not. I should have known it wasn't going to be enough.

Only my high-school guidance counselor, Mr. Martin, had an inkling about what I was really feeling about myself, what my weaknesses and deficiencies were. When I had first entered high school, he really did try to get me to join some extracurricular activity like the drama club. He gave me a copy of the school play to read and told me I would enjoy the experience. Even though I thought he might be right, I resisted. I didn't want to be on any girls' teams, either. It wasn't because I didn't like plays or sports. To be honest, I was afraid of the interchanges I would have with the others. Simply put, I was afraid I wouldn't be able to be a teenager after all, and I had yet to fail at anything in my life. Nevertheless, Mr. Martin was persistent, reasonable, and logical. He would call me in to talk with him periodically, stop me in the hallways, or repeat the advice whenever he had an opportunity to speak with my father especially.

"I know they see you as someone very different, Mayfair, and that's why they don't warm up to you," Mr. Martin told me, "but maybe if you join something and they get to know you better, they won't be so put off by your intellectual achievements."

"I don't care that much about making friends here, Mr. Martin," I said. I couldn't argue with his premise, so I tried a quick escape.

But he wasn't buying it. "Yes, you do," he insisted.

Finally, he gave up, even though I was sure that he could see in my face that I didn't mean what I told him. I wasn't always as good at hiding my feelings as I thought I was, especially from someone trained to see through the fog of excuses and fears.

Of course I would have loved to have a best friend, someone else to talk to, to share my intimate thoughts and feelings. Of course I wanted to giggle and laugh over silly things and talk for hours about things that didn't matter. But I wouldn't admit it, and I wouldn't do anything to make it happen.

Frustrated with me, Mr. Martin became intrigued with the possibility of my being accepted at the country's most prestigious colleges. While still in high school, I had been able to take a number of college classes and had enough credits to enter most universities as a junior. We had a meeting about the situation, but my father wasn't happy about Mr. Martin's priorities. He was afraid I was moving too quickly. On the other hand, it was difficult to argue against Mr. Martin's point that I was wasting my abilities.

"I know she's bored with her classes here," he told my father. "Her teachers are doing the best they can for her, but another year in high school, at least one like this, might not be the best choice."

"I'm not worried about her mental development. I'm worried about her social development," my father replied. "I mean, you were the one who brought up the problem of her not developing fully as a person if we kept her separated from her classmates. We agreed and insisted that she be put back into regular classes. Why isn't it helping?" he asked.

I was surprised to hear him say that in front of me. He sounded frightened about it, frightened that I would never be a fully rounded person and never be happy. Although he did try to get me to do some of the things Mr. Martin and some of my earlier teachers had suggested, my father never gave me the impression that he thought there was anything actually freakish about me. He was always proud of my accomplishments, but since he had married Julie and she was constantly complaining about me, he began to look at me differently.

And because he was doing that, I started doing it, too.

Hours after my tiff with Julie about lending Allison the sex manual and my sarcastic reaction to my father, I looked at myself in the mirror and thought about all this. Suddenly, I began to wonder if I really was as pretty and as sexy as some of the other girls in my class. Maybe those who gave me compliments weren't doing it simply to be nice. Even Julie had, reluctantly or not, complimented my features and expressed some envy.

Maybe it was because of the way Julie had come after me for giving Allison the book on sex or maybe it was the way my father was seeing me now, but whatever the reason, I decided to do something I hadn't much done up to now. I decided to improve my appearance to see if that would make any difference at school. Perhaps I could stop being seen as part of the woodwork, fading into the hallways and the backs of classrooms. Maybe I could sparkle, too, and from something other than my intellectual capacities. Perhaps this would lead me to socialize and be the more well-rounded person everyone seemed to want me to be. I had to start somewhere if I was going to attempt a change, and my looks were the most logical and easiest place to begin.

Whether I liked it or not, Julie was the expert when it came to that, I thought, and one thing I knew was to go to the best source for the information you wanted and needed. If I ignored her, I'd be just like any fool who refused to face facts, scientific truths, just to satisfy his or her prejudices.

I surprised her at dinner that night. She was still pouting over my giving Allison the book and my comments when she had come to reprimand me. She wouldn't look at me. Her jaw looked frozen. It wasn't uncommon for her to go into such a determined sulk so she could extract more sympathy from my father, but I could feel it was more intense. My father looked at me, practically pleading for me to mend fences.

"I want to apologize," I began.

"Oh," she said petulantly. She still didn't look at me. She was capable of childlike tantrums and could sulk for hours, if not days, until she got her way.

"Yes. A while back, I was ungrateful when you went out of your way to help me with makeup."

"What?" She looked at my father. Of course, both she and my father were expecting a different apology.

"You do all that so well," I said. "I should have paid more attention to the lessons you were trying to give me." Giving her any compliment was like swallowing spoiled milk, but I did it.

"Well, I did try to help you."

"Maybe you can show it all to me again. And I would appreciate your suggestions about my hair."

"Your hair?"

"I know the clothes I wear are blah, too," I admitted. "You're right about the colors I choose. Almost all of my clothes are not in fashion and don't flatter my figure at all."

She straightened up and nodded. "Exactly. I've tried to get you to see that, and . . ."

"You have. I was foolish to refuse your offers of

help. I should appreciate that there's someone like you so easily available to me to give me good advice. I hope you are still willing to do that."

Even though this wasn't the place my father had hoped I would go, he was beaming. Allison, however, was staring at me with suspicious eyes. I was stealing away her mother's attention, her mother's concentration on her when it came to these things, but Julie enjoyed being in the spotlight.

"Well, thank you for saying that."

"The point is, I've come to the logical conclusion that I need some help with this."

"Of course you do, and that's nothing to be ashamed about."

"I'm not ashamed," I snapped.

Her smile began to fade. Allison started to smile.

*Can't she get anything right?* I thought. I softened my tone again. "I'm simply admitting that it's an area in which I am deficient, an area in which you obviously have great expertise."

"Exactly. I've been tutored by some of the best cosmeticians and hairstylists and have followed fashion studiously all my life."

"She must like somebody who's not paying attention to her," Allison piped up, smiling with suspicious eyes.

My father looked from her to me. "Oh?" he said.

"No, that's not it," I said.

"You don't have to be afraid to admit you have a crush on someone," Julie said, enjoying my discomfort for a change. "If you have someone special in mind, it's better if you describe him a bit."

"There isn't anyone special." I looked at Allison. "If there was, I wouldn't need to be coming to you now, Julie."

"Well, there will be," she assured me. "You have the natural beauty that makes it easy to work miracles."

I could see that Allison wasn't pleased with her mother giving me compliments. I wanted to lean over and assure her that I wasn't looking for them, that I couldn't care less about what her mother thought of my looks, or me, for that matter, but I kept myself in check.

"Right after dinner, we'll do another lesson in makeup, and I'll look at your hair again." Julie sat back and looked at me as if seeing me for the first time. Then she nodded to herself. "As you often say, it's not brain surgery."

Oh, how she was enjoying this, but for me, it was like going to the dentist. It had to be done.

"I think we should make an appointment with my hairstylist this Saturday, after which we can do some shopping and see if we can make some real improvements in your wardrobe. You'll need new shoes, too, and a few decent purses. I think she needs a more feminine-looking watch," she told my father.

"Of course. I was going to get her one for her birthday, but . . ."

"You can get her another, something more special, perhaps. I think I know what you need, Mayfair."

"Thank you," I said.

"Can I go, too?" Allison asked.

"No," Julie said. "I don't want to be distracted.

I shop for you all the time, and besides, it won't be much fun for you to stand there and watch me buying things for Mayfair and not you."

Allison seemed disappointed, but she also looked at me with real envy, and I couldn't remember her doing that before. It didn't bother me. Actually, it made me feel a little better, even a little lightheaded.

My father looked like a weight had been lifted off his shoulders. I didn't want him to get too excited and happy about this. Once I had gotten what I wanted from Julie, I didn't intend to do much more with her. She would never replace my mother, and I would never call her anything but Julie. In my eyes, she was simply a good source for this particular information. I'd put her back on the shelf afterward, just as I put back a library book or clicked off a website.

However, days later, I couldn't deny that I was happy about the changes she had made in my appearance. She did have a good hairstylist, who complimented me on the health of my hair. Julie stood by and oversaw it all, concentrating on the smallest details and making me feel like some sort of celebrity. I had to admit that the cut she and the stylist chose did change my whole look, and that change began changes inside me, too. I could feel a growing confidence that came from the way others in the salon looked at my metamorphosis from someone with potential to someone who could invite cameras.

From the salon, we went to one of Julie's favorite boutiques. Everything was quite expensive, all created by one designer or another. She made me try on and model a few different styles, discussing every one with the store's sales manager, a French woman who obviously knew more than she did. At the end of the day, I had a half dozen new outfits and pairs of shoes. She even took me to get some costume jewelry, especially earrings, and made sure I had a nice watch. I had never wanted to get my ears pierced, but I clenched my teeth and agreed to have it done. I kept reminding myself that she knew better than I did about all this and it was a sign of ignorance to deny it for personal reasons.

My father brightened in a way I hadn't seen since I was very young. He didn't say it in front of Julie, but when he saw me later, he told me that for a moment he had thought my mother had returned when I had stepped into the house after my makeover.

"You have all her wonderful qualities, Mayfair. Julie's done a good job of bringing them out."

What he said made me feel good but surprisingly brought tears to my eyes. Was this physical change unchaining emotions I hadn't seen or felt for years?

I was very nervous about going to school now. Never, no matter what I did or how I was treated, was I uneasy about walking into the building. I could be indifferent to anyone and anything. But when I returned to school that Monday, I did feel quite different. Not only was my hair cut and styled, but I was dressed like a girl my age dressed, and the makeup I wore, as Julie had said, highlighted the most attractive features of my face. Those girls in my class who were jealous of my good looks to start with were absolutely beside themselves with envy now. That was easy to see and also quite pleasing. Before this, there wasn't a girl who felt threatened by me. In their opinion, my looks weren't enough to overcome the way I was viewed by boys and by other girls. Now things might be different.

I couldn't help being nervous and doubting the wisdom of what I had done. To calm myself, I told myself that it was just another sociological experiment, and I tried to analyze it that way, but as soon as I began to get second looks from boys in the corridors and classroom, the scientific, analytical approach died, and I was suddenly and finally a teenage girl whose heart began to pitter-patter with every smile tossed in her direction.

Ironically, however, it wasn't one of the high-school boys who made me feel sexy and attractive; it was one of the younger teachers, Allison's English teacher, Mr. Taylor, or Alan, as he would want me to call him later on.

He was standing in his classroom doorway when I entered the building and started for my homeroom. He knew who I was. Faculty members gossiped about their students, and I was confident that I was frequently the topic of their conversations. Whenever he had looked at me before, there was little or no excitement in his face. Like most of the teachers, he wasn't interested in having much of a conversation with me. Few wanted to know what I was researching or reading, and if any did ask, he or she would nod and smile, clearly revealing that I was into areas beyond them, reading books they didn't even read in college, but that wasn't true today for Mr. Taylor.

At six feet two inches tall, with thick, rich light brown hair and cerulean blue eyes, Alan Taylor was the most attractive male teacher in the school. He was only twenty-five and still a bachelor. All the unmarried female teachers were vying for his attention, but as far as I knew, none had won his interest. He had one of those movie-star perfect faces that hovered between handsome and pretty because of his high cheekbones and perfectly shaped nose and mouth. His good looks were complemented by his tennis-pro figure and confident posture. Just like I knew I was brilliant, he knew he was physically striking. The high-school girls who swooned over him all wondered why he was "just a teacher" and not at least on television.

"Hey there," he called to me as I started past his room.

I paused, a little surprised. "Yes?"

"What did you do with your hair?"

"I donated it," I said.

"What?"

"They use it to make wigs for women who suffer baldness during chemotherapy."

He stared a moment and then laughed.

I didn't, but that didn't discourage him. He stepped toward me, looking me over even more closely. I felt more self-conscious and had the surprising urge to bring my arms up and around my breasts as if I were topless, but I resisted. His smile now made my heart do flip-flops. I fought to hold it back, but I could feel the heat go up my neck and into my face. He took so long to speak, seeming to enjoy just looking at me, that I had to say, "What?"

He laughed again. "I don't mean the hair you had cut off. I mean you've changed your appearance."

"There's a little chameleon in all of us," I said. "You know, blend with your surroundings to survive?"

He widened his smile. I knew he was struggling to think of a response. I didn't wait. I saw no reason to linger, so I walked on to homeroom.

But I knew he was watching me all the way, and it was a different feeling knowing a man was looking at me not as a phenomenon but as a woman. I was more conscious of my body, the way I moved, even how I turned toward the classroom.

I looked back and saw that he was still looking my way and smiling. There were still feelings traveling through my body that I had longed for. I tried to contain them, but they were like wild horses that had seen an opening. My breath quickened. He nodded at me, holding his smile as if he knew I would imprint it on my memory and recall it whenever I wanted.

The moment I entered my first class, I noted the way the others were looking at me and chattering. Gossip about me already had gone through the hallways and into every homeroom. I didn't think anyone looked at me all morning without taking a second look. My history teacher, Mr. Leshman, actually called on me twice and didn't seem to mind when I went on to elaborate on the answer and get into another topic. It actually interested him, and he and I were almost alone in the room for the remainder of the period.

When lunch started and I went to the cafeteria, I quickly realized that I wasn't going to be sitting alone. Carlton James, one of the better-looking senior boys, broke away from his friends and started toward me the moment I sat at a table. From the way the others were smiling after him, I imagined some sort of a bet had been made or some sort of a challenge, and Carlton had accepted it.

"Are you a new student?" he asked.

When I had fantasized using the pictures in the sex manual, I had seen myself with him in some of the illustrations, but I would never admit to myself that I had a crush on him or anything that juvenile. And I certainly had never done anything to give him reason to think so.

"Why? Are you the official greeter?"

"I can be," he said, and slipped into the chair across from me.

Despite how much I wanted to like him, his youthful male arrogance put me off. I felt like tossing my container of juice at his wry smile. I simply didn't like being in the company of someone who had more self-confidence than I did. Perhaps that was a compromise I would have to make if I were to get into any relationship successfully. He nodded at his friends, who were still looking our way and grinning like idiots.

"What, did you draw the short straw?" I asked.

"Huh? What short straw?"

"You never heard that expression?"

He shook his head. His smile weakened.

"It was one of my grandmother's expressions." I smiled, thinking about her.

"What's it mean?" he asked, regaining his composure, obviously hoping it meant something that would please him. He couldn't imagine my saying anything otherwise, especially with the warm smile on my face.

"When a group of people decide that one of them has to do something unpleasant, they draw straws, and the one who gets the shortest straw does it."

"Oh, well, I'm not doing anything unpleasant," he said, widening his smile again. "Why would you think coming over here to talk to you was something unpleasant anyway?"

"I was born with a suspicious nature. So you're here. What do you want to talk about?" I asked.

"Just . . ."

"What?"

His smile began to fade. "Just saying hello. You know."

"Hello," I said. "Now what?"

He lost his smile completely. "What are you, gay?"

"Why do you ask that?" I was really curious, especially since I had done so much to make myself attractive to boys, or at least I thought I had.

"Because, well . . . you're, like, not interested," he said, obviously feeling good about coming up with the word and the idea. "Am I right?"

"You haven't done or said anything interesting yet," I told him. "Maybe you're just relying on your good looks. That will take you just so far in this world."

"Huh?"

"No one's ever told you that?"

He smirked, looked back at his friends, and then leaned toward me. "You're a big brain, right?"

"The size of your brain isn't what makes you intelligent." I looked around the cafeteria. "There are some very big heads in here on very stupid people."

He laughed. "Okay, how do I get you to help me with my intermediate algebra?"

"Is that why you came over here?" I asked, feeling disappointed.

"No, but I thought it might be a good start."

I smiled. That was clever, I thought, more clever than I would have thought him capable of being. "No, that doesn't work. You have to ask something you really care about, talk about something you want to talk about, not something that might just get you by."

"You sound like a dating instructor. You know, like one of those websites that's supposed to help you find someone compatible."

"You use them?"

"Absolutely not," he said, a little insulted. He straightened up. "Do I look like someone who needs to use them?"

"Looks deceive," I said. He stared at me. "Okay, you don't."

He smiled again. Then he raked the room with his eyes to be sure he was the center of attention before turning back to me. "Okay. Here's something I really want to say. What are you doing after school today?"

"Why?"

"Maybe you can come home with me and give me

some pointers about how to talk properly or something. I'm open to improvements," he said. He looked back at his friends again.

I nodded at them. "What do you win if I say yes?"

He laughed again. Then he gave me his best sexy smile. "I won't know until I get you over, right?"

That made me smile. Maybe he wasn't as dull as I had expected him to be. Yet I hesitated. I had never, ever been alone with any boy, let alone in his home. I thought about some of the conversations I had overheard in the girls' locker room. Would I have similar experiences if I went with him? I felt like a schizophrenic person arguing with herself. The feminine part of me was urging me to say yes, but that part of me that made me feel older, more mature, and far superior was telling me to say no.

I was tired of listening to that part of me.

"Where do you live?"

My not saying no immediately pleased him so much that I couldn't help but widen my smile. He looked more like a little boy to me now, a harmless, excited little boy. I was obviously making his day, and that did make me feel good. I was a big enough prize.

"On Camden," he said. "Ten, fifteen minutes at the most. And I'll take you home whenever you want," he quickly added. "I drive a BMW 335 hardtop convertible. You probably saw it out there in the lot."

"BMW? What's that stand for, Big Man's Wheels?"

He laughed. "I like that. You're pretty clever. I had a feeling you might be fun to talk to. Those idiots back there thought we'd have nothing to say to each other."

"Because they have nothing to say to each other? Nothing meaningful?"

"Yeah, I guess. No, I mean . . . I don't know what I mean. I just knew you would be interesting."

"How did you know?"

"Do you have to always ask questions?"

"That's a question."

He looked frustrated again. "I just knew, okay?"

"I'm impressed. Do you even know my name?" I asked him.

"Sure. Mayfair, like the boat that brought the Pilgrims, right?"

"No." I shook my head, not hiding my disappointment. "You're right that my name is Mayfair, but you're thinking of the *Mayflower*. The ship, not the boat, that brought over the English separatists from Plymouth, England, was the *Mayflower*. It docked in Plymouth. You must have been asleep during that history lesson."

"I'm asleep during most history lessons," he said. "Sorry. Mayfair's just as nice. You're not named after another ship, too, are you?"

"Mayfair comes from the annual fortnight-long May Fair held in London."

"No kidding," he said without any real interest.

"Do you know what a fortnight is?"

"A night at a fort?"

"No," I said, laughing. "It's a unit of time equal to fourteen days. It comes from Old English."

"You mean, like that Beowulf story we had to read in class?"

"Yes, exactly, only they don't have it in Old English in your textbook."

"Yeah, Mr. Lofter read some of it in that Old English. Dumb," he said. "No one knew what the hell he was saying. I don't know how anyone could talk like that."

"Old English was spoken in England and southeastern Scotland between the fifth and twelfth centuries. It's also known as Anglo-Saxon. It has a Germanic heritage in its vocabulary, sentence structure, and grammar. It can sound quite interesting, almost musical, when it's read correctly."

"Jeez, are you always like this?"

"Like what?"

"A teacher," he said, making it sound like a curse word.

"Are you always this reluctant to learn anything?"

He stared at me a moment and then leaned back, turning to look at his friends, who had lost interest in us and were laughing and talking with other girls. They looked lighthearted and relaxed. Then he looked at me again, this time with regret. "I just remembered I have to do something for my father after school today. Maybe some other time, when I'm hungry for knowledge," he said, getting up.

Disappointment surged through me and curled under my breasts.

He paused and leaned toward me with his hands on the table. "But it was nice studying with you," he muttered, and walked away.

I watched how his friends greeted him with

laughter. He shook his head and spoke, describing our conversation from his perspective, and then they all looked my way and laughed again, especially the girls.

*Yahoos*, I thought.

They surrounded me. If I wasn't careful, I might catch the disease of ignorance. That's what I told myself, but deep inside, I did feel a sense of disappointment and defeat.

Before the bell rang to end the lunch hour, I left for the library. I wasn't even going to bother to go to math class. My teacher, Mrs. Samuels, would simply check with the librarian later to see if I had gone there. I wanted to go on the computer and see what I could find on the mating habits of primates. I had told my science teacher that I was going to do a paper on the subject, and he'd looked very interested.

I was almost at the library when Mr. Taylor appeared, seemingly out of nowhere. It was almost as if he were lying in wait for me.

"Hey," he said. "How's your day going?"

"Like a blur," I said, and he laughed.

"Where are you headed?"

"The library. I'm doing a research paper."

"Come into my room for a while. I've got a free period," he said, shifting his shoulder. "C'mon. I'm not going to bite you."

"Why?"

"A little intelligent conversation," he said. "I'm starving for it. I spend most of my day talking to junior-high students. Don't you know this is the front line in the big battle called education?"

"What about the other teachers? Don't you talk to them?"

He shrugged and smiled wryly. "I said *intelligent* conversation."

I looked back when the bell rang. The students would be bursting out of the cafeteria like a herd of wildebeests in seconds. Half of them would knock into me. Maybe that, more than my curiosity about Mr. Taylor, made me turn in his direction. Whatever the reason, I did.

I'd always wonder if it wasn't something meant to be, not that I believed in fate or fixed destiny. If I did, I couldn't be much of a scholar, because it was too easy to fall back on that rather than study and do research for an explanation, but I couldn't help secretly hoping it was fate.

That way, all that had happened to me, to Allison, and especially to my father wouldn't have been my fault, not my fault at all. All the blame and guilt would fade, and I would be the object of sympathy, not anger and disappointment. But deep in my heart, I knew that to hope was to dream, and to dream was to deny what was real. Maybe that was all I had ever wanted to do. Maybe I was guilty of everything I had accused most other people of doing.

I wasn't profoundly gifted after all.

I was profoundly dumb.

# 7

Mr. Taylor went behind his desk and put his feet up. I stood just inside his classroom doorway with my books cradled in my arms. I wasn't about to fool myself. It wasn't the prospect of having any sort of intelligent conversation that brought me into his room. I had really come in because I was far more interested in how a mature man thought of me than I was in how one of the boys in my class thought and behaved. I already felt a difference in my own reaction. It was more exciting, because his flirting and my responding seemed like something forbidden. After all, he was a teacher, and I was a high-school junior. There were all sorts of news stories about teachers who exploited their young students, even female teachers seducing young boys.

I did think to myself, however, that if we weren't who we were, it would be different. Suppose it were a couple of years from now. If I were a woman six or seven years younger than he was, and he were a businessman and not a teacher, no one would think anything of it. People could say a teacher had an unfair advantage over a student. He or she had great powers of influence. Students supposedly looked up to and listened to their teachers. That was certainly true for most.

But I had gone through almost all of my school years and never really been influenced by a teacher. I didn't need any teacher to encourage me to study or be responsible about my schoolwork. I didn't need any teacher to inspire me to have interests in science or math or English or history. If anything, I occasionally found myself inspiring one of them. How many times had I heard one of my teachers say, "You know, Mayfair, you have me thinking like a college student again"?

I certainly wasn't looking for their compliments. Nothing I did would change, whether they gave me a compliment or not. Maybe that was the arrogance I would be accused of possessing. To me, it was just a simple truth.

There were teachers I respected, of course, but many I didn't respect. I didn't do anything disrespectful to them. I was simply indifferent. In those teachers' classes, I looked beyond them to the challenge of the work.

Still, there was no way around this. I was standing there fantasizing about a teacher and actually hoping he had some fantasies about me. For the moment, at least, I was in exciting new territory, certainly more interesting territory than I was in with Carlton James in the cafeteria. If I had too many more experiences like that, I would probably give up on boys altogether, I thought.

"Sit. Take a load off," Mr. Taylor said.

He put his hands behind his head and looked at me. There was something about the way his eyes moved over me that made me hesitate. I told myself I was feeling the natural instinctive fear a female had of a male. I had read enough about it to know what it was.

Then I told myself to stop being so damn analytical and enjoy this. *You can analyze it later. For now, just soak up the experience. You've never been with a man who looked at you more as a woman than as a brilliant brain. You don't have to romanticize about it. You're really here, and he's really here looking at you and saying these things to you.*

"You've got to learn how to relax, Mayfair," he said. "You're too intense about everything."

"How do you know that?"

I was never in his class. He had come to teach junior-high English when I entered ninth grade, nearly three years ago. Allison had him for English now, but I really had no contact with him.

"I watch you, see you moving about the school. When you walk through the hall, you barely look right or left. You don't let anything distract you. I never saw anyone as intense. A bomb could go off, and you'd keep going in the direction you were headed if you had some purpose, some goal to fulfill," he said, and widened his smile. "Not that there's anything wrong with the way you walk," he added.

"What's that mean?"

He looked thoughtful for a moment. Did he realize he already had gone too far? I regretted coming back at him so fast and hard. He shrugged, took his feet off his desk, and leaned forward. "Well, you move with a great deal of confidence. Great posture," he said. "Even now, standing there, you don't slouch like so many of the girls your age do. I have to tell you that you fascinate me, and I don't mean because of your off-the-charts IQ scores." He nodded. "The way someone walks can tell you a lot about that person."

"I'm not conscious of it," I said. "I don't think about walking like that. Walking is a habitual action. We might be conscious of it occasionally to impress someone, but generally, we don't think about it. Everyone has a unique way of walking."

"Exactly. That's my point. It's part of who you are. Insecure people have a far different way of walking from secure people, and you don't look at all insecure, ever."

"What's wrong with that?"

"Nothing. Stop challenging every comment I make. Relax," he repeated. He paused and leaned back again. Then he nodded at me and smiled. "Until today, I didn't think looking this way was important to you," he said, holding his right hand out, palm up.

"Looking what way?"

"Attractive. I don't mean to say you weren't a very pretty girl before, but now you have your hair styled. You're wearing makeup. Quite intelligently, I might add. And you're wearing clothes that complement your figure. You don't mind me telling you these things, do you?" he quickly asked.

"Mind? No. I just didn't expect it."

He shrugged again. "Why not? I'm no hypocrite like some of my fellow male teachers who will swear on a stack of dictionaries that they don't lust after any young, beautiful teenage girls."

I think I was more surprised than he was at my smile. "I don't doubt it. I'm just surprised to hear you say it."

"Hey, we're all human," he said. "When I see an attractive woman, I don't pretend I don't see her just because I'm a junior-high English teacher. Which reminds me." He lifted a pile of papers. "Spot English grammar quiz. It's good to give them. Keeps the kids on their toes, but I hate correcting them. Care to help?"

"I really do have to get to the library, Mr. Taylor. I have a paper I want to finish this week, and I have lots of reading left to do."

"Oh, too bad. Well, maybe when you have time, you can stop by once in a while after school and help me with some of this dull work, huh?"

"Why would I want to do dull work? You shouldn't think of what you teach as being dull."

He laughed. "I knew it would be an interesting challenge talking to you, Mayfair. You really are a breath of fresh air for me."

"Why is that? What makes me so fresh?" I knew I was asking too many questions and challenging him too much, but I couldn't help being interested.

"You're not distracted with yourself. I think that's why you didn't do all these cosmetic things until now. You have your feet on the ground. You're head and shoulders above your peers, and I don't mean just because of your IQ. There's something very mature about you. I can have a conversation with you." He paused, stood up, and came around to the front of his desk to sit back against it, folding his arms. "I bet you wouldn't mind speaking to someone more mature, either. You must be starved for meaningful conversation at this school."

"That's not why I come here," I said. Instinctively, I brought my books up against my breasts. The way he was looking at me made me feel as if I were standing naked in front of him.

He shrugged. "Maybe not, but everyone wants some social contact with other people. I've noticed you don't have all that many friends here. You don't join any clubs or teams. You don't sit with anyone in particular in the cafeteria or walk with anyone in the hallways. You don't even talk to other students at the lockers in the morning. You float through this place as if you're on the way to somewhere else."

"You sound like you're watching me all the time."

"As much as I can," he said with that disarmingly soft smile again.

His honesty didn't shock me as much as it excited me. Again, I felt myself smile as if there was another part of me taking me over. I didn't want to resist.

"Actually, I overhear the students gossiping from time to time and pick up things the guidance counselor says. No one's saying anything terribly negative about you," he quickly added. "It's just comments, observations."

"I'm sure," I said dryly. "They all have my interest at heart. I confuse them."

"I'll say that's true, but you don't have to explain to me why you don't socialize much with your classmates. As I said, I know you're head and shoulders above them. Miles ahead of them, in fact. I'm sure what they do, what interests them, is unimportant to you."

I wanted to say that wasn't completely true, but I didn't. I didn't want to continue standing there talking to him. His words and the way he continued to look at me were starting to make me unsure of myself. I think it was because he was touching places inside me that I usually protected, like my loneliness. Now I thought it was a mistake to play with him like this, to allow myself to have such fantasies.

"I've got to go," I said, and turned toward the door.

"Okay. Please stop by anytime you want to talk or take pity on a poor junior-high English teacher buried in drudge work. Even though I love my subject matter, there's still drudge work," he added quickly. "No matter what exciting thing you end up doing, you'll see there's always the drudge work."

I glanced back at him. He held that licentious smile. It sent a tremor of excitement through my breasts. I felt myself blush.

When I had woken up this morning excited about my new look and how my classmates and other students would react to me, what was furthest from my mind was how the best-looking male teacher in the school would react. How did I miss that? I hated not anticipating something, especially something directly related to me. Although I would have had to be blind or completely oblivious not to have noticed him before, I never dreamed my changed appearance would mean that he would be the one I would draw out.

The one thing I hated most was surprise. I spent most of my time researching, investigating, and understanding everything I saw, did, and touched. I was always prepared, but I would be the first to admit that I wasn't prepared for this. He nearly had taken my breath away.

This whole experience had me confused, not just about him but also about myself. I hated anyone causing me to be unsure about myself. It rarely happened at school, but I wasn't leaving his room because I was dying to get to the library. As hard as it was for me to admit it, I was leaving his room because I was a little frightened of my own reactions.

I was acting and thinking like one of those girls in my class whom I ridiculed.

I hurried out and didn't look back, but just like before, I instinctively knew that he was standing in his doorway watching me walk away.

And he wasn't interested in my good posture, either. I had first thought that this skirt Julie had chosen was too snug and too short, but it was the way many of the other girls were dressing. Give the devil her due. Julie knew fashion, knew how to be attractive. She had captured my father's interest and his heart, hadn't she? What good did it do me to deny it?

I did almost nothing in the library. I couldn't get the conversation I had with Mr. Taylor out of my mind, nor could I stop thinking about the way he looked at me. When the bell rang and I left to go to my next class, I anticipated him being in his doorway waiting for me to walk by again. At first, he wasn't there, and I felt a combination of relief and a little disappointment, but before I'd passed his room completely, he appeared.

"How'd your research go?" he called out to me.

"Fine," I said, only glancing back at him.

"Best posture in the school," he called after me, and laughed. I kept walking, walking faster but smiling to myself.

I was thinking so hard about him that I completely forgot about the incident in the cafeteria with Carlton James. It wasn't until I went to PE class that the consequences of that disappointing conversation were brought home to me. I was just getting my uniform on when Joyce Brooker stepped up behind me.

"We heard you blew off Carlton today," she said.

I turned and looked at her. I couldn't remember the last time she had spoken to me or I to her. She was probably the prettiest of the girls with whom she hung, or I should say clung. They always looked more like a clump of girls clinging to one another than a group of close friends.

Joyce had almost doll-like facial features, stunning green eyes, and thick amber hair. She had the best figure, too, but she behaved just like someone who knew all this would behave. Talk about a walk, I thought, recalling Mr. Taylor's comment about me. Joyce didn't walk; she moved as if she were on a fashion model's runway. If any of them would go on to become Miss California, it would be Joyce. I could just see her answering the final question.

"If you could have one wish, what would it be?"

"A better cell phone." Or maybe she'd realize she had to at least look serious and mature and say, "I would want to see an end to poverty." Even though she didn't know a single poor person.

Sometimes I felt a little envious of her, but I smothered that feeling as quickly as it showed its face.

"He never got on," I told her.

"Huh?"

The other girls joined her. They were like pigeons waiting for me to cast some peanuts.

"I couldn't have blown him *off*. He never got *on*."

She laughed and looked at the others. "Well, he tried, didn't he?"

"If so, it was a pathetic attempt," I said.

"Pathetic? Carlton James? I think it might be you who's pathetic for rejecting him. Unless, of course, you're seeing someone outside the school. Someone older, maybe? Someone in college? Figures that someone with your brains would probably be dating a college boy, maybe even a graduate student."

"Are you?" Cora Addison quickly followed. I always thought she had a face like a fox's, because it was so narrow, and her nose was so pointed and long.

I gave them all a big smile. "I never realized my comings and goings were of so much interest to all of you. I guess I should be flattered. You're interested in someone other than yourselves. I didn't think that was possible."

"Curiosity, not interest," Denise Hartman corrected. "We can't help wondering if being so intelligent means you have no love life. Men don't like brainy girls."

"There's no basis in fact for that sort of conclusion, Denise. The least intelligent organisms conjugate."

"What?"

"I'm surprised you're not familiar with that, being closer to an amoeba than a primate."

"Excuse me," she said, with her right hand on her hip. "Can you talk English?"

"Is that what you speak? It's difficult to tell."

"Very funny."

"You didn't answer the question," Joyce said.

"Was there a question? I'm still not finished translating."

"Ha-ha," Cora said. "Forget her."

"No," Joyce said, not giving ground. "The question was, are you seeing someone on the outside, and is that someone older, maybe much older?"

I half wondered if someone had reported my private conversation with Mr. Taylor or had overheard him talking to me in the hallway. Was that what she was fishing to find out?

"That's two questions," I said.

"Well, give us two answers."

"Do you write the social column here?"

"Sort of. So?"

I slipped on my sneakers and looked at the three of them. "I still don't understand why this is so important to all of you. Don't you have any lives of your own? Do you have to use other people's lives for your kicks and highs? Live vicariously?"

"Forget the big words. You don't have anyone, do you?" Cora said with a wry smile. "That's why you're not answering us. You've probably never had anyone."

"Any boy, at least," Denise said.

The two others brightened.

"Yes, that's it, isn't it? You're gay. That explains why you rejected Carlton and why no one has ever seen you with a boy anywhere."

"Believe what you want," I said. "Unlike you, I couldn't be less interested in what you think or do or what anyone in this school thinks or does, for that matter."

"Carlton's the best-looking boy in school. He could have any girl he wanted," Cora said, mostly to the other two. They nodded. "Why would she reject him if she wasn't gay?"

"Come to think of it, now that you've brought it up, Cora, I've seen the way she looks at us, especially in here when we're undressing," Joyce said.

"Oh, really? How do I look at you?"

"Like a boy looks at us."

I smiled. "You have misjudged me, girls. I am studying you, but I'm in the middle of doing a research paper on lower forms of life, and your resemblances to single-cell organisms are too remarkable to ignore. Carlton James might be the subject of every adolescent girl's wet dream to you, but he doesn't fit my criteria. I require more than a handsome face. I have to be with someone who can do more than talk about bubble-gum cards."

"Wet dream?" Denise said.

"Look it up," I said, and walked out to the gym.

The only reason I continued to take PE was my belief that it was important to get some physical exercise every day. I enjoyed the warm-up Miss Hirsch put us through, all the exercises, but only halfheartedly participated in the games, especially basketball. Whatever team I was on, the members hardly passed the ball to me. I didn't care. I was more interested in running up and down the court. Sometimes I didn't even notice who had the ball.

The three bitches from *Macbeth* ignored me for the remainder of the period and afterward in the locker room. What Joyce had been asking about my seeing someone older did make me a little more self-conscious, and I deliberately avoided walking near Mr. Taylor's classroom. I hurried out of the building at the end of the day. Allison was already waiting for her mother to take us home.

"You probably got a lot of compliments today, huh?" she asked me.

"I didn't notice," I told her.

"Yes, you did." She stared at me and almost reluctantly added, "You look very pretty now, Mayfair. Even some of my friends said some things about you, some nice things."

*Why take it out on her?* I thought. "Thank you, Allison. And yes, I did receive compliments."

"I knew you would. My mother will be very happy about it."

"That's good. It's good she's happy about something," I muttered.

I looked back as other students poured out of the building. The three bitches from *Macbeth* looked my way and then laughed as they piled into Joyce's SUV. I had hoped that my answers had discouraged them from having any more interest in me and what I did and didn't do, but as it turned out, my responses had resulted in quite the opposite reaction. I wouldn't learn about it until that night, however.

When Julie picked us up, she had almost the identical question waiting on her lips.

Yes, I had received compliments, I told her, and yes, I felt better about myself. She drove with a smile of self-satisfaction planted on her face all the way home. But thanks to the bitches from *Macbeth*, that would quickly disappear later.

Just before dinner, I could feel that something was up, but I didn't pursue it. When we all sat at the table, she didn't say much to either Allison or my father and avoided looking at me. My father went on and on about how much he enjoyed my new appearance and then talked about some big new business achievements. The whole time, Julie kept herself from looking at me. She seemed to be in very deep thought about something.

Maybe she thought I didn't show enough appreciation, I concluded, and left it at that, but about a half hour after dinner, my father called me on the intercom from the den and asked me to come down. When I walked in, I found him and Julie sitting on one of the leather settees. Both of them looked rather glum.

"What's wrong?" I asked.

My father nodded at the settee across from them. "We'd like to talk to you for a few minutes."

I hadn't done anything with Allison, nor had I spoken much to her since the sex manual incident, so I was curious about what would turn their faces into prunes.

"What's this about?" I asked after I sat.

My father looked to Julie, giving her permission to begin.

"Lauren Hartman is a good friend of mine. Maybe *was*," she added, glancing at my father.

"So?"

"You know her daughter Denise."

"I know who she is. I don't have enough interest in her or her friends to know any of them, Julie. Please stop the dramatics and tell me what this is all about."

"Lauren is very upset with something Denise and the other girls told their mothers."

"They're all pregnant?"

"This isn't funny, Mayfair," my father said.

"I don't know what it is, so I don't know if it's funny or not, Daddy."

"They claim you've been . . . I have trouble even saying it," Julie said, shaking her head.

"Write it out, then," I said.

"Mayfair."

"Well, I'm not going to sit here all night waiting for the dramatics to end, Daddy. What is it, Julie? Speak your piece or forever remain silent."

"They claim you've been watching them undress in the locker room," she rattled off quickly.

"What?"

"They said you admitted to doing that. They also said that one of the most popular and good-looking boys in the school showed interest in you, after I helped you with your hair, makeup, and clothes, and that you showed no interest in him at all. You drove him away after he issued an invitation to spend some time with you, as a matter of fact."

"Is that it?"

"Isn't that enough?"

I looked at my father. "You believe this stuff, the implication she's making?"

"Why shouldn't he believe it? You have no interest in going to parties or on dates, and we know you've been invited to some parties in the past and turned down the invitations."

"They weren't really invitations, and I know they were offered reluctantly and not sincerely," I added, looking at my father. I knew both he and Julie had engineered some of the most recent ones.

"What was the point of my doing all this for you," she said holding her hands out toward me, "if you're not going to take advantage of it? The money spent, the time and effort, why do you want this if you're going to avoid opportunities and drive away any interest in you? When I was your age, I couldn't wait for the weekend. You seem to be disappointed that school isn't seven days a week.

"And," she added after a pause, "you showed Allison that disgusting book that has a whole chapter on masturbation, even showing techniques."

I simply glared at her. Inside, my stomach felt as if a hive of wasps had broken and in their fierce anger they were stinging every organ in my body.

"As Julie said, Mayfair, Lauren's daughter claims you didn't deny their accusations," my father said. "Is that true?"

"Of course I didn't. I didn't take them seriously. I wouldn't take anything they said seriously and waste my time answering them. Who do they think they are, anyway? If there weren't any mirrors in the girls' room, they wouldn't go to the bathroom. They'd all be constipated."

He continued to stare at me. I saw a different look in his face, a mixture of worry and fear.

"You don't really believe any of this stupidity, do you, Daddy?"

"What either of us believes isn't important right now," Julie said.

"Excuse me? What my father believes about me is very important," I said.

"You're missing the point."

"That's because there isn't any."

"Let her speak, Mayfair," my father said, his voice full of fatigue and defeat.

"Okay, Julie. Speak. What else do you have to add to this idiotic conversation?"

"It's not so idiotic anymore. The other mothers are getting together and going to the principal to complain about you."

"Complain? You have to be kidding."

"I'm not kidding. They are worried about their daughters' . . . security."

"Security?" I looked at my father. "What am I now, a sex terrorist?"

"Joke about it all you want, but you can't even begin to imagine how embarrassing this is for me. For us," Julie quickly corrected. "I ask again, why did I do all that to help you with your appearance if you weren't interested in boys? Were you trying to get some girl interested in you? It's best if you tell us the truth."

"I'm not going to give any dignity to these stupid questions by answering them. Those girls never liked me. They know what I think of them. They would say anything they could that would hurt me." I stood up. "Believe me, I have more important things to do with my time right now than sit here and talk about what those girls say or think. Thinking is too high a process for them anyway."

"Mayfair," my father called as I started out.

"What?"

"You know that if you have these inclinations, you can tell us, right?"

I looked at Julie. She had her right hand over her heart as if she were about to recite the Pledge of Allegiance, and she was holding her breath. I was tempted to say I was gay just to see her have a heart attack.

How could she face her high-society friends at their lunches and charity galas? Maybe she would pack up and go, I thought. That was the biggest motivation for me to admit to it, but then I looked at my father and retreated.

"Of course I would tell you," I said. "If it's a fact, it doesn't do any good to deny it. I know I can say anything to either of you and always have. Right now, I'd like to say good night," I added, and walked out.

I left Julie stuttering and hyperventilating, but I didn't feel good about it. It didn't give me the usual satisfaction. I felt nauseated and tired. Despite the brave and angry face I had put on, I was crying inside. Look at how Julie had twisted up my father, I thought. She was insidious, inserting herself in the smallest of ways in the beginning, making changes in our house, the decor my mother had created. It was as if she thought she knew the pathway to get her out of my father's memory. She hated my mentioning her now. I had no doubt that if she could, she'd confiscate the pictures of her I had in my room. I knew my father and mother's wedding picture had been stashed in some carton in a closet.

Before Julie had come into our lives, something like this would have made my father and me both laugh. Neither of us would have worried about what the other parents thought of us or especially me. Although he wanted me to be more well rounded, my father used to believe that a very busy social life wasn't a priority, either for him or for me. It was different now. Julie had him rushing around to one social event after another. Everything was different now, and that difference was painful.

I knew this wouldn't end quickly. She was certain to moan and groan to my father about how worried she was about my influence on her precious little daughter, Allison. I realized that things would only get worse. Without telling my father, she was probably going to warn Allison not to undress in front of me or report to her immediately if I touched her. It was all very sad, but my sadness quickly turned into rage, rage against those girls in school, rage against Carlton James, whose ego I had bruised and who was surely encouraging the rumors about me now, and rage against Julie, who was like a sponge soaking up the gossip and then squeezing it out at my father's feet. She wouldn't stop until she drowned us both.

Unless I could find a way to stop her.

# 8

No one said any more to me that night, and my father didn't bring up anything about it while he was taking Allison and me to school, but you could have cut the air between us with a knife. The silence was that thick. I could see the curiosity in Allison's face. What was happening now? Apparently, Julie hadn't said anything to her yet, but despite what she might have told my father about protecting her daughter's innocent ears, I was confident that she would. It did occur to me that she actually believed it all.

I was angry enough not to put on the makeup Julie had shown me how to use and not to wear any of the new clothing she had helped me pick out, but I thought I would be cutting off my nose to spite my face if I did that. My hair was now my hair. There was no change possible, and besides, if I did revert to what I had looked like, I was sure the three bitches from *Macbeth* would see it as some sort of a victory. Maybe they would think they had forced me to come out of the closet or something and go bragging around the school about that.

When we arrived at school, my father let Allison get out first and then reached for my hand. "Just be careful how you handle this," he told me. "I know you're angry, but don't make it worse than it is."

"There's nothing to make worse, Daddy. Talk to your new wife, and tell her to chill out."

"Stop calling her my new wife, Mayfair. We've been married nearly three years."

"Whatever," I said.

"Watch yourself," he warned. "Your attitude isn't making any of this easier."

I watched him drive off and thought I was losing whatever I had left of him. Now it seemed so long ago when he had such pride in me. I could barely remember that wonderful smile on his face, that great laugh that once turned our dark days into bright sunshine. It was almost another lifetime.

Despite my bravado, when I looked at the school entrance, I hesitated. Knowing how well these girls could spread stories through their texting, phone calls, and emails, I was sure many more students were talking about me. It was like walking into a giant spider's web. Mr. Taylor was right about my ability to ignore my surroundings generally, but this was different. I could easily imagine the smug smiles, the gleeful eyes, and the waves of whispers following my every move. Yet turning and running would be just what they wanted me to do. They would be so satisfied, and so would Julie, I thought, despite the act she put on for my father.

Of course, I could stare down any of them if I chose to do so or ignore any comment. I could look right through them all. After a while, there would be nothing different about my school day here. However, I was certainly not naive enough to think that this would all go away quickly. I didn't believe they would go through with their threats, but Julie was right about the other mothers. I didn't think she knew it at dinner, but apparently, they had made an appointment with the principal this morning. Looking out the window in my first class, a window that faced the parking lot, I saw them all arrive, gather in the parking lot, and march toward the front entrance. To me it looked like they were carrying hatchets.

As I had suspected, the three bitches had begun spreading their rumors even before the day had ended yesterday and during the evening, and they were at it in a full-blown assault this morning to complement their mothers' meeting with the principal, Dr. Richards, who had a doctorate in education administration. Normally, I got along well with him, because, like Mr. Martin, our guidance counselor, he treated me as someone special and was somewhat in awe of my achievements. Many times, he'd make a point of seeing me in the library or the cafeteria to find out what I was currently reading or working on, and I could see that he sincerely enjoyed some of our conversations. But I knew that administrative positions, especially those in private schools like this one, were very political appointments. The parents who were wealthier and more powerful were usually big influences, many serving on the board of directors. Even though my father was very important, I didn't expect Dr. Richards would stick his neck out to defend me.

And boy, did the three bitches know that. They strutted with an air of confidence through the halls, attracting other students like flies to flypaper. There was so much whispering that it created a breeze, or more of a whirlwind. I could easily imagine how they were elaborating on our confrontation in the locker room and how Carlton was embellishing it with his interpretation of our conversation in the cafeteria.

I hadn't seen Mr. Taylor yet. I did pass his classroom once, but he was busy with some of his students. Because he was in the junior-high wing, I didn't think he was up on what was happening in the belly of the senior high, where all the lies and distortions were being digested.

Toward the end of third period, I was called to the principal's office. By now, almost every student in the senior high had heard something. Instead of everyone looking through me or ignoring me, now they were all watching me carefully, looking for some break in my armor of indifference. Maybe it was my imagination, but I thought even some of the teachers were looking at me differently, perhaps anticipating some sort of breakdown.

I was shocked to see Julie waiting in Dr. Richards's office. She had to have arrived after the bitches of *Macbeth*'s mothers. The mothers were gone by now, but Mr. Martin was in Dr. Richards's office waiting for me, too. For a moment, I stood in the doorway glaring at Julie. She looked like she had been crying. That didn't surprise me. She could turn on her crocodile tears as easily as turning on a faucet.

"What are you doing here?" I demanded, since my father wasn't with her.

"Come in, Mayfair," Dr. Richards said firmly.

Dr. Richards was a tall, lean man. He wasn't ugly, but he had hard, sharp facial features and rather ordinary brown eyes. Like most people who were taller than six feet four, he had a tendency to slouch. When he stood up to come around his desk, I couldn't help but think of my conversation with Mr. Taylor and his comment about my posture.

"Please," Dr. Richards said, extending his long arm and his hand toward the chair across from Mr. Martin and Julie. He took the chair beside the settee and sat across from me, too. They had a pot of tea, cups, and some biscuits on a tray.

*Isn't this cozy?* I thought.

"Would you like some tea? There are some biscuits, too," Dr. Richards said.

"No, thank you. High tea is a little later in the day for me," I said.

Julie smirked and looked away as if facing me nauseated her.

"Okay. It seems we have a little situation here," Dr. Richards began.

He glanced at Mr. Martin, who nodded. Everyone who cherished his or her job had to be in lockstep. That was for sure. When Julie turned back, she looked ready to burst into tears again. She took a very deep

breath, looked up at the ceiling, and pressed her lips
together to show us all how difficult this was and
how hard she was fighting to keep her composure.
If I didn't know her, I'd feel sorry for her, too, I
thought.

"If it's a little situation, it shouldn't be much of a
problem," I said.

Neither man smiled.

Julie shook her head slightly. "She's always like
this," she said. "Smart remarks."

"Why did you call her and not my father?" I demanded.

"We called your home," Dr. Richards began.

"Your father is at a very important meeting today,"
Julie said. "I called him and told him I would handle
this."

"Handle? What's there to handle?" I asked Dr.
Richards.

"Some accusations have been made against you.
Frankly, it's not important whether these accusations
are true or not. We're not here to find that out."

"Why *are* we here?" I asked.

"We don't want you to be unnecessarily disturbed.
We know how important a good, stable setting is for
someone like you," Dr. Richards said.

"Someone like me?"

"You know what we mean, Mayfair. You're doing
great work on your own. Everyone is proud of your
accomplishments, your test results, the reactions from
potential colleges . . ."

"What is it you want, Dr. Richards?" I asked. "It's

not necessary to set me up for some unpleasant conclusion. Get to the point."

"Can't you show some respect for your elders?" Julie snapped.

"I thought I was being respectful by making whatever this is less painful by getting it over with, like a root canal or something," I told her.

"She's right, Mrs. Cummings," Dr. Richards said. He turned back to me. "I'll get right to the point. We think that for the remainder of the year, you can be excused from PE. Miss Hirsch can give you some sort of exam later on and give you a passing grade." He smiled. "I don't imagine you're particularly excited about PE class, anyway."

I looked from him to Mr. Martin. So this was their politically correct, diplomatic solution to an unpleasant problem. I felt certain that Dr. Richards had already promised the mothers of the three bitches that I would be removed from PE and therefore any physical contact with their precious daughters. I stared, shocked for a moment, fearing a scream in my throat and thankful that it just stayed there. I swallowed it back.

"Excused from exercise?" I asked as calmly as I could manage. "No, *au contraire*, Dr. Richards. I think exercise is very important. Didn't you ever hear that expression, that healthy minds and healthy bodies go hand in hand? My brain isn't in a glass case. It's in a body that needs to be kept strong."

"Oh, yes, of course, you're right. Well, I suppose we could arrange for you to use the gym when it's free and . . ." He looked at Mr. Martin, who nodded quickly.

"Yes, there is an afternoon period when it's free."

"Good," Dr. Richards said. "It's yours along with whatever equipment you want to use."

"Isn't that dangerous? If I hurt myself without supervision, I mean? Julie might start a lawsuit."

"Don't be ridiculous," she said. "Frankly, under the circumstances, I think it's a good solution. My husband and I will sign any permission slip you need," she added for Dr. Richards. He smiled.

"Really? How surprising," I said. "So, let me understand this, Dr. Richards, understand exactly what's happened here. Some self-absorbed airheads make a ridiculous accusation against me, and the solution is to avoid confronting them, to accept what they say as true, and to find a way to please them and their carbon-copy mothers?"

No one spoke.

I looked at Julie. "This is the way you're representing my father and our interests? You'll sign a permission slip without conferring with him?"

"He doesn't need this sort of distraction right now, Mayfair. He has a lot on his mind with his business. None of us needs this distraction, and the solution is simple and avoids any more unpleasantness. Why be so obstinate?"

"I haven't found anything terribly unpleasant yet," I said. "Except the fact that I'm being judged without any sort of hearing concerning the evidence. I should at least get a trial by ordeal. Burn my hand and see if it heals in three days or something. If you want to go backward in the pursuit of justice, there are so many ways."

"Please, stop this. You know what I mean, what they mean. Why make this difficult when there's a good solution?"

"Good for whom?"

"The girls have agreed not to say another word about this," Dr. Richards said.

"There aren't any words left to say. They've said it all. They've embellished their disgusting and hateful stories so much that you'll have to wear boots to slosh through the hallways now."

"Then this will end it, get it off the front burners," he said.

"Front burners? That's an apt analogy, Dr. Richards, but I'm afraid it's already cooked."

"Please don't make this any more difficult," Julie begged, trying hard to sound as if she was really concerned about my interests. "You certainly don't care about these girls, and PE as a class is not important to you. You can exercise in our gym at home if you want. You don't even have to use the gym here at all. She can have more time to do her own thing, right, Dr. Richards?"

"Yes, that's true."

"So the conclusion here is that I should be grateful?"

No one spoke.

"You're not in the least bit curious about whether what the girls are accusing me of is true?" I asked Dr. Richards.

He smiled that plastic, political smile that administrators must practice in front of mirrors so they'd be prepared to confront boards of directors. "I think it's best we follow the military lead. Don't ask. Don't tell. Why get into such a sensitive topic? No one benefits."

"That doesn't exist anymore, and it wasn't a solution for the military anyway."

"We just want to stop it," Mr. Martin said. "Calm the atmosphere and protect you, too."

"But I just told you. They've already been spreading their lies, and they have done it in spades."

"They'll stop now," Dr. Richards said, putting on his firm face. "I can assure you of that."

"Just conduct yourself properly, and the nasty rumors will evaporate," Julie said. "Am I right?" She looked at Dr. Richards, and he smiled again and nodded.

"Precisely. I'll bring each of the girls involved in this matter into my office and spell it out to them very clearly."

"There, see?" Julie said.

I shook my head. "You're pathetic."

"It's not like you're going to run for class president," she said, sharply now. The dam had broken. There was no telling what else she would say. She was on a roll. I could see how pleased she was with herself and the solution. She might even be able to keep her friends.

"No, Mayfair has bigger things to do than that," Mr. Martin said, trying to sound like an appeaser. "You don't want to be distracted by this nonsense."

"No, I don't."

"Good," Julie said. "Then it's settled." She pounded her words down like a judge pounding a gavel to end all arguments.

She stood up quickly so there would be no question that this hearing had ended.

"Thank you very much, Dr. Richards, Mr. Martin. My husband and I appreciate the way you've handled this. Mayfair, be a good girl, now," she said, flashing a cold smile that would freeze someone's heart, and headed for the door. "I'll see you at the end of the day."

"No," I quickly replied. "I have something important after school. Just come for Allison."

"Fine," she said. She flashed another smile at Dr. Richards and Mr. Martin and then left.

"You come see me if you have any more problems with this," Dr. Richards said, returning to the chair behind his desk. "Or come see Mr. Martin."

"Yes," Mr. Martin said. "Anytime."

I rose to leave, feeling my legs half turn to lead. At the door, I turned back to them. "You didn't do those girls any favors today, Dr. Richards," I said. "You taught them that lying, being mean, is okay. They'll keep doing it until they hurt someone more than they hurt me, and they'll eventually hurt themselves."

"Don't you worry, Mayfair. We're keeping our eye on them. I'm letting them know my feelings about this. They'll behave themselves."

I smiled at them the way an adult would smile at a child who had said something very silly. "Why is it that the easiest person to fool is yourself?" I asked.

Neither replied.

I walked out. The bell had rung, and students were rushing to their next class. I felt like I was floating. I think I was in more pain than anger. I even felt like crying, letting my face flood with tears, and that surprised me. Tears did begin to burn my eyes as I fought them back. I stood still for a moment and took deep breaths to calm myself.

How could I have become the victim here? How could these tiny-minded, mean-spirited girls get the better of me? How smug would they be? I thought I looked like a clown now in my new hairdo, my new clothes, and these damn earrings in my pierced ears.

"Hey there," I heard. One look at the expression on Mr. Taylor's face told me he had found out about all this. He looked like he had been waiting to speak to me, in fact. "Keep your chin up. Stop by my classroom after school."

It was hard to understand why I would consider doing that. All I really wanted was to get as far away from this place as possible.

However, my father hadn't been here to protect me, Julie had practically brought the rope with which to hang me, and the school administrators were hiding behind closed doors, congratulating themselves on how they had squirmed out of a potentially sensational event and kept their lily-white reputations unblemished.

Who was there for me now to talk to?

"Why?" I asked.

"Just do it," he said sharply. "I'm on your side," he added, and then winked and walked away.

Before the end of the day, news about how I was being handled spread faster than the original rumors and lies. I did my best to ignore the smug smiles, but I couldn't subdue the anger raging inside me. I wasn't planning to have lunch in the cafeteria, but a girl in my class, Joy Hensley, tugged at my arm when the bell rang.

Joy was at least twenty pounds underweight, a classic anorexic. I wondered how she even had the energy to walk. Shrunken on that skull of hers was actually a pretty face starving to be fleshed out. Her eyes were a tired, dull gray, and her dark brown hair looked dry, with split ends. She was only about an inch shorter than I was. I often wondered about her, because she was probably ignored just as much as I was, for obviously different reasons.

I think the whole time I had been here, I had spoken no more than two words to her. If anything, she seemed more afraid to approach me than most people did. I had the feeling she thought I might say something even more devastating than the nasty comments other girls made. I once witnessed her being dressed down mercilessly by Joyce Brooker and Cora Addison in the locker room. They mocked her small bosom and the way her ribs pressed against her skin.

"What's your mother's food bill?" Joyce had begun. The question really took Joy by surprise, because Joyce sounded very interested and not critical.

"Why?"

"We're doing a survey for the school."

"I don't know," Joy said with the familiar look of panic on her face.

"Twenty cents?" Joyce asked.

"What? No."

Cora stepped up on her right side. "Why don't you eat?" she asked as if she cared. "Are you being used as a model at some medical school because the students can see your organs so easily?"

"No," Joy said, and tried to turn away.

"Are you getting help from the UN?" Cora asked.

"What?"

"You know, that organization that helps feed starving people all over the world?"

"No," Joy said.

"Would you like a cookie? I have an extra double chocolate chip."

"No, thanks."

By now, other girls had joined them and stood by smiling. They were like a pack of coyotes getting ready to kill and feast on a small rabbit. Joy looked around and saw that they were all feasting on her discomfort. She held her blouse up in front of her and searched for some escape route, but there was someone standing everywhere. "Leave me alone," she said.

"How do you pee? Don't you have trouble sitting on a normal toilet seat? You could fall into the water," Joyce said, and there was a roar of laughter.

I stood back, watching them as if I was observing another social ritual.

"Your mother shouldn't have to pay for gas when you're in the car with her," Cora said. "It takes energy to move weight, and in your case, a breeze could do it."

Joy shut down. She just stood there now, accepting

one derogatory comment after another, her eyes closed. When no one could think of anything more to say, they all moved away. She stood frozen for a few more moments and then hurried to get dressed and out of the locker room.

I hated what they had done to her, but I didn't particularly care to go to her defense. She had mental problems that created her physical problem, I thought. I knew she had lost her father in a terrible auto accident. I had overheard other students talking about that, but I wasn't eager to burden myself with someone else's psychological baggage at the time. I felt sorry for her, of course, but I didn't see any value in having her friendship.

"What?" I asked her now, surprised at how aggressively she had grabbed me.

"Can I talk to you, have lunch with you?"

"What about?"

"What happened to you," she said.

"Nothing happened to me."

"You're smarter than all of them, so I just wanted to know what you were going to do to get even," she said.

"What makes you think I care enough to do that?"

"I hope you do," she said. "They had no right to spread those stories about you, even if they're true."

I widened my eyes.

"I mean," she continued, "there's nothing wrong with you if they're true, right?"

It was as plain as day. She suspected that she was gay and was hoping that I was, too, or maybe that I could convince her that she wasn't. She was also hoping that somehow by avenging myself, I would be avenging her, too. "You're right," I said.

She smiled.

"Even if it was true, but it's not."

I decided to go to the cafeteria after all. Joy kept up with me and was right at my side when I entered. I looked around the room. There were many eyes on us. Conversations stopped and then started.

"I'm hungry," I said. "I didn't think I was going to be, but suddenly, I am." I went to the food line.

"I'll save you a seat over there," she said, nodding at a table.

"I doubt that you need to save it," I said. "It'll be there."

She smiled. When I got what I wanted, I went to the table. She had brought her own lunch, which was just a small plain yogurt and an apple. She started to eat her yogurt as if she had a sore throat. I could tell she wasn't even going to finish it.

"I watch you a lot," she told me.

"Watch me? What's that mean?"

"I mean, I see you working on other things in class and see how you work in the library by yourself. Nothing seems to bother you."

"Nothing here, maybe," I said. "I don't want to give them the satisfaction of thinking I care. Understand?"

"Yes," she said with disappointment.

"Time is important. You don't want to waste it on them. Work on improving yourself, helping yourself," I said. "Forget about them."

She nodded. "You're very pretty," she said. "I overheard them talking about you recently, and they were all very jealous. It must be nice to have people jealous of you for something."

I put my sandwich down. "Look, Joy, I'm no one to give anyone advice when it comes to social happiness around here, but the worst thing you can do is fall into a pit of self-pity. Get a hold of yourself. Gain some weight. Is your mother addressing your problems?"

"Addressing?"

"Getting you medical help?"

"Oh. No. My mother just tells me to finish my dinner, but she doesn't say anything when I don't. She always gives me too much."

I shook my head. *Too much to you*, I thought, *but probably just enough to anyone else.* "Okay. I'll do some research for you and get you information to give your mother. She has her head in the sand. You should be seeing a therapist, at least."

She laughed. "My mother would be terribly embarrassed if I did that."

"She's not embarrassed about you now?"

She lost her smile.

Suddenly, I thought of something. I looked around the cafeteria and saw the way some of the girls and boys were whispering and looking at us. How well known was it, I wondered, that Joy was gay? Had she had some sort of experience with someone else from school?

Possibly what I was doing now by sitting and talking with Joy was confirming the rumors the bitches from *Macbeth* had spread.

"I have to go," I told her, ironically not even coming close to finishing my own food. "I have something to do before my next class." I rose.

"Can I call you?" Joy asked.

"What for?"

"To talk," she said.

"I don't have time to talk on the phone," I told her, and took my tray to the trash bin and the shelf for trays. I didn't look back when I left.

*What am I doing?* I thought when I was halfway down the hall. I stopped. *It's like I'm running away. I'm letting them push me around.* Why was I fleeing from Joy? I was so angry at myself. *Damn them.* Maybe I would find some way to get back at them after all.

I was in deep thought about it for the remainder of the afternoon. Every chance they got, one of them would say something nasty close enough for me to hear. I didn't react to any of it, but I was fuming inside. By the time the last period ended, I felt like strangling someone. I had told Julie that I was doing something after school. I needed more time before confronting her, especially in front of my father. It was then I remembered Mr. Taylor's invitation and went to his room.

# 9

"Please, close the door," he said when I stepped into his classroom. He smiled and loosened his tie. "I need a break from the racket. Sometimes I wish I were teaching in a school for mutes."

He wasn't wrong about the racket. The students were leaving the building. Most of them always acted as if it were a fire drill, especially the junior high. They charged at the doors like prisoners released, their screams and shouts bouncing off the hall walls.

I closed the door.

"Glad you decided to stop by," he said. "I was hoping you would."

He got up and took one of the seats at a student desk. Then he patted the desk beside him, and I took that seat. Now that I was here, I felt very foolish and nervous. Why had I come? He was a junior-high English teacher. What did I expect to gain? Was I flirting? Was I so thick when it came to any of this that I wouldn't recognize what I was doing? Could he see it?

It was like I had swallowed a ping-pong ball whole and it was bouncing in my stomach. Oddly, I hadn't felt nearly as nervous in Dr. Richards's office, and he was someone who was trained to strip me mentally. Somehow, though, when Mr. Taylor looked at me, I felt naked.

"So, I hear through the grapevine that you're having a particularly bad day," he began.

"I'd say the school's having a worse day than I am."

"Well, whether you like it or not, you're part of the school. Tell me what happened, what really happened. By the time anything gets to this wing of the building, it's quite distorted, I'm sure. What actually caused all this commotion?"

*Commotion*, *situation*, whatever word was used, didn't do it justice. I looked down at the floor. His asking me about it stirred my rage the way a wild beast that had finally quieted down might burst into an angry roar when poked. My body tightened with the frustration I felt. He misread my silence.

"I'm not looking for juicy gossip," he said. "I know some of my colleagues feed on that, but I have a feeling you weren't treated fairly, and this whole thing, what's happening to you, is more important than gossip."

"Treated fairly? You've been here long enough to know that fairness is not the first consideration, not in a school where donors put in enough money to get their names on gyms and pools. Justice comes in only one color here, green."

He laughed. "Okay. What happened?" he asked, softening his tone. "How did this start?"

"How did it start? What happened was that I didn't turn into melting butter when the school's Don Juan, Carlton James, lowered himself to approach me in the cafeteria and suggest that we get together at his house after school. I believe his idea of a get-together is literally that. He thinks it's all about plugs and sockets."

He widened his smile. "That's very good. Plugs and sockets. I would have loved to be a fly on that cafeteria wall when he came on to you. I know who he is, of course. Girls trail behind him, waiting for him to drop a smile in their direction. They scoop it up like beggars hoping for a handout of love."

"You have time to notice that sort of thing?"

"I'm just being observant. We're all supposed to be observant. It comes with the job description. From what you're saying, I gather he struck out completely and left with his head in his hands."

"It was more like a balloon losing all its air. And I think he had more than his head in his hands."

"I'll bet," he said with that wide grin again. "He met more than his match when he tangled with you. And then what happened? I mean, how did it lead to all this?"

"Simple. Not being one who gracefully takes rejection, Carlton fanned the flames of hot gossip that were obediently and loyally spread by the three bitches from *Macbeth*, gossip that would make him look better, too."

"Three bitches? Not the three witches?"

"The witches at least had a purpose in Shakespeare's play, prophecy. These three just stir the pot of frogs and newts."

He shook his head. "I love it. So who are they?"

"Joyce Brooker, Cora Addison, and Denise Hartman."

"Oh, yeah. Now that you mention it, I have heard them mumbling, 'Fair is foul and foul is fair,' in the hallway. So they were the ones who mixed the witches' brew, went home, and told their parents you were making unhealthy sexual advances on them?"

"On them, I can't imagine any sexual advances possibly being healthy," I said.

He laughed again. "What fools to take you on. So?"

"We had some words in the locker room. They were trying to find out . . ."

"What?"

"If I was seeing someone from outside the school."

"Are you?" He raised his hands when I looked hard at him. Was this something he should be asking? "Just trying to understand the whole picture. Whether you are or not isn't my business. I will say I had that suspicion myself. Not that I'd blame you," he quickly added. "You're so far ahead of the boys here they probably look like tykes to you."

"Am I?"

He tilted his head. "I could tell that just from talking with you for a few minutes, Mayfair."

"I'm not seeing anyone from outside the school, anyone older," I said. "Nevertheless, they started to accuse me of being interested in *them*, assuming that if a girl turned down the school's heartthrob, she had to be gay. They accused me of paying too much attention to their naked bodies."

He unbuttoned the top button of his shirt. "I see. That's it? That was enough to cause all this commotion?"

"Mothers rushing to the defense of daughters in danger can be very persuasive, especially if their combined net worth is more than that of most third world countries."

"And what ruling has come down from the high command?"

"I'm excused from PE for the year and banned from the girls' locker room, where the alleged incidents took place. This is called a politically acceptable compromise because it's assumed I didn't want to go to PE."

He shook his head. "Makes you look like the bad one here."

"Tell me about it."

"Your parents approved of that?"

"Only my father's new wife appeared at the hanging."

"And put up no argument when they made that so-called compromise?"

"She probably cowrote it."

"Oh, I see. I'm sorry."

"That's all right. I didn't anticipate much more. Nothing to be sorry about, Mr. Taylor. I'm actually not brokenhearted about missing PE classes, and avoiding the locker room might prevent athlete's foot."

He laughed again. "Call me Alan," he said. "When we're alone in the building, I mean." Then he turned very serious. "I know that it's painful for you to see these other girls get it over on you, but joking about it doesn't help really, does it?"

"I suppose I can say it keeps me from crying, so it's the better choice."

"This sucks," he said, surprising me with his burst of anger. "It's why I keep thinking about looking for a job in a public school. There, everyone's equally abused. If there's anyone who deserves the full respect and support of this school's administration, it's you, Mayfair. I know for a fact that they brag about you whenever they can."

"Yeah, well, they will probably stop doing that. Politically risky."

He moved his hand close to mine, and before I could pull it back, he put his over mine. "You're putting on a good show, Mayfair, but I'm sure you feel as if you're all alone here, left to drift any which way, especially now. I've heard the talk about you in the faculty room. No one feels up to the challenges you present. You have to be pretty frustrated with how you're treated in and out of the classroom."

"If I gave it any real thought, I guess I would be."

"I'm sure you think about it. I don't have your IQ," he continued, "but I was pretty much at the head of my class in high school, and that cost me some popularity. It's stupid, but I intimidated some of the other students. I can't even begin to imagine how stupid you make your classmates feel."

"I don't have to do that. They do it for themselves," I said. "Stupidity is on sale here every day."

"You do have a great sense of humor, Mayfair."

"Sense of irony. There's a difference."

"Right, right."

He still had his hand over mine. Suddenly, he looked down at our hands and began to gently play with my fingers. I wanted to pull my hand away from his, but I didn't want to embarrass him or make him feel bad. I was enjoying his sympathy for me, maybe too much.

"There's no reason two people, two adult people, and that's what I consider you, an adult, can't treat each other like adults even in a place like this. I'm not your actual teacher here. For all practical purposes, I'm just like someone else you might meet on the outside. I wish you would seriously consider me your adult friend. That's what I would like to consider you."

Slowly, I pulled my hand back. "Thank you," I said.

"I mean it. I'm serious when I say that sometimes I feel as if I'm on an island here. Knowing that I have you to talk to occasionally will be something to look forward to."

"I'm not the best at making small talk, Mr. — "

"Alan."

"Alan."

"We won't make small talk. I promise. So," he said, glancing up at the wall clock, "I guess you missed your ride home. Your stepmother usually picks up you and your stepsister, Allison, right?"

Was there anything about me he didn't know? I guessed he was looking at me every chance he got.

"Bus duty," he said, seeing the puzzled look on my face. "I have to watch the critters board safely."

"Oh. Right. No, I didn't miss it. I told my father's new wife not to wait for me today."

"Why do you keep saying 'new wife'?"

"I'll never think of her as anything else."

"I see. No love lost, as they say."

"No love lost."

"Did you tell her not to wait after I asked you earlier to stop by? I mean, I'm flattered you remained after school, but . . ."

I saw where he was going. He thought I really wanted to see him, that perhaps I was hoping or expecting that he would take me home. "No. I had already made different plans," I said. I stood up. "Thanks for the talk, Mr. Taylor."

"Alan, please, when we're alone," he said. "Hearing you call me Mr. Taylor makes me feel older than I am."

"Okay. Thanks, Alan."

"I could give you a ride if you need one," he said, standing. "It's not a problem. I just have a few more things to do here, and . . ."

"That's all right. I've already made other arrangements," I said.

The disappointment on his face reminded me of Carlton James's reaction in the cafeteria. Young or old, when men didn't get the reaction from a female that they wanted or expected, they all looked the same, like little boys told to put away their toys and go to sleep.

"Wait," he said, and returned to his desk. He jotted something on a piece of paper and brought it to me.

"That's my home phone number. It's unlisted. Kids are always pulling prank calls on teachers, but you can call me anytime you want, day or night, Mayfair. I'll be there to listen, and if you want me to come get you or anything, you just call. Anytime."

Anytime? I wanted to ask him if he had a life away from this building. Didn't he have a girlfriend? How could he be so good-looking and not have a line of beautiful women at his door? Why would he be available anytime? Would it be ungrateful of me to ask?

Another thing occurred to me. Had he ever given his phone number to any other female student? Suddenly, everything about him became important. Was this his first teaching position? If not, why did he leave the first one? Where was he from? Did he have family in Los Angeles or somewhere else in California? Brothers or sisters? Had he ever been married or engaged? What sorts of friends did he have? Were they all teachers? How would he explain giving so much attention to a high-school student?

Since most of the girls here didn't talk much to me, I was at a disadvantage when it came to knowing these sorts of things about our teachers, but I did want to know more about him, if not for any other reason than to be careful.

It was so much easier for someone to get lost out there when a school was located in a city, especially one as large as Los Angeles. My imagination began to run a bit wild. Maybe after he left the building, he turned into a serial killer or was part of some sex cult.

And then I paused and thought how ridiculous it

was of me to imagine such things. It showed how this place was getting to me. I was beginning to think like some of these airheads. If any school did a good background check on its employees, it would be this one. The rich could afford paranoia, and this school catered to the wealthy.

"Thank you," I said, and put the paper with his number in my purse.

"I'm here for you," he said. "Remember that."

I nodded. He watched me leave. I closed the door behind me and walked slowly down the hall toward the front exit. I heard his door being opened, but I didn't look back to see if he was watching me walk away. It made me too self-conscious about my body. I felt as if I were in a summer thunderstorm.

Hot lightning sizzled around my heart. No man, no boy, had ever touched me the way Mr. Taylor just had. When he put his hand over mine and began to play with my fingers, it wasn't a fatherly gesture or just a friendly one. It was pure, raw sex. I could feel the heat moving through his hand and into mine. It stirred me. Fight back as hard as I tried, I couldn't keep the tingle from traveling like electricity up and down my spine and into my thighs and breasts. All sorts of sexual images flashed like lightning bolts against the darkness of my deepest thoughts. The images I had shown Allison created a stream of erotic pictures resembling a trailer for a movie with the title *Mayfair Cummings Loses Her Virginity*.

But there was thunder, too, loud crashes of warning hammering at my heart. Alan Taylor was a young man, yes, but no matter how I tried to rationalize it away, I was still legally a minor, and he was an adult with an influential position when it came to young women at the school. Besides the legal and ethical aspects, I had to confess to myself that he had an unfair advantage. He was a man of some experience who easily saw my vulnerability. How seamlessly he could make the transition from concerned faculty adviser to my first lover if I didn't heed the sound of thunder. But did I want to?

I really hated being vulnerable and innocent, because I was at a disadvantage. All the books and articles about sex that I had read did not prepare me for these feelings. I hated that more than anything. Information was always my steadfast protector, my God. I worshipped with encyclopedias, not Bibles, but here this was failing me.

And that made me angry, but to be honest, I wanted to be angry. Anger helped me avoid dealing with my inner feelings. How dare Mr. Taylor take advantage of me at one of my weakest moments? He knew I wasn't going to run to the principal or to my father to tell them about him. He certainly knew I wouldn't tell Julie. On top of what had just happened to me because of the three bitches, my creating another scandal would be too much. I wouldn't have any credibility, and it was no good to pretend that didn't matter. I still had to attend school here, and my father still had a life in this community. There was nothing to do right now but ignore what I could ignore and concentrate on my studies as usual.

I walked out and away from the building. I didn't want Mr. Taylor to see me get into a taxi after he had offered to drive me home. I sensed that he wouldn't take that as a rejection so much as a challenge. He would want me to understand that I didn't have to be bashful or embarrassed to ask him for help. Ironically, my refusing his offer would only encourage him more.

And yet I would be lying if I didn't admit to myself that I was more than flattered by his attention. The woman who had blossomed inside me couldn't help but continue to wonder what it would be like to be with such a good-looking adult man. I had read and understood enough to know that it would be quite different from being with Carlton James, even though Carlton saw himself as every girl's dream lover.

Carlton would go at it all too quickly, clumsily. The book I had given Allison explained the mechanics well. I knew that males often cared only about pleasing themselves and did so before the female even got started. In short, I knew Carlton wouldn't take love-making as seriously as a man like Mr. Taylor surely would or, at least, should. With Carlton, there would be no real romance, just groping and satisfying egos. For most of the girls, if not all of them here, that would be enough, but it wasn't enough for me. I wasn't looking to neck in the back of a movie theater or be with a boy in the rear of his car. Alan Taylor would know that, had to know that, otherwise he wouldn't have taken the risk of talking to me like this and making the subtle proposals he was making.

Shouldn't I be more attracted to that, to someone

who saw me for who I was, someone mature enough to handle this forbidden relationship?

When the three bitches accused me of being gay and making them uncomfortable in the locker room, I was angry, of course, but I couldn't deny that I had wondered about myself from time to time. I learned that it wasn't an uncommon thing for someone young to consider.

Maybe I *was* gay.

Maybe I *was* looking at those girls in the locker room.

I had read up on this once, and comments in a psychological abstract returned to me. If you thought back to your earliest memories and realized you'd always been different, you might be gay, but that didn't necessarily mean you were. However, I couldn't deny that I've always been different. I certainly didn't fit the stereotype of a gay woman, but not fitting a stereotype doesn't mean it's not true. And Albert Kinsey, a pioneer in human sexuality research, had determined that many people were in between.

Teenagers often felt strongly about members of their own sex and were aware of the attractiveness of someone of their own sex. I was keenly aware of how attractive Joyce Brooke was, but again, that didn't mean I was gay.

Did I drive Carlton away because his aggressiveness threatened me? Was I really turned off by him, or was I turned on too quickly and completely? Did I know in my heart that if I had gone with him to his home, I'd be unable to stop him from seducing me? Maybe deep down inside, that was what I really wanted, and I was afraid of myself more than I was of him.

Was I conflicted about Mr. Taylor for the same reasons?

Was Julie right? Was I infatuated with books and articles about sex because I was unsure about my own sexuality? I fantasized about boys. Wasn't that enough?

These thoughts kept the summer storm alive inside me. I didn't even realize how far I had walked until I reached the strip mall, where there were restaurants, a drugstore, a dry cleaner, and a mailing outlet. I'd call for a taxi and have the driver pick me up here, I thought, and walked toward the Italian restaurant.

Just as I stepped onto the sidewalk, I heard a car horn and turned to see Mr. Taylor pull into a parking spot. He waved and got out quickly. "What are you doing here?"

"I was going to meet someone here," I quickly replied.

"Oh. Secret date, huh?"

"Something like that. Maybe it was too secret."

He smiled and stood gazing at me with his hands on his hips. "Long walk from the school. Either you or your date were being very careful," he said.

"You're reading too much into it. Besides, walking is good for thinking, and right now, I have a lot of thinking to do."

"That it is. I don't do enough of it, of both. By the time I get home, I'm mentally drained from being on the front lines. That's what I call the junior high, the front lines. My students are like little hand grenades. When the bell rings to start class, it's like someone pulled the pin. I don't open my mouth before hands go up asking if what I said was important and should be put in their notebooks. There's enough energy in the room to launch a satellite into space."

"Sounds exhausting."

"Mentally, it is." He nodded toward the other restaurant, which was really more of a bar. "The truth is, I sometimes stop there for a while to have a drink and come back to earth." When I didn't say anything, he added, "Only one drink, of course."

It occurred to me that if he was going to stay here for a while, he would surely see the taxi arrive to pick me up. *Get out of this, genius*, I told myself.

*Unless, you don't want to get out of it.*

The summer thunderstorm inside me was gone. I felt more relaxed, maybe simply because I was out of the school building. Out here, I did feel as though we were equals of a sort. He was still a teacher, but he was never my teacher, and there were no administrators watching us from doorways.

"You're really not meeting someone, are you?" he asked, tilting his head a bit to the side and narrowing his eyes when I hesitated. "You just wanted to run away."

"I suppose," I said.

"Don't blame you." He looked at the bar and smiled. "How about we take a ride and look at the ocean? Nothing more calming than the sea on a day like this," he said. "Unless, of course, you're supposed to be home. I wouldn't want to be responsible for your getting into more trouble."

"I don't have to be anywhere," I said. "My father stopped putting curfews on me years ago."

"I bet. So?" He moved to the passenger side of his car and reached for the handle.

This was it, I thought, that great moment of decision. Should I fall back on being a teenage girl, or should I step forward and be a woman? For most of my life, I was so self-confident. I thought I would always make the right decisions, because I was so well informed and so perceptive. What I didn't count on, what I didn't consider, was what the woman in me would demand. Sometimes that had little to do with anything more than pure, raw feelings. "Okay," I said, and got in when he opened the door.

# 10

He got in very quickly, as if I might change my mind. Then he smiled, started the engine, and backed out of the parking space. Both of us glanced at the cars that rushed by, to see if any of the school administrators were driving past. I told myself that this was still very innocent. He just saw me walking along and offered a ride. They would certainly believe I had left the building in a rage.

"This looks like a new car," I said, running my hand over the leather.

"It is. I got it four months ago. I inherited a little money when my father died. He had remarried and left most of his money to his second wife. He had taken on the responsibility of raising her son, too. The kid's fourteen and a couple of handfuls, as I understand it. I haven't been close to the boy and probably won't see either of them given my father's passing."

"So you're an only child, too?"

"As far as I know," he said, smiling. "My mother wondered."

"What happened to her?"

"She died when I was in my teens, pancreatic cancer. She was just forty-five. I wasn't much older than you are. Chronological age, that is. I understand your mental age is off the charts."

"The latest research suggests that our brains never stop growing as long as we use them, learn new things, and keep challenging ourselves."

"Yes, I think that's true."

"And your father remarried, too."

"See? We have a great deal in common," he said. "Now all I need is fifty more points on my IQ."

"Believe me, you're better off not having them," I said.

"You feel that way now, but . . ." He looked at me. "And you won't change your mind later," he said, and we both laughed. I felt my body soften and defrost from the icy numbness that had overcome it most of the day.

He made some turns and headed west. As we drove along, he began to tell me more about himself. He was brought up in San Francisco, went to college in the Midwest and then took his first teaching position in a public school in Los Angeles. When the opportunity arose to teach in our private school, he jumped at it.

"I'm not making as much money, but I'm a lot happier with the class size, despite how I sound when I talk about it. At least the parents are involved.

Maybe too much," he added, obviously thinking about my day.

When we reached the Pacific Coast Highway, he pulled into the parking lot at the Will Rogers State Beach.

"You ever just walk on the beach?" he asked me.

"Rarely."

"You up for it now?"

"Yes," I said.

I really hadn't done it since my mother had died. Julie hated the beach, because the sun gave her wrinkles and the sand got into everything, including her hair. Consequently, my father never took us. Allison went with her friends occasionally, but, like her mother, she was too finicky to enjoy it and always came home complaining.

We got out of his car. There was a soft, cool breeze coming from the southwest. In the distance, I could see what looked like a cargo ship sliding along the horizon. Off to the north toward Malibu were two small sailboats. We're attracted to the sea because it takes us out of this world, I thought, off the land and far from our troubles and worries. I envied the ones on the sailboats.

"It is beautiful out there," he said, seeing how I gazed longingly at the soft blue in the distance.

"Yes."

"Ever sail?"

"No."

"I have a friend with a boat. I go out with him once or twice a month. Maybe I'll take you along sometime."

I looked at him as if he were promising to run off with me or something.

He laughed. "I will," he insisted.

We walked on.

"So, have you thought much about what you want to do? What you'll major in when you go to college? I bet you want to be a doctor, huh?" he asked as he walked.

"No, I don't think so. Maybe I'll go into bio research. I'm not sure yet."

"No hurry, I guess. I'm sure you're interested in many things. You just have to find the one that holds the most passion for you."

"Is that what you did?"

"Me? I thought I would write the great American novel but woke up days later looking at the same blank page. I enjoy teaching, though, when I have good students. At least at our school, we don't have the sort of discipline problems they have in public schools, and I don't have to spend so much time just getting the class civilized."

I laughed.

"Feeling a little better?"

"Yes," I said.

"You know, it's better if we take off our shoes and socks." He paused to do it, and so did I.

We went close enough to the water to get our feet wet.

"Yow, that's cold!" he cried, and retreated. I stayed with it a bit longer. "Aren't your ankles getting numb?"

"Maybe," I said. "I can't feel them. Does that have anything to do with it?"

He laughed, and I joined him on the softer sand.

For a while, neither of us spoke, and then I asked, "Do you have a girlfriend?"

"A couple," he said, smiling. "No one I consider serious. I'm in no rush."

"Don't any of them consider *you* seriously?"

"Maybe."

"That doesn't matter?"

He told me about a romance he had in college and how it had gone sour when his girlfriend went out secretly with a friend of his. "I guess that's made me gun-shy," he said.

His apparent honesty and willingness to talk about himself put me at ease, maybe too much at ease. When we were back at his car, he took out a towel he had in his trunk so we could wipe the sand off our feet and out from between our toes. He insisted that I sit so he could do my feet.

"Better rub them and get the circulation back since you spent all that time in the cold ocean."

"It's not that bad," I said, but he insisted.

"Nice feet," he told me. "You forgot to paint your toenails."

"I didn't forget."

He smiled, did his own feet, and got back into the car. "Still feeling better?" he asked.

"Yes, thank you."

"The magic of the sea," he said. "As long as you don't put your naked feet in it at this time of the year.

Actually, the Pacific is never warm enough for me unless I'm down in Mexico, way down."

We rode along quietly for a while, and then he slowed down.

"You have to get home?"

"I told you. I have no curfews, day or night."

"Right. I live right up here," he said. He looked at his watch. "What do you say to our getting a pizza and eating it at my apartment? I have a patio that looks out at the ocean. Of course," he said when I didn't respond immediately, "if that makes you uncomfortable . . ."

"No, it doesn't."

"Great."

He took that to mean yes, and I didn't say otherwise. He asked me what I wanted on the pizza and then called his favorite takeout place and ordered it with some salads. His car had Bluetooth, so I heard the conversation and understood that they knew him well at this restaurant.

"As you can tell," he said, "I'm not much for cooking. My best recipe is takeout. What about you?"

"I toy with it sometimes, but we have a maid who does most of our cooking and baking. We've had a few, actually. Julie, my father's new wife, as you know I like to call her, is hard on servants. She wears them down the way a driver who keeps his foot on the brake pedal wears down brake pads."

He laughed. "You sure come up with surprising comparisons."

"Not that surprising to me," I said.

"I bet. You really do fascinate me, Mayfair."

Normally, when someone said that to me, I shrugged it off. I had gotten used to hearing it, but the way he said it reached deeper inside me and stirred me sexually.

Our pizza was almost ready when we arrived. I waited in the car while he went in to get it. I had to admit it smelled delicious when he returned with it. Minutes later, we pulled into his apartment building's underground garage. He told me to leave my books in the car.

"That way, you won't forget anything when I take you home," he said.

"I never forget anything," I said, but I left them.

We went to the elevator and up to the eighth floor. He had a very nice marble-floored apartment with a living room that had a patio facing the ocean. I looked around. He didn't have any family photos up or photos of any women. The artwork was the sort you could pick up in a department store to work into your decor. I did see that he had his college diploma framed. While I was gazing about, he put on a Three Tenors—Luciano Pavarotti, Plácido Domingo, and José Carreras—CD.

"Is that all right?" he asked. "It's not rap or rock."

"I listen to it often," I said. "I enjoy many operas."

"Figured you might."

Was I that easy to read and predict? Was that because I wasn't as impulsive and reckless as most girls my chronological age?

He got our pizza ready and called me into his

dining room, which, aside from the china cabinet and one small table with a miniature grandfather clock on it, was also spartan. I saw a bottle of Chianti on the table.

"I'd rather have wine than beer with my pizza. Do you drink wine?"

"Occasionally," I said. I really hadn't drunk much wine. "Julie, my father's new wife, fancies herself a wine connoisseur, but she doesn't know the difference between a syrah and a pinot noir."

"You know about wine, too?" he asked.

"There are five basic types: red, white, and rosé; what is called fortified wine or dessert wine, which has extra alcohol; and sparkling wine and champagne. She buys sparkling wine and calls it champagne. Real champagne has to come from the Champagne province in France. I believe it's a trademarked name."

He stood with the opened bottle of Chianti in his hand, his mouth slightly open.

"And you know all this without drinking much of it?"

"I know about nuclear energy, too, but I've never created it or built a bomb," I replied.

He laughed, shrugged, and poured two glasses. "Well, I've gone this far. I might as well corrupt the morals of a minor who knows more about it than I do and give you some wine."

Maybe because he said that more than anything else, I eagerly drank the wine. I drank it too quickly, emptying my glass before his was a quarter empty. He poured me another. While we ate, he asked me more about my family life. "So tell me, why do you keep calling Julie your father's new wife? It sounds as if they just got married, but from what you're telling me, it's been years."

"She'll never be anything more to me," I said. "I don't care how many years they stay married."

He nodded. After we ate, he poured another glass for each of us, and we went out onto his patio to watch the sun setting.

"If you want to call home and let them know anything, go ahead," he told me.

I glanced at him. Was he testing me? Did he really mean I could tell them I was at his apartment having dinner and wine with him? The small smile on his face told me that he knew I wouldn't.

"It's not necessary," I said.

It really was necessary, but I wanted my father to worry. I wanted him to know how unhappy I was about what Julie had let Dr. Richards do to me. Let them believe for a while that I might have run off in a rage.

We finished the bottle of wine. It seemed to me that I had drunk most of it, because I drank faster than he did, and he kept filling my glass. He brought the empty bottle and the glasses in, and then I stood up, expecting he would now take me home. I remember feeling so relaxed. It was as if my whole body had turned into a down pillow. He met me in the living room, and for a moment, he just stood there looking at me. Maybe I really heard him say it, or maybe I was imagining it from the look in his eyes, but I walked up to him after I heard, "You have no idea how pretty you are, Mayfair, especially with a little flush in your cheeks. Don't let anyone tell you otherwise."

*I'll always regret not doing this if I don't*, I thought, *so I think I will.*

I kissed him. When I leaned back, I saw his look of surprise.

"I'm sorry," I said. "I didn't mean—"

"No," he said, putting his finger gently on my lips. "You meant it. It's all right."

Then he kissed me, but not like I had kissed him, not a quick snap of my lips against his.

I closed my eyes and still had them closed when he stopped. He didn't let go of my shoulders but brought my lips to his again, this time pressing a little harder. I felt his tongue press into my mouth. For a moment, only a moment, I thought I would tear myself out of his hands and rush to the door, but when his right hand went to my waist and his lips moved down to the side of my neck, I heard myself moan and felt my body soften even further.

"You're so beautiful," he kept whispering. "So beautiful."

He put his left arm around my waist and then his right arm under my legs and lifted me as if I were a little girl. I didn't protest. I had no doubts about what he was doing, but I didn't resist. Instead, I rested my head against his chest, and I could feel how that excited him, quickened his heartbeat. He carried me to his bed and lowered me gently.

My thoughts were spinning and tumbling over

one another in my head. He stood there looking down at me.

"Do you want it to stop?" he asked.

I shook my head. Then I watched him slowly undress, his eyes never leaving mine. It was as if his hands belonged to someone else. He loosened and took off his tie, dropping it to the floor, where he dropped his shirt, his pants, and then his underwear. He stood completely naked, enjoying the way I looked him over and reacted.

"Should I?" he asked, kneeling beside the bed and fingering the buttons of my blouse.

"Yes," I whispered. I hadn't had someone else undress me since I was three, and my mother would stand aside and watch how carefully I took off my clothes, folding them neatly.

I watched his face, the movements in his lips and his eyes, as he slowly, almost as if he wanted to tease himself, slipped my bra off me. He stared down at me so intensely.

"It's not a pot of gold," I said, and he laughed.

"To me, it is."

With continued surgical skill, he finished undressing me, taking his time to make little discoveries about my body, a dimple here, a birthmark there, the smoothness of my skin, and the soft rise of my breasts as my own breath quickened.

The wine kept me just a little confused, but I was thinking like someone who was observing and not participating. It was almost as if I were watching a medical procedure. I was fascinated with his every

move, how he continued stroking, kissing, and exciting me, and then how he stopped, remembered his
protection, which was just as much my protection,
and returned to me, again feasting on me with his eyes
first.

"You're like a Greek goddess," he said, and took
his time kissing every part of me, moving down to my
toes and then up again, pressing between my thighs,
moving over the rise of my stomach and nudging my
breasts ever so gently with his lips.

I felt as if I were sinking into the mattress, oozing
out of my body. Any thought of restraint was crushed
to bits the moment it raised its head or began to voice
itself. Every picture, every description of this moment
that I had read and seen, did it no justice. How foolish I was to believe I knew anything about my own
body when it came to what was now happening to
me. I thought this was why sex education in school
was such a weak fortress against passion and desire.
The teacher shouldn't be using textbooks. He or she
should be reading from great novels that aroused their
readers. Sex education should bring students real-life
scenes and then describe what should or should not
be done.

I did nothing to stop him, and when he was in me,
kissing me, chanting about his pleasure and my beauty,
I let myself fall back into the rush of my own exquisite
sensuality until I began to ride one wave of pleasure
after another. I was embarrassed by how I moaned and
cried. Actual tears streamed down my face. My heart
was pounding so fast and hard it seemed like one long

beat. When it all ended, I felt as if I were still dangling in space, until my blood calmed and I fell back into myself.

Without speaking, he rose and left the bedroom. I lay there, still naked, trying to recapture my normal breathing. Finally, when I had, I began to dress slowly, almost reluctantly. I watched the doorway, hesitating, hoping he would return to make love to me again, but to my surprise and disappointment, he was also dressed when he returned. He had his hair neatly brushed and looked as if he had nothing to do with what had gone on in his bedroom, almost like he was surprised to discover me in his apartment.

I hurried to dress myself now.

"How are you doing?" he asked.

"All right," I said.

"You surprised me. I really thought you were a virgin."

"I am. I was," I said. "I've never been with anyone like this. Do you want me to describe the female anatomy and why I didn't bleed?"

"No, no," he said, smiling and shaking his head. "That's a little too much information right now. Why don't you get refreshed in the bathroom while I clean up out here, and then I'll take you home. Curfew or no curfew, I'm sure you've got them wondering by now."

I didn't say anything. I went into the bathroom and looked at my flushed face. I brushed my hair, ran a cold washcloth over my forehead and cheeks, and then finished fixing my clothes. I still felt a little dazed.

He was waiting anxiously when I stepped out of the bathroom.

Because this was the first time I had been with any man, I wasn't sure what to expect. Would he start a review of our lovemaking to tell me how wonderful it had been? Would he offer some sort of apology, perhaps for moving too quickly? Would he ask me to be sure to keep this a secret? Would he say or do something to make absolutely sure I was all right with what had happened between us?

All these thoughts seemed very reasonable to me, but he acted on none of them. Instead, he began talking about the apartment, how long he had been in it, what the other tenants were like, and where he would really like to live. In his car, he went on and on about the commute to school and how it took him nearly twenty more minutes on some days.

I had to keep reminding myself that we had just made very passionate love. Was this normal? Was I making too much of it? Was that a sign of immaturity?

"One thing you can never anticipate in Los Angeles is the traffic. There's no rational way of figuring it out. Why Tuesdays are busier than some Mondays drives me nuts. You have your license yet?" he asked.

"No. I'm getting it this year," I said.

"You'll see what it's like. I know teenagers can't wait to drive, to have their own cars, but it's not long before you realize you were better off having someone drive you places."

*Suddenly, I'm back to being a teenager*, I thought. How could he turn it on and off so easily? I certainly didn't think of him as one of our school's teachers, not anymore.

"You have to give me directions. I have a vague idea where you live, but . . ."

"Turn up here," I said. "It's a faster way."

"Right. You okay?"

Finally, something that referred to what we had done, I thought.

"I'm fine," I said. "Maybe just a little tired."

"I bet. You've had one helluva day."

I looked at him. One helluva day? It was almost as if we had not gone for the ride to the beach, had the pizza and made love in his apartment, almost as if we were back at the strip mall and he was taking me directly home.

Does sex linger longer in the mind of a female than in that of a male? Perhaps that was it.

I knew what "wham, bam, thank you, ma'am" meant. Males satisfied themselves and then, as if that was all there was, left the scene. That wasn't lovemaking. That was love *taking*. In my way of thinking, it was as if they had mailed a letter with no address. They just wanted to put an envelope into a slot and leave. Whether it had any purpose or meaning wasn't important.

"What are you going to tell your parents?" he asked when I showed him our driveway. Although he tried to disguise it, I knew he was worried.

"I don't have to tell them anything."

He looked at me skeptically. "Come on. You didn't go home after school. Look at the time," he said.

"My father will just assume I went to the city library, and Julie won't even ask. I've done that before, or I've gone to museums without telling them ahead of time. If anything, Julie might be upset that I came home at all, especially after today. I'm sure she's been going on and on about how much of a strain it's been on her."

"What about dinner? Surely they'll be wondering about that."

"I told you. I've done it before and had something to eat nearby."

He nodded. I saw the way he was keeping his head tilted when he pulled up in front of the house. "Well, if they see that I brought you home, you can tell them I just bumped into you accidentally and offered you a lift."

"That's exactly what you did do," I said. I gathered my books.

"Well, I hope I helped you forget the bad time you had in school."

"What bad time?" I said, and he laughed.

"Take care of yourself, Mayfair," he said. It sounded like we would never see each other again.

*I thought that was what you were doing, taking care of me*, I wanted to say, but I didn't.

I just closed the car door and started for the front entrance of my house. I turned to watch him drive off, and then I took a deep breath and went inside.

Despite all I had told him and the brave face I had worn, I had no idea what really awaited me.

# 11

"Where were you?" my father demanded the moment I entered. He popped out of the living room, with Julie trailing behind him like a puppy. I looked at her first. If she was in any way concerned about how my father would react to what had been decided at school, it didn't show in her face. She was putting on an act, wearing the expression of a mother who had been wringing her hands with worry about a child.

"Your father has been beside himself," she said when I didn't answer immediately.

"I would have thought he would be beside you," I said.

"Don't get smart, Mayfair, and don't give me a lecture on the word *smart*, either. Where were you, damn it? After what happened today, you would think you would have come directly home."

"After what happened today, anyone would expect me never to come home. Daddy, didn't she tell you what she let them do to me?" I asked, practically shouting at him.

My father rarely saw me lose my temper. I had always relied more on sarcasm and good arguments. I had always believed that letting your emotions get control of you put you in a weaker place, but right now, I couldn't help myself. The events of the last few hours had confused me and twisted me up inside. I was feeling so many different emotions at once. It was a kaleido-scope of feelings. I had gone from anger to depression to elation. Now I had returned to anger. Julie's feigned face of concern put me over the top. I could barely con-tain myself. I felt like charging at her and slapping her and wiping that mask of false concern off her.

My father relaxed his shoulders and lost some of his aggressiveness and outrage. "As I understand it, it was a sensible compromise avoiding any more un-pleasantness for you."

"Avoiding unpleasantness for me? The only one who avoided any unpleasantness was Julie. Exactly how do you think those bitches are going to describe this to their friends in school? Are they going to tell them that I got the best of them because I don't have to take PE but I still get credit for it? Or are they going to make a big point of the fact that I was ripped out of the girls' locker room because I'm most likely gay? You're a big-shot advertising man, Daddy, how would you present this situation to the eagerly awaiting public?"

I continued, "Imagine a billboard with me on it being dragged by my hair out of the locker room and the bitches laughing. Got that image in your head?

Thank Julie for it, and then consider what it was and will be like for me in that school." I headed for the stairway.

"But we thought . . . I mean, I thought you'd be happier not having to deal with those girls every time you had PE, Mayfair," he said.

"Happier?" I turned to look at them. My father looked concerned, even a little sorry. Julie looked worried. Perhaps he wouldn't like her solution after all. I took a deep breath and continued to look wounded. I could put on a performance, too, even better than hers, I thought, if that was what it took to win back my father.

"Maybe it is my fault," I said. "It's been so long since I've been happy about anything. I probably don't recognize the feeling anymore. Besides, I wasn't afraid of dealing with them. What are they but vapid, self-absorbed Barbie dolls who spend most of their time agonizing over their choice of lipstick?" I looked so directly at Julie that someone would have to be blind not to see the connection I was making. "No, happy is not what I feel, Daddy. What I feel is betrayed, betrayed by the people who should have my best interests at heart and not their own."

I paused. I saw that my father was feeling worse every second, but I wanted him to feel that way. I wanted him to feel absolutely terrible.

"If you had been there, it might have turned out differently," I said in a softer tone. "You used to always be there for me, Daddy. I needed you today. I needed someone to defend me. My mother would have been there."

He looked up at me with as much sadness in his eyes as I had seen there since my mother's death. I started to feel sorrier for him than I did for myself. The truth was, I really didn't care what the bitches from *Macbeth* thought and said. I was angrier with Julie than I was with them. And I was angry with my father for giving her so much control over what happened to me.

But there was nothing more I could do about it right now. And I didn't want to dwell on the bad and the ugly. I wanted to think about Alan Taylor. I wanted to relive my time with him. It was still so fresh.

"Just forget about it, Daddy," I said. "It's not too important in the scheme of things. I'll live, and all the precious reputations have been saved."

"Did you have dinner?"

"I grabbed something."

"Where were you?"

"City library," I said.

Normally, I wouldn't lie to him. I had never done anything I didn't feel I could justify or defend, but this was quite different. If I began to analyze it, I was sure I would have trouble justifying and defending it to myself.

He nodded.

"I'm going to take a bath and read," I said, and continued up the stairway.

As soon as I turned down the hallway, Allison burst out of her room. Her shiny new braces glittered in the hall light. Girls her age weren't as upset about their braces as girls used to be, because every six weeks, when they went in to have them tightened, they could change the color. When that was mentioned at dinner one night, I had told my father that good advertising could make a root canal desirable, and he had laughed. That was one of our happier moments, the kind of moments that seemed rare now.

Allison wore an oversize nightshirt with a print of her astrological sign, Virgo, spread over her budding breasts and belly. Her birthday was August 24. The English translation of *Virgo* is "virgin," and for a moment, having that astrological sign in my face seemed like poetic irony.

"I'm glad you're home," she said. Those weren't words I heard her utter often.

"What do you want?" was my natural question. I wasn't disappointed. She was happy to see me because she needed something, but in this house now, that wasn't unusual behavior.

"I need help with this math assignment. It's brutal."

"Brutal?"

I had to smile at the hyperboles she and other girls her age often used. They were so dramatic, so over-the-top. Everything that happened to them, whether it was a pimple or a dead iPod battery, was tragic, practically fatal. I couldn't recall ever being like that. Although I mocked them, at times I envied them. They seemed to be able to sidestep every really important task or decision. Moaning and groaning, throwing up their hands, and bursting into a downpour of tears, they fed on adult sympathy and usually got their way. Maybe I could learn something from them after all.

Parents, especially today's parents, would do absolutely ridiculous things to placate their teenagers, including driving back miles to school to bring them an AA battery or a cell-phone charger. Later they would complain to other parents about it, but those parents would confess to doing similar things. Sometimes I felt like a modern-day Alexander de Tocqueville, analyzing society the way he analyzed American democracy. I was smart enough to do it, but it left me feeling like an outsider. Where did I belong?

"Let's see it," I said in a tired voice. I wasn't exaggerating. I was really feeling exhausted.

"Thanks!" she cried, and led me to the desk in her room.

Julie had spared no expense in setting up Allison's room, from its four-poster canopy bed with a headboard of embossed cherubs to the recently installed vanity table with a mirror straight out of a *Snow White* illustration. I half expected to hear *Mirror, mirror, on the wall, who's the fairest of them all?* automatically recited every time she stood or sat in front of it. She had a computer table and a desk and a walk-in closet that was twice the size of mine. We had similar en suite bathrooms, all marble, with whirlpool tubs and large stall showers. Of course, Allison, like me, had her own telephone, the difference being that she used hers. Mine was almost a table decoration. Most of the time, it rang only when my father called me, and lately, he hadn't done much of that.

I looked at her assignment. To me, it was the equivalent of one plus one equals two.

"This only asks you to find the fourth angle of a quadrilateral, Allison. It's basic addition and subtraction. It's far from brutal."

"I wasn't paying attention today," she confessed. "I don't remember what a quadrilateral is."

I sighed. I could never be a good teacher, I thought. It took too much patience. "A quadrilateral is a polygon with four sides or edges and four vertices or corners."

She grimaced as if I had just fed her a bitter herb. "What's a polygon?"

"Didn't you listen to anything?"

She shrugged. "Mr. Bissel talks too fast. He teaches to the kids who are really smart and forgets the rest of us."

I nodded. She was probably right. Most of the teachers I had were the same way. They looked for the easiest way to get through their classes, and ignoring the students who didn't grasp concepts and ideas quickly enough was the most convenient method.

"A polygon is simply a plane figure bounded by a closed path or circuit. It's two-dimensional, length and width. So, here, this rectangle is a polygon," I said, drawing one. "This problem tells you that the sum of the four corners is three hundred sixty degrees, right?"

"Uh-huh."

"So, just add up these three corners, which equals two hundred seventy, and subtract that from . . . ?"

"The three hundred sixty?"

"Exactly. What's the answer?"

"Ninety."

"That's it. You do the same thing with the other five problems, Allison."

"And the last one?"

"That just asks you to find the area of a square. Didn't he show you this, at least? You just multiply the base times itself."

She shrugged again. I couldn't believe any teacher would be that lackadaisical.

"What were you doing in class today?"

Her face flushed with guilt. *Today.* I should have known. Why wouldn't it all have filtered down to the junior high? The school had a total population, grades seven to twelve, of just more than nine hundred students. And everyone was in the same building.

"Someone was talking about me?" I asked.

She nodded. "I didn't encourage them," she said quickly, "but they kept passing notes to me, asking me stupid questions."

"Like what?"

I saw how reluctant she was to answer. Instead, she went to her book bag, opened it, and took out three slips of paper to hand to me.

One read, *Does she watch you take showers or baths?*

Another asked, *Does she want you to help her masturbate?*

The last one simply asked, *Does she kiss you on the lips?*

"Well," I said. "It looks like you've become quite popular. Everyone will want to be your friend to be the first to learn some gossip."

"I didn't tell them anything. I told them they were all stupid."

"Did you tell your mother about this?"

Again, she looked guilty. "I didn't show them to her. I just told her a little," she confessed.

"What did she say?"

"She said she wanted me to do my best to ignore them, but . . ."

"But what?"

"But to tell her if anything like *that* ever happened."

"Do you think it would?"

"No. You're just very smart. You're not like that. Right?"

I nearly laughed at her uncertainty. "Right, Allison." I gave her back the notes. "Save these. We might need them as evidence someday."

"For what?"

"A lawsuit."

"Really?"

"Really," I said. I started to leave.

"Mr. Taylor said something like that to me today, too."

I turned back. "Mr. Taylor?"

"Uh-huh."

"What? What did he say?"

"He saw that I was upset. I sit right up front. He's always looking at me to see if I understand things or if I'm unhappy. He gives me special attention."

"Does he? So what did he say, Allison?" I asked more firmly.

"When the bell rang, he told me to stay behind a

moment, and then he said he'd heard some nasty rumors were being spread about you and that I shouldn't
pay them any attention. He said those spreading them
would get themselves in big trouble. He's the nicest
teacher in the school, and the best-looking. I know he
likes me a lot," she added.

Something about the way she said that sounded an
alarm. "Likes you? What do you mean?"

"He likes me," she said. "He's always looking at
me and smiling and stuff."

"What stuff?"

"Just stuff," she said, and sat at her desk. "Thanks
for helping me, Mayfair. My friends think you do my
homework all the time, especially when I get a high
grade. That's why I try not to ask you too much."

"Forget your friends. If you don't understand
something, you ask me. They're just jealous."

"That's what I thought."

I hesitated a moment as she worked on the remainder of the math problems.

"Right?" she asked, showing me her answers.

"That's it. Look, Allison, I want you to tell me
what else Mr. Taylor says to you, especially over the
next few days, okay?"

"Why?"

"I'd just like that. I help you with your homework,
don't I? You can do that for me, can't you?"

"Okay," she said.

I started out again.

"Mayfair?"

"What?"

"You're not really like they're saying you are, right?"

*Look how easily someone's reputation can be ruined*, I thought. Often, just being accused of something made you guilty. Most people weren't going to be bothered with proof. Here was my stepsister, who had lived with me for years, already thinking it was possible.

"I already told you no, but stop looking so worried. Even if I were, it's not anyone else's business, and people who are like that are still good people."

I thought of something that I knew would bug her.

"Why? Are you feeling that way about yourself?"

"No!" She grimaced and shook her head vehemently.

I laughed. "See how easy it is to make you sound guilty? Don't grow up with your mother's middle-class prejudices," I said. "If you can help it, that is."

She just stared at me. I knew I was taking her too high too quickly.

But as the poet Robert Browning wrote, "A man's reach should exceed his grasp, or what's a heaven for?"

Arrogant of me, but I thought that if Allison hung around me, enough might rub off to make her at least a decent student, if not a decent person. Julie was worried that I might be a bad influence on her. *I'll be an influence on her, all right. I'll get her eyes open wide enough to see what a hypocrite her mother is.*

But I wasn't thinking about Julie now. I was thinking about Alan Taylor. Did he single out Allison because of me? Was he paying too much attention to

her? At her age, she was far more vulnerable than I
was, and today, I thought, I was most vulnerable.

I ran a bath and soaked in it, not because I felt
unclean or spoiled after having been with Alan but
because it relaxed me and let me think. What bothered
me the most was the idea that I had allowed myself
to be a victim today in so many ways. It began in
Dr. Richards's office and ended in Alan Taylor's bed.
I wanted to blame my troubles in school on those
bitchy girls and Julie, but did I let it happen? Could I
have been shrewder and more intelligent about how I
had handled it all?

Did I throw myself at Alan Taylor willingly, or did
I fall into a trap, all the while thinking I knew what I
was doing? *I'm smarter than he is. I'm old enough to
understand and handle myself,* I had told myself.

Was I suffering from what the Greeks called *hubris,* excessive pride, the fault that would bring tragedy
to the arrogant? Had my super intelligence turned me
into too much of a snob, a smuggie? Did I deserve
what was happening to me after all?

One of my grade-school teachers, Mrs. Schumer,
once voiced something to my parents that I thought
she regretted immediately afterward. They were talking about my superior intellect, the wonders I had
performed in second grade, and Mrs. Schumer said, "I
wonder if it's a curse or a blessing." She looked at my
parents' faces. This was something they had heard before from Fish Face, and they didn't like it then.

Mrs. Schumer quickly added, "Of course it's a
blessing. Look at what she will be able to do. Why,

I imagine someday, I'll be reading about her accomplishments."

She spoke as quickly as she could to override her previous utterance, but I saw it was too late. It had already taken root in my parents' minds and would flower into more and more doubt as time went by.

It had taken root in me, too. It grew like a wild vine, reaching deeper and wider inside me.

As I lay there in my bathtub filled with soothing bubbles and bath oil, these thoughts, these memories, streamed behind my closed eyelids.

And minutes later, when I opened my eyes and looked at myself in the mirror, I saw that I had been crying. Not realizing that I had been until I looked at myself was more frightening than anything.

It was truly as if there were someone else in me, a second Mayfair, who was always trying to emerge, to pop out of me and cry, *"I'm the real Mayfair Cummings, not you. I want to be normal. I want to have fun, do stupid things, eat the wrong things, make happy mistakes, laugh at dumb jokes, wear silly clothes, flirt with vapid boys, cheer my lungs out at football games, eat popcorn and watch a goofy Simple Simon raunchy movie, and neck and pet in dark corners at house parties where we all drink too much or smoke pot or take other stuff and feel like rotten apples in the morning but laugh about it on telephone calls that go on and on until our parents scream at us to get off and do something worthwhile like clean our rooms and pick up all the clothes scattered everywhere.*

*I'm the real Mayfair Cummings, not you. I'm*

*putting you back in the box and stamping it "No lon-
ger at this address."*

I put my hands over my ears as if I really did hear
my second self, and then I took some deep breaths, got
out of the tub, and got ready for bed.

There was a knock at my door.

"Not another problem, Allison," I called.

The door opened. It was my father.

"Oh."

"Hey, May," he said when he entered. He hadn't
called me that for a long, long time. I couldn't recall
when he had first started, but it was his most affection-
ate greeting. "Hey, May." Sometimes he would just
say it, smile, and go on to do whatever he had to do,
but it always made me feel good. Once he composed a
little rhyme that he would often sing for me.

*Hey, May, what do you say?*
*Hope you had a very good day.*
*If not, someone's going to pay.*

It made me smile and made my mother laugh.
Now it seemed so long ago; it felt more like something
I had watched on television or read in a book. Maybe
it was just wishful thinking, a little fantasy.

I pulled myself up on my pillow and watched him
come to my bed and sit at the foot of it, just the way
he used to before he married Julie.

"Sorry about what you went through today. I
intend to give that Dr. Richards a piece of my mind
tomorrow."

"Don't bother. It won't help. They're all probably
right. I'm better off away from those girls."

"I would have been there, but there was a major screw-up at the firm, and . . ."

"Don't knock yourself out about it, Daddy. It's over. I didn't expect that Julie would stand up for me, and she lived up to my expectations, that's all."

He nodded. "She thought she was doing the right thing."

"Believe what you need to believe," I said.

"I know it's not easy for you, hasn't been, but . . ."

"Let's just go to sleep, Daddy."

I lowered myself again. He got up and fixed my blanket. I kept my eyes closed and then felt him kiss me on the forehead. He brushed my hair. For a moment, I was afraid he might notice the change in me, sense that I had been with someone, but that was probably the furthest thing from his mind.

"Good night, May," he said. He turned off my lamp.

" 'Night," I said.

I heard him leave and close the door softly. For a while, I just lay there in the dark. I was worried that I wouldn't fall asleep, that I would stay up all night thinking about this roller-coaster day, but when I finally did close my eyes, it was as if I had fallen into a coma. I didn't dream; I didn't remember getting into bed. The light of morning surprised me the way a spotlight might catch a burglar stalking a target. It took me a few moments to realize that it was another day and I would face even more challenges, more than I, with my super intelligence, could ever imagine.

My father was quieter than usual in the morning. He always had things to say to Allison. Sometimes I thought he was sweeter to her than he was to me, but I excused that by thinking she was so much younger and more insecure. I couldn't remember being as insecure as she was, and I supposed my father never thought I needed as much reinforcement, but that didn't stop me from feeling sibling rivalry. In short, I was jealous, something I never imagined I would be.

"I'm sorry about all this happening to you, Mayfair," he said when we'd arrived at the school. "Let's just let things calm down for a while and then talk about it some more, okay? The three of us can have a family meeting."

"I don't need things to calm down to talk about them, Daddy. But I know you do," I said. "Or should I say, Julie does, which has become the same thing, unfortunately."

He didn't like that, and he didn't answer. I closed the car door and followed Allison into the school. Probably the thing I was most curious about this morning was the way Alan Taylor would look at me and what he might say. Like all homeroom teachers, he was at his doorway. Dr. Richards wanted his teachers always keeping an eye on the students as they passed through the hallways, especially in the morning. That's what Alan meant when he told me that being observant was in the job description.

He saw me coming toward him, but he didn't smile, nor did he acknowledge me in any particular way. Instead, he started to talk to a seventh-grader and turned his back on me. It gave me the strangest feeling. I wasn't angry as much as I was confused. It was almost as if I had dreamed everything that had happened between us.

Two periods later, I had another opportunity to walk past his classroom, and once again, he was in the doorway. This time, he looked at me, but it was as though he had never spoken to me and didn't know anything about me. It was the look someone would give a total stranger, an empty glance, his eyes shifting quickly toward someone he did know, and then a smile and chatter.

Perhaps he thought it was too dangerous for us to be seen talking to each other now, I thought. That had to be it. Why else would he ignore me today? Maybe, just maybe, someone had seen us together, and he was trying to show Dr. Richards that there was nothing to it.

The school day was passing quickly. I was bored and distracted in every class, and during math, I read nearly all of *Crime and Punishment.* I wasn't a speed-reader like those people trained in the Evelyn Wood methods. There was a trade-off between speed and comprehension. Long ago, during some educational psychological testing, it was determined that I had another gift associated with my super intelligence. It was the ability to gulp thousands of words and process them instantly. It was not uncommon for me at age five to read a book a day and understand each and every word, and those were books read by adults.

When the bell rang at the end of the period that I knew was the one right before Alan Taylor's free period, I strolled down to his room to see if he would beckon for me to come in. He was just leaving when I approached. He turned and saw me. I anticipated at least a smile this time. There was no one else in the hallway, but he turned again instead and hurried off toward the faculty room. I almost called to him but choked back his name and watched him disappear around the corner.

What could possibly be the reason for his ignoring me completely?

I debated remaining after school so I could confront him, but I didn't. Perhaps it was better that he find a way to contact me safely, I thought, and went out to get into Julie's car with Allison. I sat in the rear, where I normally sat, and, as usual, didn't offer a word of conversation. Julie looked more nervous than usual.

The day had turned quite overcast. A storm was blowing in from the north, and that meant rain was very possible, and the temperatures were dropping. The weather fit my mood now. I almost welcomed it.

"You were pretty hard on your father yesterday," Julie finally said, after we had been riding for a while.

I didn't respond, but Julie was one of those people who always had to have the last word.

"I know you're a very intelligent person, Mayfair, yes, probably a genius, but you really need to work on your people skills."

"And what are people skills, pray tell?" I couldn't help but ask.

"You probably don't know this," she said, "but I took a course in people skills."

"No, I didn't know there was such a course. Where was it given? The mall, Saks, Nordstrom? How many times did you have to take it to pass?"

"You're not funny, Mayfair. I happen to get along very well with most people, no matter what position they're in or how important they are. And you want to know why?"

"I have a feeling you're going to tell me, no matter what, so why?"

"Because I show people that I care about what they say and who they are. I keep an open mind. No matter what you accomplish in your life and what honors you receive, you're still going to have to communicate with others."

"I'm impressed, Julie. That's two out of three."

"Two out of three what?"

"Complete sentences. The first was an adverbial clause, what we call a sentence fragment. Allison knows what I mean," I said. "I've helped her with her grammar homework."

Allison looked at me, frightened that I was somehow turning her into an ally against her mother.

"Okay, be like that. I tried. You never gave me a chance to be a friend to you, a mother. I am your father's wife, and that's a fact that can't be denied. I love that man. I'm warning you. I won't sit back and let you hurt him."

"Don't worry about it," I said. It was a weak thing to say, but there was no doubt in my mind that she had greater influence over my father now than I did, maybe than I ever had. I hated the fact that he was a man and, like most, was vulnerable to a good-looking woman. He needed that, maybe as much as he needed me, if he did need me.

My eyes stung with tears that I wouldn't release. Now that I thought more about it, I hated the idea that in my father's eyes, Julie would care for him, protect him, more than I did or perhaps more than I could.

"And despite any of this, all that's going on in this house," she continued, almost under her breath, "Allison is going to grow up normal, because she will permit me to be her mother, to be her friend and give her the benefit of my experience. She's going to have friends and go on dates and go to parties and go to college."

"And get married, live in a house with a white picket fence, and have other little Allisons," I said.

"Exactly." She nodded at me in the rearview mirror. "Exactly. And as much ridicule as you toss over it, normal relationships give you the best chance at being happy."

"Like your first one?"

"You're just trying to hurt someone else because you feel hurt," she said.

I turned away, folding my arms and leaning against the window. Sometimes Julie's arrows hit their targets. That one did.

The rain began to fall. The monotonous sound of the wipers began.

Allison turned around to look at me, then quickly turned back so her mother wouldn't think she felt sorry for me in any way.

Right now, I didn't need her to do that anyway. I didn't need anyone to do it.

I was feeling sorry enough for myself.

# 12

When my phone rang that night, I thought there was a real possibility that it was Alan Taylor. I had given him my private phone number because I had hoped he would be calling me to arrange our next rendezvous. I had explained that he could risk a phone call because I had my privacy at home. When we had walked on the beach, I had talked about my life after my mother had died and especially after my father had remarried. By the time the evening was over, Alan certainly knew what I thought of Julie and how disappointed I had been in my father for marrying her and catering to her so much. During our dinner, I had described how little I had to do with her and even with my father at this point. I'd made it sound as if I lived in my own cave in our house.

Maybe he was calling to explain his behavior toward me in school, I thought. I was ready to accept any excuse and believe any reason he had, as long as it wouldn't prevent us from seeing each other again.

Our lovemaking had been the centerpiece of my day-dreaming.

I practically tore the receiver off the cradle, but as soon as I heard the voice of the caller, my heart felt like it had dropped into a sinkhole. It wasn't Alan. It was Joy, my new best friend whether I liked it or not. I had followed through on one promise to her. I had gotten her a good deal of information about anorexia, its symptoms, causes, and treatment. There was even a list of possible therapists in the area. I had put stars next to the names of the ones I thought might be most helpful. She had promised she would give it all to her mother, and I gave her my private phone number in case she or her mother had to ask me a question about any of it. Now I regretted it.

"How are you?" she asked.

"I saw you today, Joy. You know how I am. I'm fine."

"No, you're not, Mayfair," she said with uncharacteristic authority. "Is something else bothering you?"

"Why would you ask that?"

She was quiet.

"Were you watching me again, following me all day?"

I wondered if she had seen how many times I deliberately passed Alan Taylor's classroom and how I looked toward him, anticipating some personal recognition. If she had seen my face, she might have noticed my disappointment. Was she smart enough to suspect anything?

"I just want to be able to do something for you,"

she said. "You're trying to do something for me. My mother was impressed with the information you gave me. We had a talk. She admitted other people have said something to her about me. I will be seeing someone, one of the names you put a star next to."

"Good. Good luck."

"What about you?"

"What about me?"

"Are you sure there's nothing going on? Are those girls annoying you? Did someone say something to you, Carlton James or anyone?"

"No, and if they did, it wouldn't bother me at all. You should know that, Joy."

"I know. That's why I really thought it might be something else."

"There's nothing you can help me with, Joy."

"Oh. So there is something bothering you, but it's something I can't help you with?"

"No."

"You're sure?"

I was surprised that she hung on to my exact wording. Maybe I was rubbing off on her. "Don't be a nag," I said, and she laughed. I thought about her for a moment. She was such a lost soul. She was trying desperately to have a friend, to be needed, and to contribute something of value. I didn't have to be so hard on her right now just because I was hoping for Alan Taylor to be calling. "Thanks anyway for offering," I added, which I knew made her happy.

"If you ever need a friend for anything," she said, "please choose me."

"Okay, Joy."

"I mean it. Promise?"

"Yes, I promise. Look, I've got to go," I said. "I left a physics problem on the stove."

"What?"

"I'm just kidding, but I do have some reading I want to do tonight. Thanks again for calling."

"Okay," she said. "See you tomorrow. 'Night."

I hung up.

I couldn't imagine how she could help me with anything, especially Alan Taylor, but I had to admit to myself that it was nice hearing her offer, nice knowing someone was caring enough about me for whatever reason to sense that something wasn't right with me. I wondered what she would do if I really did confide in her. She probably wouldn't tell anyone at school, but she might tell her mother. Why take the chance? What would I gain? She certainly didn't have the experience to offer me any sensible suggestions. Besides, it required too much trust. As sad as it seemed, I doubted I would ever meet anyone in whom I could invest such confidence. Even my father had fallen into the realm of doubt.

Nothing was very different during the remainder of the school week and the beginning of the next. The bitches of *Macbeth* finally seemed to be bored with me and my apparent lack of interest in them. I imagined that everything surrounding the episode in the locker room discouraged them. I wasn't acting destroyed by it. There wasn't enough excitement in it anymore. Little did they know that my silence and further withdrawal from everything in the school had less to do with them and more to do with Alan Taylor, but there was no doubt in my mind about what they would do if they knew about that.

Alan continued to ignore me, to do everything he could to avoid looking directly at me, and he didn't say a word to me, even though there were a few opportunities for him to do so. I couldn't get myself to approach him and force him to acknowledge me. It felt too much like begging for attention, and besides, Joy was practically attached to me whenever she could be. It was like I had given birth to a second shadow. She had begun to see a therapist and was making some progress. I didn't want to do anything to detract from that. I knew my interest in her, albeit more scientific than emotional, was an important reason for her effort to recuperate. She wanted my approval. Right now, she was the only one who wanted that.

I thought about waiting around for Alan after school a few times but decided not to do it. I even wondered if he was waiting for me to do what I had done the first time and not go home with Julie and Allison but instead walk down to the strip mall and wait for him, where he had first picked me up. One day, I actually did that. He never followed me. In fact, I was sure I saw him drive right by, not even looking my way or, if he did see me, quickly turning away. In the end, I had to call a taxi.

My reaction to all this surprised me. I thought I could be more mature about it. After all, he had treated me like a mature, sophisticated woman and probably expected that I would behave accordingly. I could shake off the disappointment and go on as if nothing had happened if I put my mind to it, couldn't I? I certainly wouldn't become some lovesick teenager ready to toss herself off a bridge. But despite the confidence I had in myself, I felt myself sinking deeper and deeper into what I recognized as a serious depression. I no longer wore any makeup, didn't do much with my hair, and returned to wearing the clothes I had been wearing before Julie added to my wardrobe. Maybe I was punishing myself for being so naive and vulnerable, but I hated to come to that conclusion and think of myself as the kind of foolish, innocent young girl I often accused my classmates of being. If Julie got wind of this tryst between Alan Taylor and me and my reaction afterward, she would surely gloat.

I could see her now, lecturing my father, telling him how she could easily have predicted that something like this would happen to me. "The girl wouldn't listen to anything I said. She was always too high-and-mighty to take my advice. Oh, no, what does someone like me have to offer? What does someone like me know? Of course you should be proud of her academic achievements, Roger, but you've even said it yourself: a person has to have more than a high IQ to be a complete person, and Mayfair is far from a complete person. The fact is, she's socially immature, otherwise how could a thing like this have happened? How could a young girl living in our home be so . . . so . . . inadequate when it comes to relationships and permit herself to be taken advantage of like this?"

My father would just sit there soaking up her criticism and feeling like a total failure as a parent. Julie's hold over him and over me, for that matter, would grow tenfold, and who was really to blame for it?

Me, that's who.

It didn't matter that a teacher was involved and would take the brunt of the blame in the legal sense. He was an adult, and my chronological age made me a minor, but victims weren't given a pass all the time, even minors and especially females when it came to male abuse or exploitation. In some countries, women who were raped were punished, too.

The conclusion was almost the same everywhere. Somehow, for some reason, we always shared the blame, or to some people, we were solely responsible. We did something to tempt the male, and besides, we were spoiled now, damaged property. It was a lose-lose situation.

You'd practically have to go into the federal witness protection program to get a new start, to be innocent, pure, and fresh again in everyone's eyes.

Besides, if there was any girl who was supposed to be smart enough to avoid such a trap, it surely was me, the girl whose IQ was so far above anyone else's that it floated close to the Pearly Gates.

I had no intention of permitting this sort of criticism and ridicule to happen to me. I wasn't going to break down and cry about how a teacher seduced me, go running to Dr. Richards or Mr. Martin about it. What a field day the three bitches from *Macbeth* would have with that. They would tell every boy in school, and every one of them would approach me with some nasty suggestion. Life would be more of a living hell than it was now.

*No, swallow it all back and plod on,* I told myself. *Just try to keep yourself as busy as possible. That way, you'll worry about it less and less and stop pitying yourself. Eventually, it will all dissipate like smoke.* Of course, that was easier said than done.

How many times did I stop reading to think about what was happening? How often did I simply sit there staring into space before I realized what I was doing?

Nothing seemed to be important anymore. I was experiencing all the symptoms of deep depression. I knew it, too, but like someone sitting in a car without brakes careening down a mountainside, I couldn't prevent what was happening to me. I could only sit there and wait for the crash.

Thinking about all this made the world seem even darker and darker.

I felt like someone in quicksand who knew she was sinking but couldn't reach out for help from any of these adults and so-called professionals.

However, because I had so little contact with my teachers and fellow students, ironically no one but Joy took any particular notice of my depression. The others must have thought my silence, my self-imposed solitude, and my unhappy face were normal for me. My invisibility had grown too effective. I could collapse on the hall floor, and the other students rushing to class would step over me. Maybe they would even step on me without noticing.

Joy never stopped asking what was bothering me. She called often, and although she pretended to be calling about herself, with some question about her condition, she always brought the conversation back to me. It almost made me laugh aloud to think that someone so out of the mainstream was so observant, so sensitive to me, that she could see the subtle differences. It finally occurred to me that she really did care about me and wasn't simply trying to give herself some meaning and importance. Ironically, I was the sister she had never had. She had tuned herself in to the frequency over which my moods and feelings flowed, just like a real sister might.

Finally, I admitted to her that I was disappointed in someone.

"Who?" she asked instantly.

"I think it's better that I don't mention his name."

"Oh, so it's one of the boys at school," she concluded. "Well, he has to be blind and stupid."

"I'll get over it," I told her. "It would help, though, if you would stop asking. It keeps me thinking about it. Understand?"

She nodded quickly, grateful for the tidbit. Confiding that much in her didn't change my behavior in school at all. If anything, it made me think I had to be more careful, even a little more withdrawn.

I knew that Julie was quite satisfied with my further withdrawal. I didn't criticize or oppose anything she did or said in the house, any changes she got my father to make. As soon as I was home from school, I went into my room and stayed there until dinner.

My father was particularly busy at this time. There was one crisis after another at the company because of some bad economic news involving two of the pharmaceutical companies he represented. He was occupied with trying to pick up new business and was traveling more than usual for meetings in the Midwest and on the East Coast. We simply weren't talking to each other as often as usual.

The first hint anyone else at school had of my new mental state was my failure to turn in any required work and my not putting down a single answer on any test. I'd hand in the papers untouched. At first, some of the teachers thought they had given out too many tests and I had an extra copy or that I had lost my homework. They couldn't conceive of my not handing something in when it was due.

However, when they asked me about it, I simply said I didn't hand it in.

"Why not?" they asked.

"Sorry, I haven't done it," I said, without a note of regret.

The expressions on their faces ran the whole gamut of reactions from indifference to surprise and finally to a reprimand and a lecture telling me not to underestimate the importance of their classes.

It amused me how some of my teachers took my refusal to do any work so personally. I realized they saw it as a result of my arrogance. They believed I never thought of them as important enough to add anything to my education. I could see it in their eyes. How dare I belittle them and their subject matter and

embarrass them in front of the other students by failing or ignoring their assignments and tests?

Whatever any of them said to me in these lec-
tures went in one ear and out the other. I saw the
expressions of glee on the faces of other students who
overheard us. Sometimes I nodded and looked like I
understood and might even get back to the way I was.
They could take credit for saving me or something.
But more often than not, I simply walked away without speaking and without changing expression.

Finally, one afternoon, Mr. Martin called me to his
office to ask me what was going on. He had five different referrals now and probably had ignored them
as long as he possibly could, hoping I would get back
on track and make them all superfluous. Ever since my
confrontation with the girls in the locker room and the
subsequent meeting in Dr. Richards's office, Mr. Martin looked uncomfortable in my presence. He barely
nodded at me in the hallway and rarely took time to
speak to me the way he often had before the locker-
room incident. It was as if he had been enclosed in ice.

The moment I entered his office, I could see how
nervous and uncomfortable he was. "Mayfair," he said,
holding the five referrals up like a poker hand. "What
is all this? What's happening here?"

"I don't know what's happening here, Mr. Martin.
I wonder who does."

"What kind of an answer is that, Mayfair, especially from you?"

"I don't know," I replied. "Most of my life is spent
answering questions these days."

For a moment, he just stared at me. I could almost hear the wheels turning in his mind. I was normally a big challenge for him, but something like this involving me of all people threw him completely off kilter. I was sure he had told the principal and others that he wasn't trained to deal with a student like me as it was, because of all my special problems. Who here was?

"Is it what some of your teachers think? You think the work's too insignificant now and not worthy of your attention and efforts?"

"I suppose it's significant enough for most of the students," I said. "Although teaching intermediate algebra and calculus to some of them is like driving around with no place to go. How long can you do it before running out of gas?"

"You're not making any sense to me, Mayfair, and you're worrying a number of people here who are really concerned about you. You might not believe it, but there are many people here who think you are someone very special, someone we should do our best to satisfy and prepare for the world out there."

"The world out there?"

He looked at the referrals again and then back at me. "Aren't you feeling well? Is there something you should tell the nurse, maybe?"

I nearly laughed. "I don't have female problems, Mr. Martin, and I'm not pregnant."

Mr. Martin was a fair-complexioned man to start with. He had light brown hair and freckles that looked like spots of carrot juice on his cheeks. When he blushed, his face became so red he looked like he had a terrible sunburn. It made his green eyes practically luminous. "I didn't mean that," he said. "Is there anything, anything at all, you want to tell me?" He sounded desperate, actually interested. It was tempting.

Where would I begin? I wondered. Should I start with my need to be more accepted, surrendering to the female in me, and going to Julie for assistance, something that took away all my self-pride? Or should I begin by explaining how easily I was taken in by the school's most eligible and desirable bachelor? Maybe compare myself to the story of the fox and the hen? Despite how the parable turned out, who could fault the fox, and who didn't laugh at the naive hen? How could I do that? And besides, even if I was ready to tell someone, was he the person I should talk to, especially after he had sat in that office with Dr. Richards when the mothers of the bitches from *Macbeth* complained and then let what happened to me happen?

I realized just how much I missed my mother. For any girl, there were certain problems and subjects she felt more comfortable discussing with her mother and not her father or a best friend or anyone else. After my mother died, I did depend on my father more than most girls depended on theirs, but most of my life, I was able to analyze and solve my own issues and not bother him. Maybe that was arrogant, but I couldn't help thinking that no matter what, I could take care of myself better than anyone could take care of me, now and forever. But I really did need my mother. I needed to be cuddled and petted and told everything would be all right. When parents did it, you believed it.

Why did death have to be so damn final?

Why couldn't I at least pick up the telephone and call my mother in the great beyond and ask her advice?

Did I even believe in the great beyond?

*I'm getting childish*, I thought. *I'm losing my famous self-control.* Next thing I knew, I'd be sleeping again with my old stuffed teddy bear, the earliest gift I remembered my mother and father buying me. It was in a box, a symbolic coffin, in my closet. I put it there the day my mother died. I even dreamed of going to her grave, digging down to her coffin, and putting the bear in with her so she wouldn't be lonely.

I really was a child once. When my mother died, I became my father's little girl, at least for a short while. And I couldn't say I did that only for him. I needed his affection almost as much as he needed mine. I felt a little like that now, maybe more than a little. I battled not to burst into tears in Mr. Martin's office. I swallowed them back and balled my hands into fists so tight my nails cut into my palms and my knuckles turned bloodred.

*I will not cry*, I chanted to myself. *I will not cry. None of these people will ever get the satisfaction of seeing me cry.*

"No," I told him. "There's nothing I want to tell you."

"It doesn't have anything to do with your other problem, does it?"

"What other problem? I thought Dr. Richards brought that to a complete and satisfactory end. Both of you had it all under such control, remember?"

He nodded. I could see it in his face. He was thinking, *So this is the game you're playing with me?* "Okay,
Mayfair. I'm going to have to discuss this with your
parents."

"I don't have parents. I have only a father," I said.

"You may return to class," he said, "but please, feel
free to come here to talk to me anytime you want."

He said that so often, probably at the end of every
conversation with every student, that I wondered if it
wasn't a recording inserted in his brain by some hyp-
notist.

Of course, when he called my house, Julie took the
message and then embellished it when she called my
father. I was sure it had given her the most pleasure
anything had given her all day. The administration
of the school actually calling to complain about my
scholastic work? They were desperate for help, and
therefore they verified her view of me. If they, educational professionals trained to handle and help young
students, had so much trouble understanding me at
school, what she and others considered my world,
how could she be blamed for failing me at home?

She did such a good job on my father that he post-
poned an important business meeting to come home
early. She was very clever about it all, too. When she
picked up Allison and me, she never mentioned Mr.
Martin's call and how she had panicked my father. I
even wondered if Mr. Martin had decided to wait to
see how our little nontalk affected me. After all, he and
the other professionals were being paid to handle the
problems at school. In a private school like ours, they

did all they could to avoid laying any concerns on the parents of these privileged children. The last thing they wanted to hear was something like "Why am I paying all this money to send her here?"

Allison had been invited to a classmate's birthday party this coming Friday. The mother was one of Julie's garden party crowd, and of course wealthy and therefore, in Julie's mind, very important. She wanted to be sure Allison had a new dress and matching shoes. That was all she talked about during the ride home; she had already gone to her favorite boutique and set aside a few things for Allison to try on. She wanted Allison to have her hair done on Friday after school and had made an appointment.

"You'll have a manicure, too," she said. "You show your friends how much you care about them when you spend time on what you will wear and how you will look at their parties. It's simply good etiquette. And," she added, mostly for my benefit, I'm sure, "it's very nice that you are invited to parties, the more important parties."

Allison glanced at me to see my reaction. I just smiled at her. She looked grateful for that. Lately, she had been trying to get closer to me. She asked me even more questions concerning her schoolwork. Even after I gave her answers or helped her understand something, she lingered, hoping, I was sure, for me to say something personal. Julie usually gave her a look of reprimand if she saw that she was spending too much time with me. All that did was make Allison nervous. The truth was that despite her friends and going to parties, Allison was as lonely as I was. I sensed that she missed her father and couldn't condemn him as completely as Julie would like. It always would be a source of tension between them.

Julie was destroying her own daughter, I thought, and she didn't even know it.

Maybe, in the end, she would destroy me, too.

# 13

I was surprised to see my father's car at the house this early in the day, but then I thought about my meeting with Mr. Martin and imagined that he had reached him at work. I was still thinking that Julie didn't know about it.

"Oh, Daddy's home," Allison said, glancing at me. "He's never home this early."

Julie was watching me in the rearview mirror. "He's waiting for you in the living room, Mayfair. I called him immediately when I received the call from Mr. Martin," she said with a cold smile. "Allison, I want you to go up to your room. This is something Mayfair's father and I have to discuss with her and her only."

Allison looked to me immediately, but I gave her no hint of anything. In fact, I tried to look as uninterested and bored as I was with most things her mother planned. She got out quickly and hurried into the house.

"Couldn't wait to call him, could you?" I asked Julie as she started after Allison.

"Of course. He'd be more upset if I had waited."

When we entered, I hesitated in the hallway. I had no idea what I was going to give him as an excuse for my new academic suicide. Of course I was expecting him to be very angry, especially after the way Julie had surely presented it all to him, but he surprised me.

"Hey, May," he said when I stepped into the living-room doorway. "C'mon in. I came home to talk to you."

I nodded at him and sat, still holding my books in my arms. Allison had already gone upstairs. Julie sat beside him on the settee, doing her best to look like she really was concerned. *Why is he so blind?*

"Julie tells me that the school contacted us today," he began.

"School? How does a school contact someone?"

"No games, okay? Your guidance counselor, Mr. Martin, phoned. Julie called me to tell me, and I called him back as soon as I could. Apparently, you have been on some kind of academic strike or something, and no one can understand why. So, why?"

I looked away. There were so many other ways he should have known I wasn't happy, but it was always my schoolwork, my intellectual achievements, that drew his attention first and foremost. Didn't he notice the changes in me, my clothes, my whole demeanor? Didn't he think it had something to do with deep emotion and not something intellectual? Was he that oblivious to my feelings?

Maybe in his mind now, I was what my uncle Justin had once called me in jest, nothing more than a walking computer. Maybe he thought I plugged myself into the internet when I went to sleep, and kilobytes of information began flowing into my brain like a blood transfusion. Maybe he had given up on thinking of me the way a father would think of his daughter. I had metamorphosed into some alien creature living in his home.

*Daddy, Daddy*, I heard myself cry inside like a little girl feeling herself fall into a dark and frightening dream. *Can't you see me anymore?*

"It's very confusing to all of us, Mayfair," he continued. "As far as I know, you were free to follow your own interests as long as you did what was required, and that was never much of a challenge for you. Is this all because of what happened with those girls?"

First Mr. Martin and now him, I thought. Everyone always looked for the easiest solution.

"I told you. I couldn't care less about them and all that now. I'm not starving for friends and invitations to stupid parties. I don't care if I ever make the social page," I added, looking pointedly at Julie.

"But what happened to change your feelings about all that? You did ask Julie to help you with your clothes, your makeup and hair, and—"

"I thought it was important. I was wrong. I realized how vapid I was in danger of becoming."

"Vapid?" Julie said.

"Dull, insipid," I defined. "No one's ever called you that?"

"Stop it, Mayfair. We're here to talk about you."

"Yes, we wondered why you stopped taking care of yourself," Julie said.

"We?"

"Julie and I did discuss it, Mayfair."

"I wouldn't exactly refer to it as taking care of myself," I said.

"You know what we mean, Mayfair," my father said, looking disgusted with me.

"I came to the conclusion that it wasn't the most important thing."

"But feeling good about how you look is important," my father followed. "And I saw that you did feel better about yourself. What happened to change your mind about it? Obviously, it's affecting more than a potential social life now. Is it boy trouble?"

I didn't say anything. Why didn't he ask me this earlier? Why did it take a call from the school to open his eyes? He glanced at Julie, who kept her lips pursed and her face stiff. She didn't look at me; she just continued to face forward. I felt like getting up and slapping her to knock that mask off her face. I almost did. Maybe my father saw that in me, because his expression became a little fearful.

"No," I said sharply.

"Because if it is, that's nothing to be ashamed about, and Julie could—"

"I'm not ashamed! And I wouldn't go to Julie even if I was!"

They were both deadly quiet, almost of one face. I could hear the miniature grandfather clock on the mantel ticking, or was that the beat of my heart?

"Look, Mayfair," he said after a deep sigh, "I'm not someone who is comfortable pretending he knows more than he does or trying to do things he knows he's not qualified to do. We have a situation here, and—"

"There's that word again, *situation*," I muttered. "And that other word, *we*?"

"Yes, we, Mayfair. We're all part of this family, and when something affects one of us, it affects all of us. Now, getting back to what I was saying. I recognize there's a problem that is more serious than I first thought, and I want to do something about it."

"Like what?"

He hesitated for a moment. Julie looked at him, anticipating. "I think you should see a therapist. For a few times, at least," he quickly added. "As I said, I'm not qualified to do that sort of work, and neither is Julie. We readily admit it, but we care about you, and we're worried."

"So you want me to see a therapist," I said. "You think that would solve the situation?"

"It's a start, Mayfair. Many people, good people, successful people, are in some form of therapy or another. Life is very complex today. You're a unique individual, and you have problems and issues most people don't have, that most couldn't possibly understand."

"Because I'm so unusual?"

"Whatever," he said. "The problems are there because you are an exceptionally intelligent person. Everything in this life comes with its own baggage."

"Baggage? So now you think it's a curse, is that it?" I asked him.

"What is?"

I was disappointed that he didn't remember having once been told that I might be cursed or I might be blessed with such superior intelligence. "Nothing," I said. I stood up. "Okay. I'll see a therapist. It might be interesting. Let me know when I have an appointment."

"You have one tomorrow," he said quickly.

I spun around. "Tomorrow? What sort of therapist has an opening so quickly?"

"One of Julie's friends is good friends with a highly regarded therapist, Dr. Burns in Santa Monica. And—"

"Oh, one of Julie's friends? Maybe she is really one of his clients and not one of his friends. Therapy is in vogue, I know. It's right under getting a facial on the list of priorities for her friends."

"You're not funny, Mayfair. Your appointment is at two o'clock," my father said firmly. "I have a car and a driver arranged to pick you up at school and take you home. I'd do it myself, but I have a full day."

"Therapy car service. Probably a booming business around here," I said. "Fine." I started to leave.

"You don't believe us, I know," Julie said, "but we are very worried about you."

"Oh, I believe it, Julie. I'm just not convinced you both share the same reasons for it. Well," I said, looking at my father, "maybe that's no longer true."

My father looked at me sternly. "Two o'clock tomorrow, Mayfair," he said.

I glanced at Julie. She nearly smiled. I hurried out and up the stairs.

Allison had her door open and quickly turned from brushing her hair and looking in her Snow White vanity mirror when I approached. "I could hear some of it from the top of the stairs," she confessed.

"Good. Then I can verify that I didn't imagine it," I said.

She grimaced. "I'm sorry you're not feeling well," she said.

"That's funny," I said.

"What's funny?"

"You're the only one who is sorry." Of course she was confused, but I had no patience or interest in explaining it to her.

"What's wrong with you? Why do they want you to go to a therapist?"

"I'm round, and I can't fit into the box."

"What?"

"I don't feel like talking about it right now, Allison," I said, and went into my room. I didn't sulk like a child, but I kept to myself as much as possible for the remainder of the evening.

Julie didn't say a word to me in the morning. My father told me he would be very interested in hearing about my first therapy session as soon as he was able to give me his full attention. I told him I would make a full report in triplicate if he wanted it.

"I hope you take this seriously, Mayfair," he said. "Or at least give it a chance."

I didn't respond. Maybe I did need therapy. Maybe

he was right after all. I mean, didn't I push Joy into going into therapy? This might be one of those "Physician, heal thyself" sorts of things. Even therapists needed therapy.

Later, in school, I suddenly became a little paranoid about it, however. There were other clues. It seemed to me the bitches of *Macbeth* weren't ignoring me anymore. In the halls, in classrooms, and in the cafeteria, they were looking my way, smiling and whispering. Maybe they had overheard some of my teachers talking about me, or maybe Mr. Martin's secretary gossiped about our meeting and my behavior. Another very likely possibility was that Julie had discussed me with Joyce Brooker's mother, perhaps even telling her that I was going to see a therapist. Joyce Brooker's mother might even be the therapist's client.

If that was true, these girls could tell everyone how right they were about me. "See? She really is crazy. We told you so."

Something more was definitely going on. I could sense it. Carlton James wore a look of deep self-satisfaction. He, too, whispered to his buddies and looked at me while doing so. Then he strutted with pride and threw me a condescending smile that said, "You should have accepted my invitation, bitch. Now look at where you are."

Even Joy looked at me differently. Her "Are you all right?" now seemed planted.

"If you ask me that one more time, I won't talk to you again, understand?"

She nodded.

"Don't," I said, as she started to explain herself. "Just forget it."

She bit down on her lower lip and followed me around in silence. I thought I saw her talking with Cora, one of the bitches, between classes. Why would any of them give her the time of day? Maybe she was promised something, like an invitation to a party, if she spied on me and got them some juicy gossip to spread. My paranoia was exploding. I had to get hold of myself.

However, by two o'clock, I told myself it didn't matter that I was paranoid. I was convinced Joseph Heller's famous quote from *Catch-22* that "Just because you're paranoid doesn't mean they're not after you" was true, especially for me. All that I believed was happening was really happening. My stepmother, Julie, had sabotaged me at school. Whether it was true or not, I convinced myself that it was at minimum a credible theory.

I saw Allison in the hallway and pulled her away from her friends.

"Did your mother know you overheard the conversation with me in the living room yesterday?" I asked her. "Well?"

She nodded.

"Did she tell you not to say anything in school or to any of your friends?"

"No," she said. "I only told . . ."

"Don't tell me. It doesn't matter," I said, and left her.

In a way, Julie had done me a favor. My self-pity

turned into raw rage. By the time I got into the car
to go to Dr. Burns's office, my strategy was formed.
I was tired of being the victim here. My old self was
returning. I could feel the surge of energy and glee.

*I'll show my father's new wife how to play this
game*, I thought.

Dr. Burns had a small but very comfortable and
bright office. There was a large bay window in his
lobby that faced the ocean, so the afternoon sun
beamed through the translucent curtains and tinted
windows. There were two dark brown leather settees
that faced each other, with a glass table between them.
Everything was immaculate and neat, including the ar-
tificial flowers that were strategically placed to supple-
ment the brightness and warmth. The light blue walls
had framed prints of country scenes, fields, rivers, and
mountains. Everything was designed to make someone feel relaxed and safe, including the elevator music
piped in but kept so low it was almost subliminal.

His secretary sat in a small inner office with a
window facing the lobby. I could see the file cabinets,
copy machine, fax, and printer behind her. She had a
name plaque that read "Sylvia Jones." I thought she
was about Julie's age but less plastic-looking. She was
even permitting some gray strands to infiltrate her
neatly styled dark brown hair.

"I'm Mayfair Cummings," I said.

"Yes," she said, smiling with that superficial warmth
surely designed to let the doctor's clients feel relaxed
and calm about the fact that they were here to see a
therapist, that they were admitting something wasn't

right with them. "I'll let Dr. Burns known you're here. He's just finishing up a phone call."

"Don't I have to fill out anything?"

"No, dear. Everything's been done."

Probably by Julie, I thought. Maybe even a year ago.

I went to sit, but before I could, the second inner office door opened, and Dr. Burns called to me.

"Hi there," he said.

If a director were looking to cast an actor for the role of a modern-day psychotherapist in a play, he'd have chosen Dr. Burns. It reinforced a theory of mine that people often grew to look just like people expected them to look. Dr. Burns, who probably was no more than forty, was the new hip psychotherapist, with long black hair, wearing jeans and a light blue long-sleeved denim shirt with the sleeves rolled up to suggest he was going to get down to real work. He even had a small diamond stud earring.

In honor of Dr. Freud, maybe, he had a neatly trimmed goatee and a pair of wire-rimmed glasses that rested on the bridge of his nose. He looked to be about my father's height but much slimmer in build. I thought he had almost feminine hands. He extended his right hand, and I took it to shake, but he held on to mine and stepped back to have me enter his office, not letting go until I walked in and he could close the door. Maybe he was afraid that after taking one look at him, I'd turn and run. Perhaps he had potential clients who had done just that.

I gazed around. He had a large, dark-cherrywood

desk, a window that also looked out on the ocean, and another behind his desk with the drapes drawn closed. There was an oversize chair in front of his desk, walls of filled bookshelves, and only one picture, a print of the famous *Christina's World* by Andrew Wyeth. It showed a young woman lying in a field and looking like she's crawling or wants to start crawling toward a gray house on the horizon.

Dr. Burns saw that I was looking at it. "All my clients love that painting," he said. "Everyone has a different interpretation about who she is, why she's lying in the field, what's in the house."

"And you use that to analyze them?"

"Sometimes," he said, smiling. "Should we use it for you?"

"Won't work. I know the history of that painting. Wyeth saw a young woman with a paralyzed lower body crawling and was inspired to do the painting. He used his wife as a model for the girl's torso, even though she was much older than the girl depicted."

"You can still find some meaning in it, can't you?" he said, indicating that I should sit in the large chair as he moved behind his desk.

"I just told you what it was."

"You're very literal. Please, sit," he said when I continued to stand.

"What?" I said, looking around. "No couch?"

He laughed. "That chair has a lever on the side, and you can sit all the way back with your feet up. How's that?"

"Perfect." I sat and tried the lever.

"Don't fall asleep on me. I've had that happen more times than I care to admit."

"Then don't bore me," I said, sitting up again.

He smiled, but not as widely or as deeply as he had the first time. "Okay. Let's see if I can avoid that." He said, looked at a file on his desk. "Mayfair Cummings, nearly seventeen years old, with quite a remarkable school history. You're in very good physical health, I see."

"How long have you had all that information?"

"Oh, a little while. Preparation is important, right?"

"That's not preparation. That's anticipation. Maybe even a little plotting."

He laughed and sat back. "Okay. Let's not go through the mental fencing. I have no illusions about being subtle with you. I know how intelligent you are. You might know as much about my work as I do. Your parents are concerned that you've hit a wall of unhappiness with yourself, and we're here to see if we can understand the cause and do something about it."

"Father," I said.

"Pardon?"

"My father is concerned. His new wife, Julie, has her own agenda."

"Oh? Which is . . . ?"

"She couldn't care less about my academic achievements. She wants me to fall in line, be what she calls normal, so I don't corrupt her daughter with independent thinking or distract my father too much from paying attention to her."

"I see."

"No, you don't. You haven't heard enough, and you haven't asked the right questions yet."

"Okay. Let me try. What makes her think you're not normal?"

"I don't dwell on my appearance, my clothes, my hair. She tried desperately to get me to do that, to be more like her. For a while, I tried it, but I felt like a phony. So in her mind, I'm not normal. I don't have a boyfriend or go to parties, and I'm still a virgin." I thought I'd add "still a virgin," even though it was no longer true. It was important to my strategy.

Dr. Burns looked sufficiently shocked. "She doesn't want you to be a virgin?"

"Let's say she wants me to be more interested in sex than I am," I said. "It's clearly very important to her, and anyone who is not as interested in it as she is would be abnormal in her way of thinking."

"What has she done or said to get you to believe this?"

"She's tried to get me to look sexier, wear low-cut blouses, shorter skirts, push-up bras, more makeup. She's even tried to get me to enjoy orgasms."

He stared and sat forward. "I don't understand. How did she do that?"

"Told me how she enjoys sex, masturbation, and then . . ."

"Then what?"

"Bought me a vibrator."

"She bought it for you?"

"Yes. My father doesn't know about it. I haven't used it yet. She keeps asking."

I saw his look move from skepticism to thought-fulness. Then he wrote some notes and nodded. "Well, let's go back a little. How do you feel about the boys at your school?"

I smiled to myself. *He's buying it*, I thought. "There are some I think are good-looking, but they haven't shown interest in me. I suppose I'm a little shy. Julie makes me feel bad about that. Sometimes I wish I could please her just to get her off my back. She's tried giving me hints about how to be more enticing, how to flirt, stuff like that. I feel funny about it, but I can't tell my father these things, so I feel a little trapped. I suppose this has all been weighing on my mind lately, gotten me depressed. I didn't want to worry my father, but I just haven't figured out how to explain it to him. He's so devoted to her."

"I see."

"Yes, now you might have enough to begin to see," I said.

"Maybe you should consider psychology as a career."

I shrugged. "Maybe," I said. "I have been think-ing about that, but let's see how well you do with me first."

He laughed and leaned forward. "Tell me more about this pressure your stepmother is putting on you," he said. "I notice you don't call her that. You said"—he looked at his notes—"your father's new wife, but haven't they been married for years?"

"Well, she'll always be new in my eyes. He was married before."

"And your mother died. You resented Julie right from the start, then?"

"Classic. Of course. Any child doesn't want to see her mother completely replaced, forgotten. I think I handled it as well as could be expected. I'm not troubled by that anymore. My father made a decision he thought was best for us both, and that's that. It's just that . . ."

"Yes?"

"With all this concentration on boys and sex, she seems more like an older sister to me or an older girlfriend."

"Go on about that," he said, nodding.

I continued, elaborating on the details I had planned to describe as vividly as I could, describing evenings when she came to my room to tell me about her own sexual exploits, explaining how it would make me stronger to have such experiences and help me decide when it came time to settle on one person.

"She said it wasn't fair that boys were expected to have many girlfriends, many sexual experiences, but girls who did the same were frowned upon, labeled with nasty names."

He nodded and took lots of notes, scribbling away for practically the entire session.

It was going just as I had planned.

# 14

"Well?" my father asked. "How did it go with Dr. Burns?"

He had come to my bedroom. I was lying on my bed and reading *The Art of Persuasion*. I was surprised at just how many techniques had come to me instinctively when I was in Dr. Burns's office. Ironically, I thought, my father would be very proud of me under any other circumstances. I was in his world of advertising and persuasion, a world where the truth was easily twisted or completely buried.

Julie wasn't home when I returned. She had taken Allison to try on outfits for another party, so she couldn't give my father a preliminary report concerning how I looked or acted after my therapy session. I had planned on giving her a little of her own medicine, phony smiles and sweetness.

I lowered my book. "I like him," I said. "He has a good sense of humor, and he's not heavy."

"Heavy?"

"I don't mean his weight, Daddy. You know, too demanding, pushing, getting too quickly into your head."

"Oh, right. Well, what about progress? You think you can make some with him?"

I nodded. "He helped me see some things. I won't deny that it's good to have someone who wants to listen to you, even if he gets paid to do it."

"Well, as I said, someone who is trained to help is important," my father said. "As you always tell me, a little learning is a dangerous thing. Go whole hog."

He really couldn't see how unhappy I was about all this, I thought. It wasn't that long ago when he could sense something was bothering me with just a look or a few words. I wasn't inscrutable when it came to him. I wouldn't even try to fool him back then. Maybe Julie was influencing me more than I would willingly credit her for. After all, I had a master of disguise right under my feet. Learn from your enemies, and distrust your friends enough not to be disappointed. That had become one of my new rules of life.

"I couldn't agree more. Amateur psychologists don't do anyone any good."

He smiled with relief. "I'm not an amateur psychologist. I just don't like to see you unhappy, Mayfair."

"I don't like to be unhappy, Daddy," I replied, and he laughed.

"Maybe we'll all go out to dinner Friday night, huh?"

"Allison has another one of her socially important parties. Julie will want you to take her and pick her up."

"Oh, right. Well, we'll figure it out," he said.

"I'm sure we will," I replied. *As long as it fits what Julie wants*, I thought.

He nodded, smiled, and left. I looked at the empty doorway and wondered for a moment if I was doing the right thing with Dr. Burns. I could lose my father completely. We were alienated enough from each other as it was without me adding to it, but it was too late. I had gone too far. I was confident of what would happen next, and sure enough, it did.

Julie did not ask me anything about my therapy that night at dinner or the following morning on the way to school. It wasn't that she was afraid to ask or didn't want to know. I had a different sense of it. Something told me she was confident that she would know everything whenever she wanted.

When I arrived at school, I continued to feel this new sense of energy that had been born out of my anger. I returned to the vigorous pursuit of my academics. I aced a math test, answered questions in social studies, and got into such a deep discussion with Mr. Feldman about *Huckleberry Finn* that it seemed as if there was no one else in the classroom but us. He was very happy, even exhilarated. He told me he felt like he was back in college, discussing great literature with his professor. Half of the class hadn't even read the portions he had assigned.

He said a nice thing to me. "For one bright moment, I remembered why I had gotten into teaching in the first place."

The result was electric. Before the day had ended,

my teachers had reported my academic resurrection to Mr. Martin, and he was eager to show how effective he had been, even with someone like me. I knew he especially wanted to please my father. Before the day ended, he had obviously called Julie and reported to her. She commented about it when she came to pick up Allison and me.

"I was pleased to hear you've returned to doing well in school again, Mayfair. I'm glad I recommended Dr. Burns to your father. Therapy can be helpful," she said.

"Yes, it can be. You should try it yourself," I told her, and her look of self-satisfaction evaporated.

The real result, however, my intended result, occurred after I had two more sessions with Dr. Burns, elaborating even more on what I had told him the first time, providing practically pornographic details.

It was one of Julie's girls' nights out, and she had gone to dinner, which was supposed to be followed with a movie, but instead, she had come right home. She made quite a dramatic entrance.

Allison rushed in to tell me. "My mother's back early," she said, gasping.

"So?"

"I was downstairs watching television, and she came home very upset, slamming the door and crying."

"Really? Think she had a fight with one of her vapid friends?"

"What's vapid?"

"Ask your mother."

She looked at me strangely and then returned to

her excited report. "I don't know if she had a fight with anyone. She wouldn't let me stay there with her and Daddy," she said. "She told me to go up to my room, and Daddy agreed."

Julie had insisted that Allison call my father Daddy, both as a way of killing any relationship she might still have with her real father and as a lesson to me, for I still refused to call her anything but Julie. Nevertheless, Allison was always a bit hesitant to do so when she was alone with me. She thought I might resent it, when, in fact, I was more unhappy for her father than for myself.

"I never saw her so angry and upset, even when she had bad fights with my father," she told me.

"Well, I'm sure it's nothing terribly serious. Women get hysterical over small things sometimes. It's part of being a woman," I said.

"It is?"

"According to most men," I added. Allison was lost. I smiled to myself and returned to my computer.

I was intrigued with some experiments being carried out at Oxford University involving the transplanting of human brain cells into monkeys to improve their intelligence. Out of the corner of my eye, however, I saw that Allison was quite shaken and didn't want to leave my room. Julie must have gone quite over the top, I thought, frightening her own daughter with her antics.

"You can stay here and watch television, if you want," I told Allison. "Just keep the volume low."

"Okay."

She turned on my television and sat watching it. Fifteen minutes later, my father arrived. He asked her to leave us alone. She glanced at me and then turned off the television and hurried out.

"You frightened her, Daddy," I said. "She's frightened enough as it is over how her mother apparently behaved. The child has enough damage from Julie's bitter marriage and divorce. She should be the one seeing Dr. Burns. As a matter of fact, if—"

"Forget Allison for the moment, Mayfair," he replied sharply, and closed the door. He just stood there looking at me and shaking his head.

"All right. What is it now?" I asked, and turned completely around in my computer desk chair.

"Why did you make up all those lies about Julie?"

"Excuse me?"

"The things you told Dr. Burns," he said. "Absolutely crazy lies."

"How do you or anyone else know what went on between me and Dr. Burns? Are you telling me that Dr. Burns violated the confidentiality between himself and his client?"

"I'm not interested in that, Mayfair."

"Well, I am. Do you think I would have been so forthcoming if I thought he would gossip about me? What did he do? Call you? Call Julie?"

"How she found out isn't important."

"Stop saying that. If anything, you should be on the phone with your attorney and not up here talking with me. He told one of her friends, didn't he? What, is he having an affair with her?"

He just stared at me.

I smiled and nodded. "That's it," I said. "It makes sense. That's why Julie was able to get me the instant appointment. Her friend's having an affair with him. I can see it now. He revealed things about my therapy session while he was sleeping with her, and she couldn't wait to tell Julie, right?"

He sat, looking overwhelmed. "You've misinterpreted everything. Julie's concern for your looks and your social happiness isn't out of some mean motive. She's beside herself. She was only trying to help you so you'd be happier and we'd all be happier. You know she's gone through this terrible marriage and horrible divorce. Her former husband belittled her, had affairs, and even brought a woman into their home, into their very bed, while she was away. She's trying so hard to have a happy marriage now, a happy family. I'm so disappointed in you, Mayfair." He looked down and shook his head. "I really don't know what else to do. A vibrator! To tell Dr. Burns she bought you a vibrator?"

He sighed deeply and rose.

"Needless to say, your therapy is over. Nothing will change until you want it to. That's clear. I've forbidden Julie to make any more efforts."

He stood for a moment looking at me.

"I don't know you anymore," he said, and walked out slowly.

I had never seen such a look of disgust in my father's face. She had played him well, I thought. She had him in her complete control now. Why wasn't he angry

about how she had manipulated me into this therapy
session, where she knew she would find out everything
about me and use it against me? It wasn't right. I was
being abused. Why wasn't he defending me, outraged
about what had happened to me? Why couldn't he see
that I had simply turned the tables on her?

Maybe it was hopeless. If anything, I hated her
more than ever. She was down there sobbing, and he
had probably returned to her side, holding her and
comforting her, when he should be up here comforting
me. Maybe if he had done that, I would have told him
more, told him about Alan Taylor, and the loving ties
that were splintering between us would have grown
stronger again.

He'd be my father.

I'd be his daughter.

There was a tiny knock on my open door. Allison
had returned, still looking very frightened. "What
happened?" she asked. "Why was Daddy so angry?
Are you in trouble? Is my mother still very upset?"

"It was just what I told you. One of your mother's
friends said something unpleasant to her that upset
her. She'll be all right. Don't worry about your
mother. She'll always be all right."

"I wish everyone thought I was grown-up enough
to know about everything," she said, sitting on my
bed. "I know about a lot of stuff my mother doesn't
know I know about."

"I'm sure you do."

"When you're not home yet and she can't see me, I
read some more in the book you gave me."

"Oh? Well, that's good."

"If you're going to fall in love, you've got to know about that stuff."

"That's very adult of you, Allison. I thought you were old enough to appreciate it. That's why I gave it to you and was disappointed when your mother took it away from you."

She beamed. I never realized how much my compliments meant to her. "Do you think someone my age could be in love?"

"I don't know if age has much to do with it. Why? Do you think you're in love?"

"I don't know. Maybe. Jamie Baron says that when you are in love, you can't think of much else, and sometimes you look dopey."

"Jamie Baron sounds dopey."

"You never fell in love, right?"

"No."

She looked disappointed.

"Why is that important, Allison? You're who you are, and I'm who I am. We don't have to have the same feelings and thoughts about everything. In fact, you don't have to have the same feelings and thoughts as your friends do, either. You'll end up being a clone if you're not careful."

"What's a clone?"

"An exact replica with no independent thought. In short, a nobody." I wanted to add "like your mother and her friends," but I thought I had gone far enough.

She shrugged. "I just thought that if you fell in love, you'd know more so you could tell me for sure.

I trust you. I mean, you know so much that I would believe what you said."

"Well, I don't have to be in love to tell you that it has to be something that lasts longer than a week."

She nodded. "This has lasted all year, practically," she said as if she was in a confessional booth.

"You mean for you?"

"Yes."

"It also helps if the person you fall in love with falls in love with you."

"And wants to be with you a lot?"

"Yes, of course."

"And likes to touch you?"

"Exactly."

"And smiles and looks bright every time he sees you . . ."

"Now you sound as if you could write an advice to the lovelorn column," I said. "You going to see this boy at the party Friday?"

"Oh, no."

"No? Why not?" I grimaced. "I get it. He's not what your mother calls popular or acceptable. Is that it? He wasn't invited."

She pressed her lips together.

"Well?" I pursued. "Which is it?"

"None of that. He wouldn't come to a kids' party."

I sat back. "Wouldn't come to a kids' party? Who is this mysterious lover of yours?"

She pressed her lips together again. She certainly could look just like her mother at times. "I can't tell you," she said, and slipped off the bed. "It's a very big secret, the biggest secret of my life."

"That's more reason to tell me. Something that big could mean big mistakes, too. Who is it?"

"Allison?" we heard.

"My mother's calling. I'll see you later," she said, and hurried out.

Why was I wasting time listening to an adolescent's fantasy? I asked myself and returned to my research on the internet.

The following day, I could see that Julie's new approach toward me was going to be simply to ignore me. She didn't mention a thing about my conversation with Dr. Burns, nor would she talk to me or look at me unless it was absolutely necessary. Maybe she thought that if she acted like this, I'd break down and apologize to her. I knew she was hoping for some reaction, because after a while, the silent treatment was ricocheting back on her. It was too uncomfortable in the car and at the dinner table. However, she was too proud to play the victim. She was more comfortable on the attack, and she was at least smart enough to know where I was most vulnerable.

The day after that, she finally turned to me in the car and said, "You have no idea how much you've hurt your father, Mayfair."

I didn't respond, but she had launched her attack, and every chance she had, she repeated it and other accusations.

I was an unnatural child.

I didn't appreciate anything she and my father were doing for me.

I had never given her a chance.

I was resentful from the beginning, and actually, despite my high intelligence, I was very immature.

The best one was "Everyone has hardships to bear. You have to be more considerate of that."

I didn't have to ask her to elaborate. She was off and running.

She had a horrible first marriage and had to provide all the parenting for her daughter. Allison might not be a quarter as intelligent as I was, but she was a decent, good girl. They had a wonderful, trusting relationship compared to what I had, and what I had or didn't have was my own fault.

My ability to turn her off the way I used to seemed diminished. Something had weakened me in that regard. I felt like putting my hands over my ears. It seemed to be the only way, either that or shout back at her until she stopped.

Over the next few days, there was no doubt that my father was more upset with me than he had ever been. He acted like someone defeated and devoted more and more of his time to his work. I knew he was trying to find ways to avoid me, avoid the tension in the house.

In school, I had completely stopped trying to catch Alan Taylor's attention. I no longer even glanced his way, and I avoided passing his doorway. What had happened between us seemed so much like a dream now that I began to wonder if I had fantasized it all.

Finally, after another week had passed, I was going to the library just after his free period had begun, and

I had to pass his room. Just as I drew close, he stepped out.

We were alone in the hallway. There was no way to avoid each other.

"How are you doing?" he asked.

"Are you talking to me?"

He smiled. "Listen, I know how it must seem to you, but I thought it all over that night. We both crossed a line, and it's better if we pretend nothing happened."

"Better for whom?"

"Both of us." He hesitated and then added, "Probably more so for me. I'm thinking of getting engaged, by the way."

"I thought you didn't have a serious girlfriend."

"I didn't think it was as serious as she did—does—and after a while, I realized she was the right one for me. You'll be all right," he added. He flashed a smile and walked away.

*I'll be all right?* What, was he comparing what happened between us to a common cold or something?

I stood there watching him and wondered why he had to be my first experience. Why couldn't I have been with some intelligent, good-looking college boy, at least, the sort of boy the bitches suspected I might have been seeing? Even if that had ended disastrously, I wouldn't feel as much like a victim as I did right now.

When I glanced at myself in the glass of a trophy cabinet, I cringed at the expression on my face.

"Stop feeling sorry for yourself, damn it," I told my image.

As Suzie Bubble Brain loved to say, "Cry me a river. Build a bridge and get over it."

I started to walk on but stopped with surprise when I saw Allison standing in the girls' room doorway, which was just across the hall from Alan Taylor's classroom.

"Hey," I said. "Why are you just standing there like that?"

"I was watching you talk to Mr. Taylor."

"So?"

She shot away and walked quickly toward her classroom.

"Allison?"

I hurried to catch up with her when she paused. When she turned back to me, I saw she had tears streaming down her cheeks.

"What's wrong?"

"I heard what he said to you."

A chill ran through me. "What did you hear him say?"

"He said he was getting engaged," she replied, and turned to walk away a little faster, flicking the tears off her cheeks as she did so.

He thought he was getting engaged? Why was that so devastating to her? What was I missing here?

I walked slowly to the library, thinking about her and Alan Taylor, and when I entered the library and set my books on a desk, it hit me. I didn't realize I was laughing out loud until Mr. Monk called out to me sharply. The other students all looked up, surprised.

"Sorry," I said, and sank into my seat, wondering

just how far along and how deep Allison's fantasy went.

That little discussion we had about love in my room the other night now made more sense. This was why the love of her life wouldn't attend her girlfriend's birthday party. If Julie knew what sort of fantasies her precious, perfect daughter had, she surely would have heart failure. Maybe she'd even agree to send Allison to see Dr. Burns.

Again I laughed, but this time to myself.

I turned on the computer and took out my notebook. I was still doing research on the transplanted human brain cells and some of the statistical results that were being posted. How ironic, I thought, that scientists not only in England but here and in most industrialized and technologically sophisticated countries were doing research in an attempt to improve and increase intelligence in animals instead of all these human airheads. One of these days, I might get a call and be asked to donate some of my own brain cells.

That, too, brought a smile.

But something was nagging at me about Allison and her fantasy. She was so overly dramatic. I knew girls her age often were, but there was something different about her, something more. I paused and recalled the exact conversation we had, and then I felt my eyes widen.

How did that conversation go?

"It also helps if the person you fall in love with falls in love with you," I had told her.

"And wants to be with you a lot?"

"Yes, of course."

"And likes to touch you?"

"Exactly."

"And smiles and looks bright every time he sees you."

*Likes to touch you?* She did say that. How much of this *was* fantasy? I wondered.

I was at a disadvantage. Unlike most girls who went through puberty, I never had a crush on a teacher. I never idolized a rock star or a movie star. I never swooned over anyone. What were you supposed to feel and think? How far was this to go before it became ridiculous, even dangerous? I'd seen other girls break out crying for no apparent reason and then discovered it was because some boy or some teacher looked at them the wrong way or didn't return a smile as warmly. I never paid much attention to it, but this was different. At least, it felt different. Maybe, just maybe, I wanted it to be different.

I watched the clock and left the library about a minute before the bell to end the period would ring. I waited just outside the door of Allison's classroom. She came out talking with some of her girlfriends, but she still looked despondent. When she saw me, she stopped and said something to the other girls. Normally, I rarely spoke a single word to her during the school day after we had arrived, and sometimes I said nothing to her all the way home.

"Are you waiting for me?" she asked.

"Yes. I'll walk with you to your next class. Hang back, so the ones with big ears aren't so close to us."

"What? Why are you waiting? What do you want to talk about that's so important?"

"When you were in my bedroom and we were talking about love, you meant Mr. Taylor, right?"

She kept walking until I grabbed her arm.

"You meant Mr. Taylor, right?"

She looked around to be sure no one was close enough to overhear us. "Yes," she said. "Are you going to tell my mother?"

"What for? Besides, she wouldn't believe anything I said now, anyway. Stop worrying like a child, Allison. You're having grown-up thoughts. You're maturing, developing. You'd better act grown-up now and catch up with your body. Girls who don't are usually the ones who get themselves into trouble."

She looked at me, impressed, and nodded.

"I'm really the only one who's close to you who understands these things. You know that, right?" I asked.

"I guess," she said.

"Don't guess. Know it. I gave you the right things to read and always will."

"I know."

"You're right to be worried about your mother hearing about this. She'd have a nervous breakdown, and it would be your fault. When you were in my room, you said he likes to touch you. Were you making that up?"

"No."

"Don't lie to me, Allison. I'll find out," I said, grabbing her arm at the elbow and stopping her. She couldn't look me directly in the face. "You made all of it up, didn't you? You just told me those things to seem older, more sophisticated, right?"

"I *am* more sophisticated," she said with defiance. "He thinks so, too."

"Who does?"

She turned and looked down the hallway. Alan Taylor was standing in his classroom doorway as usual. She didn't say his name. She simply nodded in his direction for me and kept walking.

I looked at him, too. He seemed worried.

I caught up to her again and grabbed her arm, a little harder and tighter than before. She cried out. I pulled her farther away.

"You hurt me, Mayfair."

"That's nothing. Stop behaving like a child, now." I looked at Alan Taylor again. "Have you been telling me about Mr. Taylor? Was he the one you said loved you and touched you? Tell me, Allison," I said, with as determined and angry a face as I could manage.

"Yes," she said.

"Yes." I glanced at him again. He was still standing there watching us. "What are you saying? Have you ever been alone with him?"

She looked down.

"Just tell me. It's very, very important, Allison. Have you been alone with him?"

"Yes," she said, pulling her arm away.

"When?"

She kept walking.

"When, Allison?"

She paused and turned back. "I'll tell you later, maybe. Or I'll show it to you."

"Show it? What's that mean? How can you show it?"

"I wrote it all down," she said, and kept walking.

She was walking toward Alan Taylor. He was watching us closely. I stopped her again. "You wrote it all down?" I said under my breath. "Wrote what?" I couldn't raise my voice. We were too close to him now, and he was obviously very interested in whatever we were saying to each other.

"Everything," she replied.

"Everything?"

She walked away quickly.

Alan stepped aside to let her enter the classroom but kept his eyes on me. Maybe he heard what she had said.

I felt like a dozen firecrackers were going off inside me.

# 15

I couldn't concentrate on much else for the remainder of the school day. Of course, I couldn't talk to Allison again about it while Julie was driving us home. I'd had no other opportunities to pull her aside in school, so I had to hide my interest and as usual pretend to be in some deep thought about something too far above Julie to mention.

"Where did you write those things?" I asked Allison after we arrived home and went upstairs. I couldn't help lunging at her as soon as I had the opportunity.

"What things?" she asked, coyly now. Did she think she had something over me because she had something I wanted to know very much? Or did she realize the implications of what she had said and regretted it?

"You know what I'm talking about, Allison. I'm talking about Mr. Taylor. Don't try to be your mother and act like you don't know what's going on when you do."

"My mother doesn't do that."

"Okay, she doesn't do that. Where did you write the things about Mr. Taylor?"

"I wrote them in my diary, but I can't show it to you."

"Why not?"

"No one is allowed to read my diary. Not even my mother. I'm sorry I said anything about it. Leave me alone," she replied, and went into her room. Before I could respond, she slammed her door closed.

I should have thought she'd write something like that in her diary. Now she was embarrassed. I had never kept a diary. I did keep a journal when I was her mental age and for a while after, but it was filled with scientific observations of my experiences with insects and animals and very little about my feelings about them or about people.

When my father first married Julie, I started a journal about her. I was like an attorney building a court case. I kept track of every unpleasant thing she said or did. When I realized that nothing I wrote would please or perhaps even interest my father, I tore the pages out and burned them.

Somewhere I read that girls keep diaries because they can express their innermost thoughts without having to worry about anyone's reaction. Some analysts believe it's a form of therapy, a cheap form. Maybe I should have kept a diary about myself like Allison's diary. It's cathartic. It gives you relief. You get all the inner pain and tension out.

And I surely had a lot to get out. And I certainly didn't do it with Dr. Burns.

I had seen Allison writing in her diary only once and was so uninterested I barely paid any attention, but at least I had a good recollection of what it looked like. It was a leather-bound ruby-red book with a gold clasp. I imagined she kept it in her desk drawer, and I was sure she was writing in it right now, crying her river but building no bridge to get over it. Like most of the overly dramatic teenage girls around me, she wallowed in her own sadness even without an audience. At least she could feel sorry for herself if no one else would.

However, the depth of Allison's depression surprised me as much as it did Julie and my father. She was so unhappy at dinner that she barely ate a thing, and no matter how her mother prodded her with questions, Allison would not reveal the cause of her unhappiness. Unfortunately, Allison glanced at me during the questioning, and her mother became even more suspicious.

After dinner, when Allison had left for her room, Julie pulled me aside. "Did you say anything nasty or unpleasant to her that would make her so unhappy?"

"What would I say? What are you going to find wrong with me now?"

"Do you blame your father's disappointment in you on me? Is that what this is about? Because if it is, you have no right to take it out on poor Allison."

My father stood off to the side, looking meek but waiting to see what I would say. Years ago, he would have told her the idea was ridiculous and not to bother me with such a question.

"No," I said, glancing at my father. "I blame his disappointment in me on him."

My answer took them both by surprise. Julie's eyes nearly exploded, and he looked like he was in physical pain.

Before either of them could respond, I went upstairs and, like Allison, slammed my door shut. I didn't have a good night, either. It was uncharacteristic of me, but I sulked and raged inside myself. I didn't do any significant work and couldn't read. I watched a few minutes of television before shutting that off in disgust and just lay in bed, staring up at the ceiling. I felt tied up in knots, frustrated with myself as much as with everyone else.

We were so much better off before my father married Julie, I thought. Of course we both missed my mother. Because of who I was, what I could do, people might believe I missed her less. Some of that was understandable. Being a man, he was more lost and lonely. I could understand why a man as young as he was at the time had a need for a relationship with a female. I just couldn't understand and probably never would understand why he chose a woman like Julie. Maybe he should have had a heart-to-heart talk with her ex-husband and learned what the divorce was about from his point of view. People like to find out who drove the used car they're considering and what they thought of it before they buy it. Why couldn't he have given a new wife at least as much thought and caution as a used car?

I didn't get more than a few hours of sleep. My father had to leave very early for a business trip. Julie took one look at me at breakfast and did her best to avoid looking at me after that. She was quieter than ever in the car, and with Allison still acting depressed and me behaving like a clam in a shell, it was more like riding to a funeral than to school.

"Remember, I'm going to Lisa's house to study for tomorrow's history test and have dinner," Allison told Julie just before she got out of the car.

"Oh. Right. Call me when you want to be picked up, but don't make it too late, Allison."

She finally turned to look at me.

"I'll be here to pick you up," she said.

"Don't bother," I said. "I have things to do after school and will take a taxi home."

"Oh. Well, then, I'll do some shopping down in Newport Beach with some friends," she said. I could hear the relief in her voice. She didn't have to be alone with me, even for fifteen minutes. I could shut her out easily, but it was a relief for me, too, not to have to bother.

It was an unremarkable school day for me, except that every time I saw Allison, she continued to look despondent. I noticed that when her friends were laughing, she wasn't even smiling. How could a fantasy about a teacher, even one as good-looking as Alan Taylor, cause a girl Allison's age to be so depressed? Why couldn't she see how ridiculous it was, and why would it take her so long to get over it? I felt sure she had fantasized about other teachers, boys, rock stars, and the like. She had gotten over them.

Could it really be that it wasn't a fantasy? Was

Alan Taylor's involvement with me simply part of
his characteristic behavior? People, especially young
girls, had the incorrect idea that only unattractive
men took advantage of young girls. But I knew that it
had nothing to do with their looks; it had to do with
their mental state. Maybe, even for Alan Taylor, older
women were too much of a challenge, too threatening,
and this claim about his impending engagement was all
a cover story.

Too curious now to ignore what was happening
with Allison, I decided to go right home after school.
It wasn't the first time that the behavior of other teenage girls interested me. I couldn't help feeling like an
outsider. The things that made them laugh and cry,
seized their complete interest and devotion, were
mostly meaningless and silly to me. I took time to
study and analyze them, knowing all along that it was
a way to analyze myself. What was I missing? Why
had my super intelligence made me so different? Did I
enjoy being different?

Julie was gone for the day with her friends. My
father was away and wouldn't be home until dinner.
Our maid had left. The house was dead quiet. It was
my house, but because of what I wanted to do, I suddenly felt like an intruder.

After I put my things away, I went to Allison's
room. I wanted to read that diary, but I was surprised
not to find it in her desk drawer. I had to be careful
rifling through her things. I didn't want anyone to
know, especially Julie, that I was doing this. I could
just imagine the issue she would make of it.

It wasn't in any of Allison's dresser drawers, not even under the clothes, and it wasn't on the floor of her closet or on the shelf in it that was stacked with her board games. I checked her old toy box, with its dozens of small dolls and discarded electronic games, and then, frustrated, I even looked in the bathroom cabinets. If I hadn't seen her writing in it, I would believe she had made it up.

Did she carry it with her always? She probably did, I thought. Many girls her age probably did that. They were all afraid of forgetting to write down some major event in their lives, like their dreamboat boyfriend casually brushing against their budding breasts or something.

I was about to give up when I glanced at her shelves of children's books. Why hadn't I realized that for Allison, her diary was as important as a world-famous title? There between *Alice in Wonderland* and *The Wonderful Wizard of Oz* was the gold-trimmed, ruby-red leather binding. How appropriate that it was located between two of the world's most famous fantasies, I thought as I plucked it off the shelf. I listened to be sure no one had come home yet, and then I sat at her desk and opened the diary.

The first page was titled "My Life by Allison Cummings." Although my father still hadn't legally adopted Allison because her real father wouldn't give up custodial rights, Julie insisted that she go by his name. She was Allison Cummings now. It wasn't legal, but Julie told her it would look dumb to use her real father's name. I didn't know whether that bothered

Allison very much or not. She never said, and I never asked her.

From the dates on the pages, I realized she hadn't begun to keep this particular diary until early this year, but she began by recalling her feelings and thoughts after her mother had married my father and they had moved into our house. I was almost as interested in that as I was in what she had written about Alan Taylor.

Her writing was simple but surprisingly grammatical. Of course, she began each section with "Dear Diary" and dated it as if she were writing to someone who would actually listen or care. I suppose in the diarist's mind, she was sending a letter off into something like cyberspace. It was all floating out there but never touched by any other eyes.

What seized my attention, of course, was her opinion of and feelings about me. She liked my father very much and even thought he loved her almost as much as her real father loved her. I could understand that. My father did have a warm, wonderful smile. It was why he was so successful in business. I, however, was another story.

*Dear Diary,*

*I always wanted to have a sister, even a brother, but when Mommy told me Mayfair was to be my new sister, I wasn't very happy.*
*The first time we met, she was very polite, but she looked at me so hard with those scary*

273

33333

eyes that she made me feel funny. She was very quiet and read even when we were all in the car or in a room together. She never asked me any questions or came into my room.

I remember she wouldn't let Mommy kiss her.

She still won't.

She didn't even kiss her father that much. He always kissed her, but she never threw her arms around him and kissed him like I would kiss Daddy.

I like her father very much. Someday I'll just start calling him Daddy, I'm sure. He'll probably love me more than he loves Mayfair, because I won't hesitate to kiss him or let him kiss me.

Maybe her daddy is sad about having a daughter like her. Maybe he pretends he's happy that she's so smart. Maybe he wishes he had a daughter more like me.

Mommy always thought Mayfair was very strange. She told me her father said she was more intelligent than any other student in the whole school. She told me Mayfair might be smarter than any student in the whole state and that we have to forgive her if she seems different because she's always thinking.

She's still that way. She can't help it.

Her brain won't stop.

Mommy said she thinks Mayfair even thinks when she sleeps and doesn't dream.

*Dreams can't fit in her head because it is so crowded with thoughts and facts.*

*Mayfair never had a doll or at least never showed me one or told me she had one.*

*Mayfair doesn't have any real friends. Even now, I never see her talking with any girls except one girl named Joy who looks like she just got out of a third world country where people are starving to death. I don't think many girls or boys call Mayfair unless they need help with something in school. She usually doesn't get invited to other girls' houses after school or on weekends. I don't think she's ever hung out with friends at the mall or gone to a movie with them.*

*I can't remember if she was ever invited to a real party, but she doesn't seem to care.*

*Mayfair reads books Mommy can't read.*

*Mayfair never tells me about boys she likes.*

*She never wants to do anything with me. I asked her many times to do things, even just go for a walk, but she's always too busy.*

*But she is really very smart, even smarter than my teachers.*

*I ask her to help with my homework. Sometimes she does, and sometimes she's too busy.*

*I don't know why she's too busy. She is either on the computer or reading or writing things.*

*No one makes her do it. She does it because she wants to.*

*Mommy thinks she does it because she can't help it. Her brain makes her do it.*

*I still wish I had a sister.*

*Mayfair is like having another adult in the house. She doesn't even want to go to the movies with me and tells me every movie I want to see is silly.*

*Mommy says Mayfair might be the smartest kid in the whole world, but she would rather have me for a daughter and that secretly her father wishes the same thing.*

*She said Mayfair will never be happy. She said she wanted to see if she could help her.*

*That was when she tried to show her how to put on makeup and fix her hair.*

*Mayfair wasn't very interested, and Mommy gave up.*

*Here's what I remember about Mayfair when I first came to live with her and her father.*

*She never spilled anything at the table. She never ate too much or too little, and she always wiped her lips after every sip of what she was drinking.*

*She didn't care about her dresses or her shoes very much.*

*She never had a nightmare or cried.*

*She smiled sometimes, but it wasn't a big smile, and I can't remember when she laughed at something I laughed at.*

*She asked Mommy questions that made*
*Mommy want to get away from her.*
     *Everything in her room was always neat.*
*She liked taking care of her own room and*
*didn't like the maid doing much in it.*
     *She never told her father that she loved him*
*in front of me.*
     *I don't remember him going into her room*
*much and never to tuck her in at night.*
     *I remember thinking that maybe she was*
*made in a laboratory and she wasn't a real girl.*
     *She was in some of my nightmares.*
     *That's what I remember about Mayfair*
*when I first came to live here in her and her*
*father's house.*

I stopped reading for a moment. Nothing Julie had
told her really surprised me, but reading Allison's im-
pressions of me did give me pause. I loved my father
more than she thought I did. Her mother had filled her
with these ideas. The idea that she thought she could
replace me in my father's eyes was disturbing. Maybe it
was just a little girl's dream, that of a little girl who really
didn't have a full-time father, but it still bothered me.
     A second realization was how much Allison
wanted me to like her and for her to like me. She
really needed a sister. My father wasn't wrong when
he said I wanted a sister, too. I wouldn't let myself get
close to Allison. It was too much like accepting Julie.
I didn't have to wonder why Julie never had any more
children. Her husband probably realized that bringing

another one into the world with her would be unfair to the child, maybe unfair to the world.

I looked at the diary again, this time flipping through the pages that described more about her early years with my father and me, how much she missed her own father back then, and what she thought about her new school, her new friends, and our house itself.

I was beginning to be discouraged and imagined that she had made up what she told me on the spot. She never had written about Alan Taylor, or at least not in her diary. But then I turned a page and saw the title: "The Day My Life Began."

Again, I listened to be sure no one had come home yet. The house was still as quiet as before, and I felt like a real intruder. My eyes returned to her writing.

*Dear Diary,*

*Mr. Taylor looked at me differently today.*
*I wasn't wearing a training bra anymore.*
*And I had my first period last week.*
*He knows I'm a young woman now.*
*Mommy said I was.*
*I think he knows how much I like him. He always spends extra time with me, and today when he stopped at my desk, he put his hand on mine and kept it there the whole time while he talked to the class. I saw how my girlfriends were looking at me, all of them excited and jealous.*
*I had a hard time listening to what he said. My heart was beating so fast. Then he ran his*

*hand over the top of my head and down the
back of my hair as he walked away.*

*I thought about him all day, and
whenever I walked past his room during the
change of classes, he was standing there and
smiling at me.*

*He was looking only at me.*

*His smile was only for me.*

*Dear Diary,*

*Today Mr. Taylor put his hand on my waist
when he leaned over to read my composition.*

*I love his aftershave lotion.*

*He brought his face so close to mine we
almost touched cheeks.*

*I know he likes me more than any other girl
in his class, maybe all his classes.*

*He spends more time with me and never
touches any of the other girls.*

*And he always waits for me in his classroom
doorway so he can see me and smile at me
when I go to other classes and pass his room.
Today he even called to me and said, "Hey,
how are you doing, Allison?"*

*I almost couldn't talk. I said, "Fine," and
he laughed.*

*I love his laugh.*

*Dear Diary,*

*I knew it. I knew he likes me a lot and would find a way for us to be together more.*

*Today he asked me to come in during his free period and help him correct some quizzes.*

*How did he know I had study hall and could be excused?*

*He checked and made sure. He wouldn't have done that if he didn't really like me and want only me helping him.*

*My heart was pounding again when I walked into his classroom. He asked me to close the door, and then he told me to sit next to him at his desk. He put a chair there for me.*

*When I sat, he told me how much he liked the way I was wearing my hair and how much he liked the clothes I wore. He said the skirt I was wearing looked especially soft. He took some of it in his fingers and said, "Yes, this is very soft."*

*He didn't let go of it. Instead, he moved his hand under the material and kept saying it was the softest material he had ever touched. When he lifted it some more, he looked at my legs and said they were very pretty.*

*He touched my thigh and said my skin was so soft, too.*

*I didn't say anything. I wished he would kiss me, but not on the cheek, on the lips.*

*And then he moved his fingers up my thigh and touched me between my legs.*

*He wanted to know if I liked that, and I said yes, and he lifted my panties away.*

*Then he kissed me on the lips.*

*He told me he liked me very much because I was more grown-up than the other girls.*

*And I told him how much I liked him, too.*

*He said he wasn't all that much older than I was and the difference in ages between many wives and husbands was either the same or even more than the difference between us.*

*He had me move closer to him.*

*He moved his fingers all over me, and I closed my eyes.*

*Afterward, he said we should correct some papers just in case anyone asked.*

*Then he told me to come back on Thursday.*

*Dear Diary,*

*On Thursday, Mr. Taylor locked his classroom door after I came into the room.*

*Then he took me into the book closet at the rear of the room, and he kissed me again.*

*He wanted to take all my clothes off, and I wanted him to do it.*

*When I was naked, he kissed me everywhere and told me he knew he would keep loving me.*

*He said our love would get stronger and stronger as I grew older, and even when I was away in college, he would still love me.*

*And when I came home from college, he would take me out.*

*By then, no one would think it was wrong, and we would get engaged.*

*He said the most pleasure in the world for him would be watching me grow into a more beautiful woman.*

*Afterward, he had me get dressed quickly. He told me he didn't want us to do much more just yet.*

*He said we had to go more slowly, and I had to get more prepared.*

*He said he knew just how to do it and that I shouldn't worry about the details of sex.*

*Dear Diary,*

*I've been with Mr. Taylor almost ten times now. He said that we have to think of a way to meet outside the school.*

*He said he would think about it and I should think about it.*

*It's hard because it's such a big secret.*

*I wouldn't even tell Mayfair, even though she knows most everything and would make the best suggestions.*

*I promised him I would never tell anyway, and he said that if I broke a promise to him, he would never love me again.*

*Today I wrote his name nearly five hundred times in history class. No one knew because I didn't write his whole name. I wrote, A--n T---or.*

⁓⁓

*Dear Diary,*

*Mr. Taylor and I finally met after school.*

*I was at my friend Lisa's house, and when her grandmother left, I told Lisa about Mr. Taylor. I couldn't help it. I was bursting with it and had to tell someone I trusted. She swore first on her brother's, mother's, father's, and grandmother's lives that she would never tell anyone. After that, I told her everything, and she believed me, and I left.*

*Mr. Taylor knew what time I would leave and came by in his car.*

*I got in, and we drove around just talking.*

*Then he stopped by an old deserted house he knew, and we parked behind it where no one could see us.*

*I took off all my clothes, and this time, he took off all his and we just held each other.*

*He said it would be good for me to know about men, and he told me how to touch him.*

*I didn't want to tell him, but I knew a lot already because Mayfair had given me a book to read, and I was reading it even after my mother took it away.*

*He said we still had to be careful because I could be spoiled and ruined if I went too fast.*

*I saw what sperm was, and then we got dressed quickly and he dropped me off back at Lisa's house.*

*Lisa wanted to know everything that happened. I'm glad I have a friend like her, but I saw she was a little jealous. I made her swear again on everyone in her family's lives never to say anything, and she did.*

*I promised her that if she was true to me, I would always be true to her and I would tell her more when it happened.*

*Then my mother came.*

*Dear Diary,*

*A terrible thing happened today. I can hardly write it, but I had to write it.*

*I heard Mr. Taylor tell Mayfair that he was going to get engaged.*

*I think my heart must have stopped.*

*I'm sick to my stomach.*

*Now, when he sees me, he doesn't act any
differently from how he acts with the other
girls in the class.*

*I don't want to hate him, but I can't
help it.*

*I feel like running away or dying. All I
do is cry when I'm alone, and when I'm not,
I cry inside.*

*I think I'll cry for the rest of my life.*

*Only Lisa knows and understands why I'm
so sad.*

I closed the diary and sat there.

Were these just the fantasy ramblings of an adolescent girl? They convincingly described the slow and deliberate approach of a sexual predator, the gentleness, singling her out, touching her innocently at first, just the way he had first touched me, and then the credible advances. Look at how easily he had turned himself on to me and then turned himself off when he had gotten what he wanted. Reading her diary made me feel as if I had been violated again.

I went from being fascinated by it all to blind, bloody rage.

Allison was just the type of girl who could be easily victimized. She was searching for a father figure since her parents' divorce. My father was providing something for her, but it wasn't really enough for a girl who was just blossoming into her full female emotions. The first part of her diary described someone desperate for significant, loving relationships. Julie certainly couldn't compensate for what Allison was missing, and I hadn't done much of a job of it.

Alan Taylor had pounced on her the way he had pounced on me.

Of course, it reinforced my opinion of Julie, too. How could any mother miss all this? A mother as self-centered as Julie could. I stared at the diary. Yes, to anyone else, it might just be the ramblings of a love-sick teenage girl fantasizing, but to me, it was as good as a legal brief.

I had to help her, I thought, and in doing so, I would get my own revenge and justice.

I laughed to myself, because an added bonus would be shaking Julie out of her tree of selfishness, arrogance, and insensitivity. Maybe then, maybe finally, my father's eyes would be opened and the hold she had over him would evaporate.

I knew just what I had to do for Allison and for myself.

I never liked believing in the power of coincidence or fate, but even I had to admit that something, maybe the spirit of my mother, had put me in a position to do what had to be done.

And I would do it.

# 16

Maybe I should be a writer of fiction, I thought as I sat in my room after putting Allison's diary back on the shelf. I loved to plot. The obvious occurred quickly. I couldn't reveal that I had sneaked into Allison's room and read her diary, and whether it was my pride or something more, I couldn't get myself, even now, even with this added potential evidence, to tell my father and especially Julie why I had a good reason to believe what Allison was claiming. For now, maybe forever, that would have to remain a deep secret buried in the darkest place in my heart. Too often, the messenger gets punished for the message, anyway. Julie would accept no favors from me. That was for sure. She would find some way to blame me and convince my father that she was right. At a minimum, she might point to the things I told Allison and the book I gave her to read.

"You put sex in her mind and all this has resulted because of it," she might say, as ridiculous as that was.

Suddenly, I would become the biggest influence

on Allison, and whatever I would have done to her, I would have done out of some meanness, some anger against her mother. Look at what I had done with Dr. Burns, how I had used him. Nothing I did was by accident. I was far too intelligent to do anything accidentally.

I could hear it all now.

No, this had to be done more subtly. It was a matter of planting seeds and using the system, which had also let me down when it came to what the bitches of *Macbeth* had done to me. This truly looked like the way to get back at everyone.

And I knew just how to start.

After Julie had picked up Allison and brought her home, Allison went directly to her room. I waited a few minutes and then knocked on her door. She was getting ready for bed and was already in her pajamas.

"I need to talk to you," I said. "It's very important." I closed the door.

She sat on her bed and waited with a look of concern. "What is it?"

"I know you're upset about Mr. Taylor. You have a right to be upset. What else did you hear him say to me besides telling me about his engagement?"

"Nothing else," she said. "I mean, I wasn't listening until he said that word. Engagement."

"Okay. Did you talk to anyone about what you heard him say to me?"

She started to shake her head.

"You'd better not lie about this. It's very serious. I'll tell you why, but you have to tell me the truth."

She looked sufficiently frightened.

"You told your best friend, Lisa, right? If I had a best friend, I probably would have told her, too. Well?"

She just stared at me.

"Look, Allison. You know you can trust me, and you know I'm smart enough to help you if you get into big trouble."

"Why would I be in big trouble?"

"Just tell me the truth, or I'll turn around and walk out of here. I mean it," I said sharply. "Did you tell Lisa or anyone else about Mr. Taylor, about being in love with him and his being in love with you?"

She still hesitated.

"You're luckier than I am, because you have a best friend you can trust, don't you?"

She nodded.

"Okay. Did you tell her anything about Mr. Taylor?"

She thought for a moment and then nodded.

"Do you know what happens to people, especially young girls, who make up stories about their teachers and what could happen to their parents?"

She shook her head.

"For starters, all sorts of legal troubles and lawsuits, not to mention what would happen to your mother's and my father's reputations. Now, if you didn't make up any stories, you wouldn't get yourself or your mother and my father into any trouble. Did you make up any stories about Mr. Taylor, stories you might have told Lisa?"

She shook her head quickly.

"Are you sure, Allison? This isn't some kid's game, now."

"I didn't make up any stories," she said. "Besides, I wouldn't even try to lie to you, Mayfair. You're too smart to fool about anything."

I widened my eyes. *Forget the compliment*, I told myself, *she does sound credible*. "What makes you think Mr. Taylor liked you so much that you would think he loved you?"

I saw that she was reluctant to answer.

"Did he favor you in class, touch you?"

She nodded.

"Did you help him correct quizzes or something with no one else in the room but you and him?"

She widened her eyes. "Yes."

"Did he touch you then? Tell me," I demanded.

She nodded. She looked like she might start crying, so I decided to stop.

"Okay, okay. Don't be frightened. You have nothing to worry about. You just listen to me. Even if you elaborated on something that happened between you and Mr. Taylor, embellished what happened a little because you wished it was more like that, don't ever say you made up any stories, understand? No matter what, don't ever say that, because once you say one thing is not exactly how it happened, they'll believe that nothing was, understand?"

"Okay. But why? Why are you asking me all this and saying all this?"

I paused and sighed as if it were a great effort for

me to talk about it. "I heard lots of gossip today. I think some of the older girls wanted me to hear it. Did you ever hear that expression 'Two can keep a secret if one is dead'?"

"No."

"Well, people can't keep secrets. Sometimes they don't even mean to reveal them, but they do accidentally. Lisa might have done that. She might have told other girls about the things you told her."

"No, she wouldn't. She's told me her secrets, and I wouldn't tell anyone."

"Whatever. If someone asks you about it, though, you'd better be sure you don't say you made things up. Okay? I can't stress this enough."

She nodded. "I'll ask her if she told," she said.

"And she'll say no, because she doesn't want you to be angry at her, or she might admit that she thought she could trust someone just like you thought you could trust her. She might have another friend she thinks of as a best friend, right? But she might think you'll be jealous, so she might not even tell you that. It probably won't do any good to cross-examine her."

I could see she was thinking.

"Right?"

She nodded.

"All right. Don't worry about it. I'm here for you. I'll make sure nothing happens to you and, that way, nothing happens to your mother and my father. Okay? It's too late for us not to expect some trouble."

She stared at me, her eyes filling with panic. "When?"

"Relax, Allison. I said I would protect you, and you know I can do that, right?"

"Right," she said.

"I'm trusting that you're telling me the basic truth about all this, Allison, trusting you the way an older sister would trust a younger sister. You realize that?"

She nodded. Again, she looked like she was going to burst into tears. I had pushed her far enough, I thought.

"Okay. Just go to sleep, and don't say anything to anyone about this, especially your mother, because once you tell her, she'll be very disappointed in you and maybe get sick or something. And that will be entirely your fault. It's better if you don't ever tell her you and I talked about it, either. Can you promise not to do that?"

She nodded.

"I don't hear you."

"I promise," she said.

"Good. This time, we have a secret," I said. "And I don't tell anyone anything that I don't want them to know," I added sharply. "You know you can depend on me, and I want to believe I can depend on you. That's what sisters do for each other."

She looked sufficiently impressed that I had referred to her twice as my sister.

"Good night," I said, and started out, stopped, and then returned to touch her hand. I saw how much that pleased her.

"Thank you, Mayfair," she said in a loud whisper.

I looked at her and smiled. She didn't know it, but

it was I who should be thanking her for not only helping her but helping me.

Allison's depression was replaced with abject fear
the following morning, but it had the same appearance
as far as her mother was concerned. She was just as
quiet as the day before, maybe more so, because she
was afraid to say anything about school in case she
would make some mistake. She looked to me every
time her mother asked her a question. I tried to answer
for her, but I could see Julie was getting very concerned now.

That was good.

That was perfect.

I would go directly to stage two of the plan. I felt
confident that I could carry it all out for both of us.

After my third period in the morning, I went to
Mr. Martin's office and told his secretary I had to see
him. I tried to be as dramatic as I could, emphasizing
how important it was. She was impressed and went
quickly to his inner office. Seconds later, she was out,
telling me he was finishing a phone call and would
see me immediately. For her benefit, I tried to look as
troubled as I could.

"Mayfair?" Mr. Martin said, coming to his door
moments later. "Come in. Please."

"Thank you," I said, and entered his office.

"Have a seat," he said, closing the door. "How can
I help you today?"

"It's not me," I said. "It's my stepsister."

"Oh?" He sat behind his desk.

"Mr. Martin, I'm going to tell you some very

personal things so you will understand why you have to protect me."

"Protect you?" He sat forward. "What's this about?"

I looked down for a moment and then pulled myself up more firmly in the chair. "I was never happy about my father's remarriage," I began. "Julie knew that from the start, and consequently, we've never had a good relationship. I do what I can to keep the peace for my father's sake, but as you saw when she came in to talk about my situation with the other girls and their families, she was not what you would call a real advocate for me."

He didn't respond, but he didn't have to. I saw his agreement in his face.

"I'm not here for that," I added quickly. "I'm here for my stepsister, Allison. What goes on between her mother and me is not her fault. I've tried to be as good an older sister to her as I can be with her mother running interference all the time. She simply doesn't trust me with Allison. Allison, however, would like an older sister and does turn to me for help, not only with her homework but with other things."

"Well, that's very good," he said. "I'm sure in time Mrs. Cummings will realize —"

"The point is, what I'm about to tell you can't come from me. It has to come from Allison, but she is understandably terrified, especially about talking to someone else."

"Terrified? Of what?"

"Mr. Taylor," I said after a long pause.

"Mr. Taylor? Good heavens, why?"

"Even her mother doesn't know any of this yet," I said. "Allison is too frightened now even to tell her, but I can see how much she is suffering emotionally and psychologically. This is why I decided to come to you."

"Even her mother doesn't know about what?"

"Allison, my stepsister, has been sexually abused," I said.

His mouth opened and closed and then opened as he sat there dumbly.

"I didn't find out the details myself until recently. I've given it lots of thought, of course. I questioned her closely, and I read what she wrote in her diary without her knowing I had read it. In my opinion, there's validity to her stories. They're more than just some young girl's fantasies. I thought that because you and I have a good relationship, I could trust you with the information, and you would know how to handle it. I want to repeat, however, that if you use me as the source here, it will create new and more difficult problems, not only for my father and me but also for Allison herself. Her mother might never believe her, and that would be tragic. There are too many similar situations we all read about every day," I added, emphasizing the word *situations*.

"I see," he said. He looked like he was having trouble breathing.

"I don't have to tell you how hard mothers and fathers try to avoid facing reality when it comes to their children being responsible for something unpleasant, and in this situation, Allison has been involved in something quite unpleasant. Like you, I've read many of the extracts on the psychology of parenthood, the protective instinct of mothers and fathers, whether they be birds or people."

"That's true," he said. I could see his mind was reeling with the possibilities, the bad publicity, and his own responsibilities. He wasn't even listening to what I was saying now.

"Mr. Martin!"

He snapped out of his thoughts and looked at me. "Yes, yes, I'm listening, Mayfair."

"In this case, my case, Allison's mother would spin on me and try to blame me as long as it would all go away. She would be blind to what is really happening, and Allison would be victimized twice. If you can appreciate that, I'll go on."

"I understand your problem," he said.

"This isn't going to be hard, Mr. Martin." I leaned forward. "My stepsister is a very young, impressionable teenage girl just entering adolescence."

He nodded.

"Naturally, she has a trusted girlfriend."

He continued to nod.

"When I questioned Allison, she revealed that she had told her friend things, too, and I'm afraid that girl might have told another girl, who would tell another. You know how that can explode into something that would create quite a scandal for this school."

"Yes, of course." The worry in his face was practically oozing out of his eyes now.

"However, this gives us an opportunity. If you called Allison in and told her you've heard some things involving her and Mr. Taylor, she might just tell you everything herself, and that would make it easier for you. And for me and my family," I said.

The reality of what I was suggesting landed with a thump in his brain. He widened his eyes. "This is a very, very serious thing, Mayfair. An accusation like this against a teacher . . ."

"That's why I came to you first. Might I suggest, Mr. Martin," I added with a look of firm determination, "that as serious as it might be for a teacher, it is twice as serious for a young girl like Allison. Her whole emotional life could be damaged here. Her parents, my father especially, would be very, very upset."

"Of course," he said. "But young girls like Allison often form crushes on their teachers, and they fantasize, too."

"Absolutely. It will be up to you and whoever else to investigate and determine whether it is true or not. At some point, you'll have to ask for her diary to read the details or, if and when it comes to it, inform the proper authorities to request it." Before he spoke, I added, "Please keep this as quiet as possible for now, until you and whoever do a proper investigation."

"Yes, that's very important."

"You can be assured I won't talk about it. I've already explained why."

"Good."

"Mr. Martin, if you betray me, I'll make sure my stepsister clams up, and things will go far worse for

everyone, especially the school administration. There
are too many examples almost daily now of young
people being abused and authorities sweeping it all
under the rug to keep from being embarrassed."

"I understand. I'll handle it," he said quickly, and
stood up. "Thank you for your trust," he added.

I rose. "No. Thank you for helping us. I'm leaving it
entirely in your hands," I said, my voice full of warnings.

He nodded, and I left his office.

I didn't think I'd ever felt stronger, taller, and more
powerful than I did at that moment. Anyone seeing
me walk down the corridor would think I had just
taken over the school.

My timing was good. The bell rang for lunch, and I
intercepted Allison on her way.

"Take a walk with me," I said, pulling her away
from her friends.

"What is it?"

"Mr. Martin called me into his office to ask about
you, about the stories he had just heard. He has a very
high regard for me and has often asked my advice
about things, but this is quite different and the most
serious thing of all."

Blood rushed into her face.

"Don't worry. I handled it well, as I promised.
When he calls you in, tell him the truth. Can you remember some of the details you wrote in your diary?"

"I guess so."

"When you wrote in your diary, did you include
dates so someone would understand when these things
actually happened?"

"Yes."

"That's good, very smart of you, Allison. It's like proof when it's written like that. I'm proud of you. So just tell those things if you're asked. You can tell him what you told Lisa, too. Did you tell her everything you wrote in your diary?"

"Not everything."

"Then just start with what you told her exactly. He might call her in, and it's important that she tells him what you said just the way you said it."

Her eyes began to tear up. She bit her lower lip. I think she was actually shaking.

"It's all right to look frightened, but if you're told you could get into great trouble by making false accusations against Mr. Taylor, don't start crying and say you made it up. This is a big embarrassment for the school and especially for the administration. They'll be hoping you're lying. They'll try to pressure you to say you were, but I told you that you could hurt us all, because they wouldn't stop with you. They'd call in my father and your mother, and other people would know about everything, especially Mr. Taylor. Okay?"

"Yes."

"When Mr. Martin calls you in, come look for me afterward to tell me what happened. I'm in the library all day today. All right?"

She didn't answer.

I shook her arm. "All right, Allison?"

"Yes," she said.

"Good. Go eat lunch, and act as if nothing is wrong," I told her, and sent her on her way.

I watched her in the cafeteria. Her friends were their usual boisterous and dramatic selves around her, but she sat like someone made of stone. When the bell rang to return to classes, she looked like she would need help to stand, but she did. I saw her walk out talking with her friend Lisa. Maybe she was warning her.

Toward the end of the following period, she came into the library. She looked pale and fragile. I was keeping an eye on the door, so when she appeared, I got up quickly and indicated that she should go back out.

"Into the girls' room," I said, and she followed me in. "Okay. Tell me everything that went on. Don't leave anything out."

"It wasn't just Mr. Martin. Dr. Richards was there, too."

"Yes?"

Finally, she started to cry. It was as though the tears had been pushing on her eyelids like a wild river pressing on a dam. They streamed down her face. Her lips trembled, and her shoulders shook. I put my arm around her and took her into a stall, put the toilet seat down, and had her sit. Then I handed her tissues and waited.

"It was just like you said it would be. Mr. Martin said he heard I was spreading stories about Mr. Taylor. He said it was a very, very serious thing and I could get into very big trouble if I was saying things that weren't true about a teacher."

"And?"

"I didn't say anything. Dr. Richards was nicer. He

smiled at me and said I shouldn't be afraid. I should tell them anything I wanted. So I did what you said. I thought about my diary and told them some of the things I had written in it."

"What exactly? You never showed me the diary, remember?"

"Like when Mr. Taylor started touching me and when he asked me to help him with marking quizzes. I only had study hall, so I could do it."

"He gave you a pass out of study hall to come to him?"

"Yes."

"Well, they can check that out easily enough. Very good, Allison. That was good thinking."

She smiled through her tears.

"What then?"

"I couldn't say some of the other things. I told them I was too embarrassed to say them, so they took me in to see Mrs. Milligan."

"The nurse. Very good. I should have anticipated they would do that," I added, but more for myself than for her. "What did she do?"

"She asked me all kinds of stuff, like what was in the book you gave me."

"And you told her?"

"She saw I couldn't say it easily, so she said she would ask me a question, and if it was true, I should say yes or, if I couldn't talk, just nod."

"I didn't hear everything in the gossip. What sorts of things did you say yes to? Him touching you between your legs, under your panties? It's all right to tell that. Those things often happen when someone takes sexual advantage of a young girl. Well?"

She nodded. "Even more," she said.

"Good. What did she tell you to do now?"

"Go back to class."

"You don't have to go back to class," I said. "You're too upset. We'll return to Mrs. Milligan's office. Don't worry. I'll go with you now. You'll say you came to look for me. It's all right."

"I'm scared," she said.

I put my arm around her. It felt as surprising to me as I'm sure it did to her. I had never embraced her like this before, but in a way, I felt I was embracing myself, comforting myself. I even kissed her on her forehead the way my father might kiss me to give me a sense of security. "You don't have to be the one who's scared now, Allison. Besides, I'm with you. C'mon," I urged, and walked her out.

I brought her to the nurse's office and told Mrs. Milligan she had come to me and was too upset to return to class. I asked her to let Allison rest in one of the small rooms she had in her office area, and of course she did.

"Did she tell you any of this?" Mrs. Milligan asked me.

"I'd rather not talk about it now," I said. "Besides, it might be legally unwise to do so. You should have kept her here. How could you expect her just to carry on as if nothing unusual had occurred after you cross-examined her? This is a major emotional and psychological crisis for a girl her age."

She recoiled. My sharp tone was like a slap to her. She nodded and went about some clerical work without trying to defend herself. I looked in on Allison, held her hand for a few minutes, and told her to be brave.

"Remember, you're doing this for all of us, Allison, especially your mother and my father. You're okay?"

She nodded and squeaked out a tiny "Yes."

I returned to the library. It was better to keep busy and behave as though nothing unusual was going on.

Stage three was about to start.

It began right before the end of the day. Julie was called to the school, and my father soon followed. They were in Dr. Richards's office when the bell to end the day rang. Dr. Richards's secretary came looking for me and told me to report to his office. I waited in the outer office. When the door opened, Julie had her arm around Allison's shoulders. Allison had been crying again, but now that was fine. The more she cried, the better it was, in fact. She would get the credibility she needed.

My father looked at me and shook his head. "You know what's going on here?" he asked.

I nodded. "She came to me after she was called to the office, and I took her to the nurse's office because she was so upset." That was all true. I wasn't lying to him.

"Let's go," he said.

Since he had met Julie at the school, they had two cars. I was to ride home with him, and Allison rode with Julie.

"What a mess," he said as we drove off behind Julie and Allison. "When did you learn about this?"

"I had some suspicions, but mostly last night."

"Why didn't you say something to Julie about it?"

"I'm not exactly Julie's favorite person right now, Daddy. I wasn't going to be the one to start something like this. What if it's not true? It has to be handled correctly."

"It sure looks true. You know that old expression 'Where there's smoke, there's fire.'"

"Yes, Grandmother Lizzy always said that," I replied. He turned and saw me smiling at the memory.

"What a mess. I wouldn't mind having Lizzy around to help with it."

"Where are we going?" I asked when I saw Julie miss a turn that would take us home and he turned to follow.

"We've arranged for Dr. Baer to see her."

"What? Why?"

"Julie wants her checked out to see . . . you know, if she's been sexually violated."

"That's disgusting. That will make her even more upset. That could cause serious emotional damage, Daddy."

"It's got to be done. This is a criminal situation now."

"But she never said things went that far."

"Who knows what she'll tell and won't tell, Mayfair, even to you. She's a very frightened little girl."

I sat back. This shook me up a little, because I hadn't anticipated it, and I should have. I really did feel sorry for Allison. I would hate to have had something like this done to me after being with Alan Taylor.

At the doctor's office, we waited in the lobby while Allison and Julie were in the examining room. When they came out, Julie looked at my father and shook her head. For a moment, I wasn't sure what that meant. It occurred to me that Allison might have somehow lost her virginity without telling me about it. Girls could have their hymens broken in other ways, too. I was a prime example.

We stood up, and Julie stepped closer.

"She's still a virgin," she told my father but also for my benefit.

I looked at Allison. She seemed to be walking in a trance. My heart twisted with regret. I didn't want to see her in so much emotional pain, but my anger was directed fully at Alan Taylor for both our sakes now.

"Let's go home," my father said.

The fact that she was still a virgin didn't contradict what I had read in her diary. She had never described penetration, so I didn't let that fact detract from the validity of the rest of it. What I had read and how she had reacted to my questioning were convincing enough for me, especially when I added what my own experience had been with Alan Taylor.

The story began to spread that night. Julie's friends were on the phone with her for hours, each taking a turn. Allison was too upset to come to dinner. Something was brought to her room. At dinner, my father and Julie said they had decided that Allison should stay home from school the next day.

"I don't think that's wise," I told them. "It will
only make things more difficult for her when she re-
turns. They'll be talking about her all day tomorrow.
Besides, it will give her more strength if she follows a
normal routine."

"I won't have her behave as if nothing unusual
is going on. It's too much to expect of her. She's not
you!" Julie practically screamed at me. "She has real
feelings."

"Well, she can't be taking after you, either, then."

"Mayfair," my father said softly.

I thought about what she had said. I had no trouble returning to school on the days following my tryst
with Alan and trying to confront him. His attitude
and avoidance were just as traumatic, but I didn't stray
from my normal routine. Was Julie right? Did that
mean I didn't have real feelings?

"I'm only trying to help. I've studied these sorts of
traumatic events, Daddy. I know what has been found
to be helpful and what has not. It's not a matter of
feelings, Julie," I said, trying desperately to sound as if
I did care about her and what she was going through,
having her daughter involved in such a thing. "It's a
matter of what's more effective. I'm only thinking of
Allison."

"She's not going there tomorrow, and that's that,"
she said firmly.

I looked at my father and then finished eating
without saying another word.

Julie mumbled through the remainder of dinner.

"I'm not burying my head in the sand, letting the school take any convenient way out of this. I'm going to make sure that justice is done. Those administrators know it."

I couldn't resist. "I hope it's better justice than what occurred after those bitches from *Macbeth* soiled *my* reputation," I said.

Julie bit down on her lower lip. My father shook his head.

"Maybe that was a terrible injustice," Julie confessed. "I was only trying to do what was best for you."

"She knows that now," my father said, looking at me pointedly.

I didn't have to say anything. Stage four had begun. Julie was going to charge ahead like a wild bull again, and Dr. Richards, unlike me, couldn't lock his door against her.

There was nothing left for me to do but wait.

In the morning, I saw that a substitute was replacing Alan Taylor. It would remain that way until the matter was resolved, but it became very clear that no matter how it was resolved, his future at the school was in jeopardy. Julie and her friends were simply too powerful for anyone, even if he were innocent, to overcome them. This was, after all, a private school that was dependent on tuition and donations from wealthy parents and friends of the school.

Of course, in my mind, no matter what he did or didn't exactly do with Allison, he was not innocent.

Perhaps I was more of a victim. It didn't matter now. It was better this way. Julie was taken down more than a peg or two. I was getting two birds with one stone.

I did have moments of self-doubt and even moments when I thought I had gone too far for justice and revenge, but I always overcame those feelings with cold logic, convincing myself that I was surely not the first or the last high-school girl he had victimized, and Allison wasn't the first young teenager.

Before the week was over, Alan Taylor and his counsel appeared at the school for a meeting in the principal's office. The moment he was spotted, the news flowed like an electric current through the halls, classrooms, and offices. How he found out I was alone in the laboratory, I didn't know, but when I looked up from some slides I was studying under the microscope, he was in the doorway. For a long moment, we just looked at each other.

"You put her up to it, didn't you?" he asked.

"Did I? Or did you?"

"You can't believe that."

"I believe in what I can prove and what I know from my own experiences. Nothing else."

He nodded. "You don't have to admit to it. I know. I didn't treat you well. I'm sorry." Then he surprised me by smiling. "What was it William Congreve wrote?"

"'Hell hath no fury like a woman scorned,'" I answered.

"Exactly. I guess I should have remembered that.

Well, have a good and interesting life," he added, and walked away.

I returned to my slides, but I wasn't focusing on anything. My vision was too cloudy. I had my victories, but I was disappointed in my reaction.

I had trouble seeing through the tears.

# 17

The famous moments of the calm before a storm followed. It was especially dark and silent in our house. Dinners were like funerals. The clanking of silverware and dishes had never sounded as loud. Even the maids seemed to be tiptoeing wherever they went and speaking in whispers. Allison was forbidden to use her phone. She had been told to speak to no one about any of this now that an actual criminal trial was looming. Julie didn't even want her to mention it in the house. In fact, thinking about all this, Julie was so disturbed one day that she charged up the stairway and disconnected Allison's phone so it wouldn't ring, practically ripping the wire out of the wall. She was constantly laying down threats. I thought she was close to having a nervous breakdown.

Whether he had to or was just looking for some relief from the heavy atmosphere in our home, my father worked longer hours and took three overnight trips during the week. Julie went to dinner with friends all three nights, soaking up waves of sympathy, I was sure. In my mind, despite the act she put on in the house for us, she probably enjoyed the extra attention she was receiving from her friends.

And then, just as there was an opportunity to take a deep breath, another crisis exploded.

The district attorney informed Julie that he had to have Allison's diary. Just as I had advised her to do, Allison had revealed to Mr. Martin that she had written everything that had gone on between her and Alan Taylor in it, along with the dates. He had informed the district attorney. When the assistant district attorney arrived at our home a day later to get the diary, my father wasn't home, but I was downstairs. Julie had been at her wit's end about it because Allison wouldn't let her read it first. She had hidden it in a better place, which amused me at first and then, when I gave it more thought, worried me.

Was she simply embarrassed or afraid of her mother's reaction to the things she had written? Even though I had never written anything I didn't want anyone else to read, I realized that especially for a girl like Allison, someone else, even a mother, reading her intimate thoughts was truly like exposing herself, parading naked and revealing every blemish. Everyone needed some sort of privacy. If you couldn't even protect the sanctity of your thoughts, what did you have left? On top of everything else that had been done to her, especially the vaginal exam, Allison could easily have a nervous breakdown herself, and who knew what the result of that would be?

"Once we have it, we'll have to turn it over to Mr.

Taylor's attorney," the assistant district attorney told Julie.

She looked absolutely shocked. "What? How many people will read this? I won't permit it."

"We can't withhold evidence from the defense attorney," he explained calmly. "And that diary has now become evidence, Mrs. Cummings."

Of course, Allison didn't want to hand over the diary. She cried, and Julie made the assistant district attorney promise her that only the people who absolutely had to read it would be permitted to read it. Allison wanted to rip out the pages that had nothing to do with Alan Taylor, but the assistant DA said that would not go over too well.

"I haven't even read it," Julie said, and she looked angrily at Allison. "She's hidden it from everyone."

I was sure Julie was wondering what Allison had written about *her*.

"I'm sorry," the assistant DA said. "We'll ask the judge to restrict access to the document. That's the best we can do."

That didn't make Julie any happier, but there was nothing she could do about it. I was surprised when she looked to me for help.

I shook my head. "If the district attorney believes it will help make the case stronger, Julie, you shouldn't resist turning it over," I told her. "We want Allison to have all the support she can get."

She glared at Allison. "She never kept so many secrets from me. I never knew she had been writing in such a diary."

"Didn't you?" I asked.

I thought she had hit all the stops on her way to fe-male adulthood. How many times did she describe the dances she had gone to, the boyfriends lining up, the proms, the clothes, the hairdos, all of it spun not only to rub it in my face, I thought, but also to convince Allison that her mother was some sort of a star?

"Didn't you have a diary when you were Allison's age?"

"It wasn't something I expected would end up in a courtroom," she snapped back. Her eyes quickly cooled because of the assistant DA, who now looked uncomfortable. Then she added, "But none of us ex-pected any of this, I suppose. Go get the damn thing," she told Allison. "Now!"

Allison brought it down, fear and trepidation vivid in her eyes.

"I promise you'll get it back when it's no longer needed," the assistant DA told her when he took it from her reluctant fingers.

"We won't want it back. We'll want it burned," Julie told him.

Two days later, I waited in the living room for my father and Julie, because I knew the district attorney had called them to his offices to discuss the case. From the looks on both their faces, I could tell something wasn't right. Allison was up in her room doing her homework. I had just helped her understand some of her new math and explained some grammar problems. I was truly feeling sorry for her, but I also wanted her to be strong for what was to come, strong for both of us.

"I need a drink," Julie said almost the moment she stepped into the house.

My father glanced at me, shook his head, and went to the bar. Julie sat on a stool and lowered her head to her hands. Neither spoke. Watching them, I felt the tension building in me, too.

"What's happening?" I asked. "Why are you both so upset?"

Julie turned to look at me. I had been reading a book on child psychology and was still holding it. A crazed smile broke across her face, twisting her lips. One thing I had to say for her, she rarely looked ugly. Even when she was in a rage, she had the sort of beauty that was even more striking. Right now, she looked like someone suffering from Bell's palsy, a form of facial nerve weakness, with half her face distorted.

"That might be the right book for all of us to read now," she muttered. "I guess I'll have to borrow it when you're finished."

"What? What's going on?" I asked my father as he served her a Cosmopolitan, the vodka drink she favored.

He stood back and watched her drink half of it in one gulp.

"Daddy?"

"They've recorded the events and dates that Allison entered in her diary and continued their investigation based on that. Lisa Morris was interviewed yesterday, and the date that Allison claimed to be at her home when Mr. Taylor came by to pick her up is not right. Lisa's mother had taken her to the orthodontist that day. Allison couldn't have been there."

"What's the big deal? Maybe she just got the dates confused," I said.

"This is a criminal case, Mayfair. It goes to court. You can't claim dates and events that don't prove true and undermine Allison's credibility. It makes the diary nearly worthless."

"Didn't Lisa describe the things Allison had told her, though?"

"The assistant DA said she did describe some of those things but in a very vague and confused way. He said she isn't going to be a good witness. She is in Allison's class, and when she was asked if she had seen any of the things Allison claimed were happening in the classroom between her and Mr. Taylor, she said no. Apparently, they've quietly questioned some of the other students and have yet to find one who corroborates any of the things Allison claimed. It doesn't seem like he singled her out."

"But they had the pass he wrote for her to get her out of study hall, didn't they?" I asked. "Allison told me about that just the other day," I quickly added.

"Yes, but that only confirms that she helped him correct quizzes. Apparently, he did that with other students in his class, many of them boys. It's not something no other teacher in your school does, anyway, Mayfair."

Julie sucked back a sob and drank the rest of her Cosmopolitan. "Make me another, Roger," she commanded.

"What else did the district attorney say?" I asked. I could feel my stomach tightening into a knotted ball of rubber bands.

My father sighed. Julie uttered a small moan. He prepared another drink for her. "In light of this," he said, "but something he probably would have done anyway, Taylor's attorney, who saw a wide hole to drive through, asked the court to assign a child psychologist to interview Allison."

Maybe they'd assign Dr. Burns, I wanted to say, but any attempt at humor to lighten the moment would surely go over like a lead balloon.

"A girl as young as Allison, under such pressure and emotional tension, is easily capable of getting some facts confused," I offered.

Julie turned to me. "You think so?"

As if I had it underlined in the book I held, I lifted the volume for emphasis. "Of course. All those young girls are under great pressure. They're afraid to say anything that would involve them in any way with what's happening. Many might have been warned by their parents to keep their mouths shut. If the district attorney is good, he'll know how to navigate and build his case."

Julie looked a little relieved, but my father only offered a knowing smile, like someone who realized I was humoring a desperately worried person.

I left them.

I wanted to go right into her room and ask Allison more about Lisa from what I knew she had written, but I was still reluctant to reveal that I had read her diary, and my father had already asked me to try to help calm things down by avoiding any conversations about what had occurred.

The only thing I did discuss with Allison, a few days later, was her upcoming session with a court-appointed psychologist. She knew I had gone to Dr. Burns, of course, so she relied on my experience.

"It's just a lot of talking, Allison," I told her. "He's not going to make you feel bad. Tell him the truth, and tell him what makes you feel better to tell someone. Just the way you revealed everything to me, in fact."

She told my father and Julie that I had given her older-sisterly advice about her upcoming interview, and my father came to my room to let me know how proud he was of what I was doing to make the situation easier for Allison.

"Julie just said that it's at times like this when she really appreciates how mature and bright you are, Mayfair. I think she wanted me to express that to you, too."

"Did she?"

"Yes, she did."

He hugged and kissed me on the cheek before leaving. Secretly, of course, I was very frightened for Allison, as I was for myself.

The proverbial other shoe dropped two days after Allison's session. The district attorney called Julie and my father in again, this time to tell them the psychologist's report was going to be devastating to any prosecution. The heavy depression that had fallen over the house only seemed to get thicker.

"This is getting to look more and more like a disaster for all of us," my father declared.

"He's just got a very good lawyer," I told him and Julie. "Lawyers would defend Satan if they were paid enough."

Neither of them cared to argue or had much more to say about it.

One night soon after, my father came to my bedroom to tell me the school board was requesting that he and Julie attend a special closed session to discuss the matter. Julie said she felt like someone who had stuck her head out the window of a 747 jet. Previously, she had gathered a half dozen of her friends, mothers of other students at the school, and they had demanded a special session with the school board and administrators. The big question was how something like this could occur at a school as small as ours and right under the eyes of other teachers and staff. The conclusion the parents came to was that someone obviously was not supervising properly. My father attended the meeting, too, and I heard them discussing it afterward at home. The promise was made to conduct a vigorous investigation. But there was also the big possibility that some heads would roll.

This time, things went quite differently. I heard them arrive back home and waited in my room. Allison was already asleep. I think she had fled to bed out of fear more than anything. I went downstairs. They were both in the living room. My father was having a Scotch and soda, and Julie was sitting on the settee looking stunned.

"What's happened now?" I asked.

"It wasn't pretty," my father said.

Julie cried, "How can I ever look my friends in the face?"

"There'll be a story in the paper," my father said. "Of course, Allison's name won't be mentioned."

"But everyone will know what's happened and who it's happened to," Julie moaned.

"I don't understand. What went on?" I asked.

"Alan Taylor's lawyer was present," my father said. He could easily start a lawsuit, but Mr. Taylor's not interested in prolonging this. Under the circumstances, everyone else was quite relieved."

Alan Taylor was going to act like he was doing everyone a favor, but I was sure what he was really worried about was it going any longer and my coming forward. Allison's diary inaccuracies and fragility were one thing. If I were the witness, it would be a totally different situation. I could describe details of his apartment, where we got the pizza, even the wine he had served me, and both Julie and my father would remember that was an evening I did not call or come home for dinner. Maybe he'd be concerned that someone had seen us together. If the police really investigated, it could come to that. No psychologist or misdated diary was going to change it, good defense attorney or not.

Of course, there was the possibility that people would still think I was out to avenge my family, my stepsister, and anyway, I didn't think my father and Julie were up to another barrage of depositions, investigators, and public scrutiny.

"Damage is done to the school as it is. It will be mentioned in the stories, of course, and this sort of thing is not good for a private school always looking for potential new students with parents who have fat checkbooks," my father said.

"Mr. Taylor didn't ask for anything in return?"

"A good recommendation, apologies. He's already lined up a new job, apparently."

"You didn't apologize to him, did you, Daddy?"

"No."

Julie sobbed harder. She looked up at me. "You believed her," she asked with some note of hope in her voice. "Why?"

All of a sudden, my opinion was very important to her. Was this my time to make my case, start them at Alan Taylor again, and once more turn the school topsy-turvy?

I looked at my father. Should I do it? Should I tell them both exactly why?

"There's no point in doing this sort of thing to ourselves," my father said, sensing my reluctance. "Let's not go over it and over it. It's done. Over. Let's just work on our recuperation. Get things back to normal as quickly as we can." He looked to me for confirmation.

I said nothing. I turned and went up to my room.

In the days that followed, Julie seemed to wither right in front of me. Her arrogant posture and condescending tone were gone. She practically tiptoed, slouched over, and was unusually quiet at dinner. My father was upset and did the best he could to cheer her up, but she often broke into periods of sobbing.

This time, I took the opportunity to suggest that she go see Dr. Burns. "If there was ever a time when someone needed some therapy, Julie, it's now, and it's you."

After she flew out of the room, my father told me he didn't think that was funny.

"It's not meant to be funny, Daddy," I told him. "She's obviously in a bad depression and needs either some medication or counseling. She's not eating properly. She's spending too much time sleeping. Next thing you know, she'll abuse alcohol or drugs."

He frowned, but I could see he was taking me seriously and wondering if having her see someone for professional counseling wasn't indeed necessary.

Both he and Julie were worried about Allison, too, but oddly, when Allison returned to school, her friends treated her more like a heroine than a girl who had done something evil. Allison told me about their conversations. She claimed that many of her friends refused to believe it hadn't all been true. I understood that they could talk about Alan Taylor openly, since he wasn't in our school any longer. Now that they weren't in front of a district attorney or giving a deposition, they comfortably swore that Mr. Taylor did single Allison out and spent more time with her than he did with them. Some even claimed to have had similar experiences. It was like one of those mass-hypnosis situations. Maybe they thought it made them look older or more sophisticated to have been titillated, teased, and inappropriately touched. So Allison had gone a little too far with her accusations. So what? She did what she had to do, didn't she?

I stood back and watched her in school and laughed to myself when I saw how popular she had become. It made me feel a little better about the outcome. Everyone wanted to know the details about her being questioned by the district attorney and a psychologist and about the things she had said. She got away with it by admitting that she had exaggerated a little, but saying Mr. Taylor had still been after her "bod." In any case, after a while, I thought she had outdone her mother when it came to being a little arrogant. She was the one strutting around the house, not Julie. Her phone was always ringing, and invitations for parties and dinners with friends were constantly being offered to her.

I was the one who had new troubles in school. I had forgotten about the bitches of *Macbeth*. They boiled their venom and came at me whenever they could with their snide remarks about how bad an influence I was on Allison. Most of the time, I ignored them, but one afternoon outside the library, I decided enough was enough.

"Your little stepsister is quite the liar, isn't she?" Joyce Brooker asked me. She practically put her face right up against mine. "I guess you trained her well."

"Afraid she's competition for you?" I replied, not backing up a step.

"Just whose fantasies were they?" Cora Addison asked, stepping up beside her with her hands on her hips. "Yours or hers?"

I spun around on her and smiled. "I think she told me she overheard you dreaming out loud and got her ideas from that."

"That was a silly question, Cora," Denise Hartman said. "They can't possibly have been *her* fantasies.
They involved someone with a penis."

They all laughed.

That brought some other students around to listen
and watch, and then more gathered to see what was
happening to cause such interest.

"From what I hear, you're the one around here
who's involved with more penises than an urologist,"
I replied.

"A what?" Cora asked.

"Oh, I forgot. You're a little slow and need someone to translate English for you."

"You're such a freak," Denise said. "No wonder
your stepsister is so screwed up. Who wouldn't be
screwed up living with you?"

"What did your father do to have someone like
you, take drugs?" Joyce said.

"No," Cora said over their laughter. "He has to
take them now, now that he has to live with her and
admit to being her father."

"Unlike your father, who's not sure he *is* your father, is that it?" I fired back.

"Bitch," she said.

"That's what I hear the boys around here call you,
'my bitch,' " I said.

Everyone howled, and Cora turned bright pink.
She looked at her audience and then, without any
warning, swung her pocketbook at me and caught me
on the left side of my head. She must have had something heavy in it, because it dazed me. I stumbled and

then lost my footing and slipped on the short step at the library door. When I fell, everyone took off in every possible direction.

I heard Mr. Martin call my name as I was struggling to my feet. "What's going on here?" he asked, helping me up. "My goodness, your head's bleeding, Mayfair. What happened?"

I felt my temple and looked at my fingers. The amount of blood didn't surprise me. "It's all right. Head wounds usually bleed like this," I told him.

"It's not all right. We'd better get you to the nurse. C'mon," he said, taking my arm. I was still a little dizzy. "What happened?" he asked again.

"The debate team lost control of itself," I said.

"Who hit you?"

"Does it matter?"

"Absolutely," he said.

We entered the nurse's office, and Mrs. Milligan sat me down immediately and hurried to get a wet cloth.

"Did she fall?"

"No, someone hit her."

"With what?"

"A pocketbook loaded with cement," I said.

She began to work on the wound.

Mr. Martin stood there staring at me. "Who did it? What was the argument about?"

"CSI will confirm Cora Addison," I replied. "I'm sure there's some of my DNA on her pocketbook."

"Was this about your stepsister?"

"It seemed to be more about Cora and her friends, but that's just my opinion."

"This is quite a deep cut," Mrs. Milligan said. "She might need stitches. We need to be concerned about a possible concussion."

"I'm not going to sleep, and there's nothing one could do about a minor concussion, anyway, Mrs. Milligan. I'll be fine."

"I don't know." She looked at Mr. Martin. "I'll clean it up and cover it, but I really think she needs stitches. I'll run her over to the urgent care. And I'd feel better if she had an X-ray."

"I don't need all that," I protested.

"You're not a doctor yet," Mr. Martin said. "Do what you have to, Lila," he told the nurse. "I'll inform her parents," he said, and left.

I tried to resist, but Mrs. Milligan was determined.

"It's out of your hands and mine," she said. "The insurance company would insist."

When we went out to her car, I could see students gaping at us from classroom windows. Mrs. Milligan saw them, too.

"You've attracted a crowd," she said.

"I'm glad I can provide them with desperately needed distraction from their boring classes," I told her, and she laughed, which surprised me. Could it be she liked me after all? Even after the things I said to her when I brought Allison to her office?

Less than an hour later, Julie arrived at the urgent care. I did require stitches, and an X-ray was taken. I had no concussion.

"How could such a thing happen now?" Julie asked Mrs. Milligan immediately. From the way she asked it, anyone would think she was blaming me, no matter what.

"I failed to duck, bob, and weave," I said.

Mrs. Milligan told her as much as she knew. The rest would come later.

"I guess we're going to have to seriously consider whether both of you should continue at this school," Julie told me on the way home.

I didn't say anything. My head was throbbing, and despite what I had told Mrs. Milligan and Mr. Martin, all I wanted to do was go to sleep.

My father was very upset when he heard about the incident. He came home as soon as he could and hurried up to my room.

"Hey, May," he said, sitting on my bed and taking my hand. He looked at my wound. "Nasty. I heard what you told Julie. I thought I taught you how to duck."

"I guess it was one of the few times I wasn't paying enough attention."

"You want to tell me how this happened?"

"It was the same girls who made those stupid accusations about me in the locker room, remember?"

"Oh."

"They were emboldened by the resolution of that situation, and now we're seeing the fruits of the politically correct compromise."

"I'll look into it myself this time," he promised. "This time, there'll be no politically convenient solution."

I shrugged skeptically, but he did look determined.

He went down to his home office to make some calls and returned in a little less than half an hour to report that Cora Addison had been called to the principal's office and suspended from school. Her parents would have to go in with her when she returned.

Although Mr. Martin and Dr. Richards saw this as just punishment because Cora had resorted to violence, I knew it would not do me any good with the rest of the student body, especially the other two bitches of *Macbeth*.

This was far from over.

# 18

If there had been anyone who would say hello, smile, or be in any way friendly to me before this at school, he or she was gone, probably forever. My academic achievements, my freedom in pursuing advanced studies, and my self-imposed isolation from school activities already had done much to single me out as someone too different. Now I was surely going to be not only too different but also too much trouble, someone never to be trusted. I knew I would feel like I was walking around school wearing not a scarlet A like Hester Prynne in *The Scarlet Letter* but a scarlet R for *rat*. Or a scarlet C for *creep*.

I didn't look forward to it.

Later, at dinner, when my father talked about my violent confrontation with the bitches of *Macbeth* again, Julie looked like she had always expected it and wondered why something like this had never happened before. I could squeeze as much sympathy out of her as I could squeeze water out of a rock.

However, Allison felt sorry for me, and after dinner, she came into my room to tell me so.

"That was very mean what they did to you," she said. "They ganged up on you."

"That's the way people like that are, Allison. They can't do anything unless they're part of a gang. They're really cowards."

"It's all my fault, isn't it?" she asked me.

"Why is it your fault, Allison?"

"I heard they were saying bad things about me, and you told them off."

"They were saying bad things about both of us, mostly me, Allison. Forget about them. They're not important. I could sketch out their entire lives for you. They'll end up eating their own hearts."

I didn't want to tell her they would probably become women just like her mother, but she brought up Julie herself. "I told my mother how you defended me, how you tried to help me with everything," she said.

I put down my book and looked at her. "What do you mean, everything?"

"You know," she said. "When you told me what to do and what to say and what not to say when Mr. Martin called me into his office that day."

"But you and I had a secret," I said. "You made me a promise you would never tell anyone, not even your mother, about our conversations."

"I wanted her to know how much you helped me," she said, raising her arms. "I wanted her to know how we were becoming real sisters and that she should feel sorry for you about what those girls did."

"Okay," I said.

What else could I say? But it was like sitting there listening to the ticking of a time bomb.

Allison returned to her own room. I closed my eyes. The throbbing had stopped but now suddenly began again. This time, it wasn't coming from the wound. It was coming from my anticipation.

After nearly an hour passed, I thought nothing more would occur this particular evening, but I was wrong. I heard the knock on my door, and before I could say "Come in," my father opened it, stepped in, and closed it behind him. The look on his face was enough. I didn't need to hear anything.

He stood there looking at me for a moment. Then he shook his head and came closer. "Let me begin by telling you that Julie is quite hysterical downstairs."

"Inordinately so?"

"No, King's English this time, Mayfair, and no sarcasm. I'm warning you. I'm trying to understand this. You went to Allison and told her that the stories she had told her best friend about Mr. Taylor were being spread around in the school?"

"So?"

"Did you do that?"

"I did, after she was so upset about overhearing him say he was going to get engaged. You saw how depressed she was during those days, how she hardly ate and wouldn't talk."

"Yes, I did. Julie tried to talk to her about it. We both assumed it was boy trouble at worst but certainly not man trouble."

I looked away. Why was he so sensitive to Allison's emotional pain and so insensitive to mine? When was the last time he looked at me and wondered if I was happy or if something had upset me? Was it my fault? Because I was so intelligent, with an off-the-charts IQ, he believed I would always be smarter at solving my own problems than he would be? Did my brilliance make my father feel unnecessary?

Or had Julie turned him away from me completely so that all his fatherly attention and concern were directed at Allison? Whenever I had been alone with them, Julie's conversation was usually centered on Allison. There was never any time to talk about me, ask about me, and care about me, unless it somehow supported her beliefs about who I was and what I needed on her terms and her terms only. She was the sun in this house, and I was barely just another planet.

I sincerely felt bad about it all, but another part of me was smart enough to ask if I wasn't simply trying to rationalize and excuse my bad behavior. The bottom line was that I shouldn't have used Allison to get my revenge on Alan Taylor and punish Julie at the same time, even though I still thought Allison had also been abused.

"According to what Julie is saying Allison told her, you advised her to tell Mr. Martin and Dr. Richards these fantasies and warned her not to say that any of it was a lie, no matter what. You told her to tell them what she had written in her diary. You pushed her into this situation, this confrontation, Mayfair. Is this true?"

"I gave her the best advice I could," I said.

"You know that's not true, Mayfair. The best advice was not to tell her to deny that anything was untrue but instead to only tell the truth. Did you know that what she was saying was untrue from the start?"

"I did not and I still do not know that to be a fact, just because she confused a date in her diary and her friend, who's probably a young airhead, can't remember details. Any psychologist can twist a girl like Allison into knots and get the district attorney to back off, especially if there's a smart lawyer involved."

"But . . . you didn't know any of this to be a fact, and you're the one who's always preaching facts first, feelings second. I can't believe this, Mayfair. What about this poor guy? You could have destroyed his career, his life. You nearly ruined him forever and, no question, put the school in a terrible position. Why did you take such an active role in this and manipulate Allison, and not only her but us? Me?"

I turned my gaze sharply on him, my eyes burning with the pain I felt inside. My father was betraying me, but he did not know why he shouldn't. Maybe I was too smart for my own good; maybe I was my own worst enemy. "Don't worry about him. He wasn't lily-white pure, Daddy."

"How would you know that?"

"I know," I said firmly. "Personally."

He flinched and then looked stunned. "What are you saying?"

"I have factual, positive proof that he took advantage of a student besides Allison."

"What? Who? What are you saying now?"
I stared at him.

His eyes washed over me, and then it was almost as if I could see a cartoon light bulb go off above his head. "Let me understand this, Mayfair. Are you now saying that you were the one sexually abused by Mr. Taylor?"

I turned away. "I have trouble thinking of it as sexual abuse, Daddy. I'm old enough both chronologically and mentally to know what I was doing. It's the aftermath that I consider abuse, and that's why I was so easily convinced that Allison might have been another victim," I said. I didn't want to mention any other motive, especially my chance to expose Julie so he would see her for what she was.

"I can't believe this. Why wouldn't you come to me if that was true?"

"As I told you, I didn't see myself as a victim then, and when I did, I felt more foolish than violated. We know who would enjoy seeing me embarrassed the most."

"You don't mean Julie."

I didn't reply. Then I thought and said, "Among others, especially the bitches from *Macbeth*."

"You're not eighteen," he said. "Of course you are a victim."

I smirked. "You know my opinion of chronological age versus mental age, Daddy."

"Your opinion isn't important in such a situation. There are legal opinions here." He shook his head. "This is too much. I don't understand what you did here or why. You hid what happened to you and decided instead to use what Allison told you to get back at this man? Is this the gist of what you're telling me?"

"I guess so," I said.

"You guess so?"

"Yes! That's the gist of it!" I felt my eyes flooding with tears, something I hadn't felt for some time. "Yes, yes!" I cried. "That's exactly what I did."

He sat for a moment, stunned. "Why, Mayfair? You're so much brighter than most people, brighter than anyone I know. This wasn't the right way to handle things."

I wiped tears off my cheeks. "Maybe intelligence isn't everything after all, Daddy. Maybe we underestimate the power of feelings. I was hurt, and logic didn't make it any better this time."

"What exactly happened between you and him?"

I sat for a moment looking out the window, wishing I were like a cloud that could be blown toward the horizon and not have to linger in one place.

"Mayfair?"

"What usually happens between men and women?"

"When?"

"The day Julie sold me out in school, that day, that afternoon and evening."

He thought a moment. "The time you said you were at the library?"

"I guess it qualifies as research now and nothing more." I turned to him. "I don't want you doing anything about it now. It's too late."

"You should have come to me. You shouldn't have tried to get revenge or justice this way, Mayfair."

"Should have and could have are probably the most used concepts since the invention of the wheel."

He nodded. "Well, Julie is rightfully upset, Mayfair. My marriage is in real jeopardy here."

He knew my feelings about his marriage. He didn't have to hear it. "I wouldn't call that jeopardy," I muttered nevertheless.

"She makes me happy, Mayfair. It's not up to you to judge that. I have a life to live, too. I mourned your mother's passing. I suffered. I was ready to give everything up and not care, but I wanted to be strong for you until you could be strong for yourself, and when I thought you were, I looked after myself somewhat, too. I don't feel guilty about it, and you will never make me feel guilty about it.

"No father could ever be prouder of a daughter than I was of you. I was right there for all your amazing awards. I bragged about you until my business associates wanted to take me out to be shot. My office walls are covered with your plaques, citations, and letters from every respected institution that involves academic accomplishment.

"During those early years after your mother's death, I tried to be your mother and father. I did the best I could. You've gone way too far this time, Mayfair. Not this school and certainly not Julie and I are capable of giving you what you need, apparently."

He lowered his head and sat quietly for a long moment. The tears that burned inside my eyes boiled over. I turned away quickly, and then he rose and left my room.

When I was very young, reading books that college-age kids were struggling with and doing math problems that high-school teachers wouldn't attempt, much less try to teach to seniors, I used to wonder if I had really been born like other children. The possibility occurred to me, especially after reading *Frankenstein*, that I might have been created in some laboratory. I asked my mother.

At first, she laughed, but then she saw that I was really thinking it might be so.

"Oh, no, no, Mayfair," she cried, and hugged me. "You were born on a very sunny morning. I was dreaming of giving birth to you and woke up when my water broke. Your father was so nervous and excited that he was very funny. He put on two completely different shoes and never realized it until he was at the hospital.

"It was only five fifteen in the morning, but on the way there, he stopped at that traffic light at the base of our road, the one everyone complains about because there's so little traffic that it barely needs a stop sign, and he just stayed there waiting for it to change while I was moaning. He suddenly realized how silly and nervous he was acting and shot ahead. These were wonderful memories for us after you were born.

"The moment I looked at your face, I knew you were going to be something special. Two days old, and you looked at me and listened as if you were already two years old. You were the favorite of the maternity nurses, too.

"No, my darling, wonderful little girl, you were

not created in a laboratory, unless you want to call my womb a laboratory."

She held me and laughed.

I could hear her melodic laugh now. I hadn't heard it for so long. It had been buried under too much in my brain, maybe, but when I remembered it now, it didn't make me smile. It made me cry.

I held myself and curled up in my bed, wishing I had someone who loved me holding me instead. I rocked and cried like a little girl.

Finally, sleep caught up with me, but I welcomed it. Thankfully, it was the weekend, and I didn't have to get up early and go to school. My father had decided yesterday that he was going to take us all for a ride to the Fashion Plaza in Newport Beach, where Julie could enjoy some shopping. We were all to go to lunch in Laguna Beach, but I didn't feel like getting up, much less going for a ride and spending a day with Julie and Allison now. I was anticipating her look of disgust and condemnation, even though she had probably promised my father she would not mention anything. When I didn't go down for breakfast, my father came up.

"Are you sick?" he asked. "Are you in pain from that cut on your head or anything?"

"No."

"Well, are you going with us today?"

"I'm tired," I said.

"Suit yourself," he replied, and left quickly. He had no patience for me and no forgiveness yet. I wondered if he ever would.

Later, I rose and had a little to eat. I wasn't happy being alone in the house this time. Normally, I could distract myself with reading or research, but I couldn't concentrate on anything. Impulsively, I dressed and called for a taxi to take me to Santa Monica. I had no idea why until I got out and walked on the beach. It took me only moments to realize I wanted to relive what had been the most exciting day and night of my life. It was the first time I could really say that I felt more like a young woman than a super-brilliant prodigy.

I took off my shoes, folded my arms under my breasts, and walked down the beach, sometimes stepping into the water and remembering how it had felt that afternoon when I was walking with Alan Taylor and how we had laughed about it. I recalled how I had begun to relax and become more and more fascinated with him, with how he opened up to talk about himself, which only encouraged me to do the same. I was telling him things I hadn't told anyone else, some things, in fact, that I had never told my father.

I remembered thinking, *I can do this. I can have a relationship with him secretly but intensely.* He was complimenting me in ways I had never been complimented and touching me in places that longed to be touched. As we walked, it really seemed like we passed through an invisible wall into a new world of possibilities. What he was back at school, what I was back at school, drifted behind us, blown away by our smiles and laughter. We were simply a man and a woman enjoying each other's conversation, each other's company, and the beauty surrounding us.

I had no idea how long I had been walking now. I suddenly stopped and realized I was close to Alan Taylor's apartment building. For a moment, I just stood there staring at it, the sea breeze threading through my hair. I turned off from the beach and stopped at a bench along the walkway to put on my shoes. I sat there thinking, remembering. The images and feelings were as vivid as ever, especially since I was so close.

Just as I was about to get up, walk back a little, and then call for a taxi home, I saw Alan coming up the sidewalk. He was holding hands with a very attractive strawberry-blond-haired woman who was only about an inch shorter than he was. She wore a pair of designer jeans, with glittering jeweled patterns on the sides of the legs, and a pink short-sleeved blouse. She had the svelte figure of a model and wore a pair of very fashionable sunglasses.

I froze and watched them. They were laughing at something and looked very happy. Perhaps he was telling the truth about becoming engaged, I thought. I didn't wait for them to enter his building. I turned quickly and headed down the walkway. The sight of him looking so fresh and young, in his dark blue jeans and tailored white shirt, seemed to rattle my brain. I hated feeling the excitement rush through my body. I felt like some lovesick teenage girl, more like Allison, and I wanted to pound my legs with my closed fists. I was walking quickly but slowed down to catch my breath.

For a few moments, I stood looking down and

then raised my head to look out at the ocean, just as I heard him call my name. Had I imagined it, wished for it so much that I convinced myself I really had heard it? Very slowly, I turned and saw him standing there alone.

"Why did you come down here?" he asked.

"Oh, is this private property? I hadn't realized it," I said.

"You know what I mean, Mayfair."

"I had to get out of my house for a while, and I wanted the sea air. I haven't been spying on you, if that's what you think."

"It did occur to me."

"Yes, I imagine it would. Your ego has enough room for all favorable possibilities."

He nodded, looked back at his apartment building, and stepped closer. "You're right to hate me, and I deserve your wrath and all that happened as a result. I did feel sorry for your stepsister. But she's not any more impressionable than any of them."

"Them?"

"Girls her age. I did consider the possibility that you might have believed I abused her, but I never intended to abuse you."

"What would you call it?"

"A man's weakness, I suppose. And you're right about my ego. I rationalized that I was giving you something special, too. What I told you is still true, Mayfair. You're a beautiful young woman with an amazing mind. You fascinated me, and for a while, I did fool myself into believing it was possible for us to carry on, but as difficult as it might be for you to believe, the mature man in me finally got control. I should have handled it differently. I was a coward."

I looked away. As much as I wanted to, I couldn't hate him.

"Why didn't you turn me in instead of using Allison?"

I didn't answer.

"I'll tell you why," he said, and I turned to him.

"Oh, you will? Tell me."

"Pride. That's going to be your one weakness, Mayfair, your *hubris*. See, I know my classic tragedy, even though I only teach junior-high English. You're constantly told how high up you are. You can't let yourself admit to being human, because that's what having a weakness means, being human."

My eyes felt as if the tears that had been building up were frozen.

"Don't judge every man you'll meet by what happened between us, by what I did and didn't do. Be kind. Be forgiving. You don't want to be with a man who is your equal. You want someone who will need you and whom you'll need, Mayfair. It's not a sin to need someone. I wish you luck," he said. "I really do." He smiled and walked away.

My chest ached. I couldn't swallow. I watched him disappear, and then I turned and walked for another hour before I called a taxi.

I wasn't prepared for the depth of depression I fell into that night. My father called from the freeway to tell me they were staying longer than anticipated and would stop for dinner before returning to Los Angeles. When I didn't even utter a grunt to acknowledge him, he asked if I had heard him.

"I heard you."

"What have you been doing all day, Mayfair?" he asked suspiciously. For a moment, I wondered if he had decided to have me watched or something.

"Nothing out of the ordinary for me," I said, which was cryptic enough.

"All right. Tell Martha what you would like for dinner," he said.

"Okay," I replied to end the call.

I didn't tell our maid anything. I took an apple upstairs with me and, after sitting and thinking for a while, went to sleep early. I didn't even hear them come home. If my father checked on me, I never noticed that, either. I was up before everyone the next morning, however. I had some coffee and buttered toast and went for a walk before sitting at the pool. It was nearly an hour and a half later when my father walked out to see what I was up to.

"How's your head?" he asked.

I laughed.

"What's so funny, Mayfair?"

"That's probably always been the most important part of me in your eyes and everyone else's," I said, which clearly upset him.

"You're acting like a girl half your age, and I don't mean chronological," he replied. "I'm taking Julie and Allison to the movies this afternoon to see the new Nick Razor blockbuster. Would you like to join us?"

Nick Razor was a detective in the future who was nostalgic for the past. The films were filled with special effects and nonstop action, what my father called popcorn movies. When I was a little girl, I did go to those sorts of movies with him and my mother, but I hadn't for some time.

"No, thanks," I said.

"Everyone's trying, Mayfair, but if you don't, this will go nowhere."

"I'm already there," I said.

He nodded, bit down on his lower lip, and turned and walked back to the house, his shoulders slumped. I closed my eyes and nearly fell asleep again. I knew my depression was continuing even more intensely after confronting Alan Taylor the day before, but I felt helpless, really helpless, for the first time in a long time. When I returned to the house, everyone already had left for lunch and the movies. I went up to my room and tried to do some reading, but my mind wouldn't absorb anything. I couldn't even watch television. Nothing held my attention. I went out again, walked again, and remembered that I hadn't eaten anything since my coffee and toast. It was only the realization that drove me to eat anything. I wasn't really hungry.

Afterward, I went up to my room and dozed until I heard my father, Julie, and Allison return. No one bothered me until just before dinner, when my father sent Allison to my room to tell me to come down to eat.

Reluctantly, I did. Everyone else seemed nervous. I was too numb to be nervous. They talked incessantly, it seemed to me, about the movie. I ate mechanically and then announced that I had a headache and was going up to rest.

"Maybe we should take you to a doctor for that," my father said.

"It's not from the injury," I replied.

"She would know," Julie quipped.

I didn't bother to respond.

When I went up this time, I was drawn to my closet to look in the carton that contained some photo albums, birthday cards, and old report cards. I sat on the floor and looked at everything slowly. The pictures of my mother and me, all three of us, brought back some of my warmest memories. I didn't cry, but I pretended I was back there and wished that I could magically turn back time. I wasn't one to fantasize or dwell in my imagination long, unless I was trying to project what something might be like after more technological advances.

When I was the little girl in those pictures, I wondered why I didn't react to toys in a similar way to how other girls my age did. I knew I wasn't much fun for them, and after a while, none really asked for me. I went to their birthday parties, but I guess I never looked like I was having fun. I was smart enough already to know that other girls' mothers considered me quite strange. Some were even worried about their daughters playing with me. I probably said things to them that confused and maybe shocked them, things they told their mothers. I recalled how hard my mother had tried to get me to enjoy myself. She would even say, "Remember, Mayfair, they are just little girls," as if she thought I might be more understanding and gentler with them, something only someone much older would do.

It never occurred to me back then that my mother might be sad or unhappy about me, maybe even disappointed. She probably feared that I wasn't going to be the young daughter she'd dreamed of having, the one she could dress up and slowly guide into a wonderful adolescence filled with new discoveries about myself almost daily, discoveries she remembered having and was so determined that I would enjoy. Mothers relived their own youth through their daughters, and even the short time we had together could have been something more wonderful for her.

How my heart ached now, for so many reasons.

I closed the albums and put everything back into the cartons and then the closet. I prepared for sleep and went to bed wishing I needed to suck my thumb or something. I curled up in the fetal position and hugged my oversize pillow, but nothing helped me sleep. I dozed and woke, dozed and woke, until the morning light slipped around my curtains like fingers of gold searching for a way to touch me.

Everything on me ached. I guessed I had been too flippant about the head injury. My neck was sore. I moaned and just fell asleep again. I never heard Allison come into my room, but I did sense her presence and opened my eyes.

"What?"

"Mom wants to know if you're going to school today. You'll have to hurry."

"Mom? Tell her no. You just go on without me."

"Are you sick?"

"Sick of."

"What's that mean?"

"Forget it, Allison. Tell her I'm taking the day off."

"Daddy had to leave early."

"Lucky him," I said, and turned over.

I thought that was it for the day, but a little more than an hour later, my phone rang. It was my father.

"What?" I said. "Don't worry. I don't need to go to a doctor."

"I'm not taking you to a doctor. I'd like you to get dressed and be ready to go to the school with me in about an hour. We have a meeting with Mr. Martin."

"Mr. Martin? What about?"

I imagined I was to make some sort of confession, but he surprised me.

"Your educational future," he said.

"What, is he a fortune-teller now, too?"

"Mayfair."

"Okay, Daddy," I said. "I'll be ready."

"Good."

I got dressed. Julie was nowhere to be found, which didn't make me unhappy. I wondered if she would be with my father when he came for me, but her car was gone, and she didn't return before he arrived.

I stepped out just as he opened his door, and I ran around to get in.

"What is this really all about, Daddy?" I asked as he backed out of the driveway.

"A solution," he said. "For all of us."

# 19

Mr. Martin handed my father and me copies of the Spindrift School brochure.

"It looks more like an old mansion than a school," I said. "An eclectic Queen Anne. How can it be a school?"

"Everything about it is unorthodox. You'll see as you read," he said.

I glanced at my father to show him my skepticism. Not that I was afraid of going to a school away from home, but a part of me was hoping he would say, "It won't be that long before she's completely away from us. Why rush it?"

"As you can see, the grounds are beautiful," Mr. Martin continued in a seller's tone, as if he were getting a commission.

It occurred to me that maybe he was. Maybe I was being exploited and victimized once again.

"It's fenced and walled in, a very private place with the most sophisticated technological security.

As you will see, it has most anything any really good school or college would. Turn the page. See that modern laboratory, that computer room, and look at that library. There are a thousand volumes, covering law, science, literature, anything you can possibly think of researching, plus the most up-to-date internet access, of course."

"Impressive," my father said.

"This is actually a specially designed school for students like you, Mayfair. It's a school at which you live and work in a totally unorthodox learning environment. The principal is a renowned child psychologist, Dr. Jessie Marlowe. You might have already read some of her studies."

"Yes, I think I have. I have some questions about some of her conclusions."

"I'm sure you have," he said, smiling. "Anyway, they take in only fifteen students."

"Only fifteen?" Daddy asked. "All this for only fifteen?" Now he sounded like the one getting a commission.

"Exactly. Frankly, there are not many students who would meet the criteria, Mr. Cummings, and Spindrift is very selective about choosing from the list of those who do. However," he added, "I already know that Mayfair would be very welcome. I took the liberty of getting them some preliminary information. No sense in wasting your time or theirs, right?"

"Where is Piñon Pine Grove?" I asked.

"It's in the Coachella Valley, not more than two hours from Los Angeles. Not that far from home."

"Maybe it's not far enough away," I muttered, and glanced at my father.

"How long has this school been in existence?" he asked Mr. Martin, ignoring my comment.

"It was started ten years ago as the brainchild of someone who would have benefited greatly from it, Dr. Norman Lazarus, now one of the world's most renowned biochemists."

"Lazarus? Did he rise from the dead?" I asked.

Mr. Martin smiled. "Maybe his ancestor did."

"I think we should be a little more serious about this, Mayfair," my father said. He looked at the brochure and read some more. "You're right, Mr. Martin. These students are very protected, apparently. There is a great deal of security. No one can just walk in on them. I like that."

"Exactly. The philosophy is that their students are very valuable national assets. The graduates of Spindrift have gone on to do wonderful things in all fields. A number of them work for NASA. Many are doing things that are kept top secret."

He turned to me. "The big point here is that you'd be studying and researching with students at your level of learning, students equipped the way you're equipped, Mayfair. I don't think it's much of a secret that your skills and intellect are not being challenged here.

"This recent incident you had with some of the other girls is characteristic of what happens with gifted students everywhere," he continued, talking more to my father. "Other students either resent them or see them as . . ."

"Weird, freaky," I finished for him.

He smiled. "I was just going to say unusual."

"It's not cheap," I said, noting the tuition. "Are all the other unusual students from wealthy families, too?"

"Most are. They do give out one scholarship a year to a candidate who fits the criteria but whose family can't afford to send her or him. One of the former graduates, who wants to remain anonymous, donates the tuition."

"Walled in, high security, guards at the gate—probably makes it quite a curiosity to the locals. Piñon Pine Grove sounds like an exciting little city," I said, reading from the description on the last page of the brochure. "Twenty-five thousand people, a few home building supply companies, other small factories, a mall and movie complex, and a senior citizens gated-home community with four thousand people. Wow. It's overwhelming."

"The students at Spindrift don't have much, if anything, to do with the people in Piñon Pine Grove. There's a sizable entertainment area in the school, with a big-screen movie theater and all the music you or anyone there would want. There's a gym and an indoor pool. As you see, they even have an impressive telescope for astronomy. You probably wouldn't want to leave."

"You sure this really isn't a mental institution?" I asked.

"Hardly, unless you call a place for developing your mind to even higher levels a mental institution," Mr. Martin said.

"Very good. How do you just happen to know so much about it, Mr. Martin?" I asked.

"I have a good friend in the state education department who told me about it."

"After you told him about me?"

"Exactly," he said, and smiled. "No sense trying to put one over on Mayfair," he told my father.

My father nodded and turned to me. "Well, what do you think?"

"Do I have a choice?"

There was no doubt in my mind that Julie was waiting for his call, waiting to hear that I was headed out of the house and especially away from Allison.

"Do you want a choice? Do you want to stay here in this school?"

I looked again at the brochure. "Spindrift," I said. "From where we can look down on everyone else."

"Which is exactly what you've been doing here," my father said.

It stung.

I closed the brochure and looked out the window.

There were graduates of our school who had returned for visits from colleges they attended. They often gravitated to me because they could have a more intelligent conversation than they could have with other juniors and even seniors, not to mention many of their former teachers. We talked about the courses they were taking, the books they were reading, and the demands on their time for study and research. All of them always commented on how much they respected me for being so far ahead that when I went to college, it would seem like kindergarten. But many of them, especially the ones who were college freshmen, voiced some nostalgia.

"I wish I was a carefree high-school student again," they might say. They'd look around and add, "I never thought I would miss this place, but I do. I had some happy times here."

I didn't, but I wanted to very much. I wanted to miss this place someday, too. Would I ever be nostalgic for anything anymore?

It was going to be easy to walk out of this building, out of this school world, but ironically, that didn't make me happy. It made me feel empty. Oh, there were a few teachers I would miss because we had some good discussions, but those talks were too few and far between to amount to much, not enough to give me that sense of nostalgia those returning college students showed.

I had joined no clubs, had been on no teams, and had never been in a school show or the school band. I had no good memories of any social event. Probably, in weeks or even days after I left, I would be forgotten, and if I weren't, I'd be remembered as some sort of freak or monster to which students could compare each other when insulting each other.

"You want to be another Mayfair?" they might say.

Or they might turn my name into a verb. "You're Mayfairing me" or, simply, "You're Mayfairing."

Poor Allison. If she weren't taken out of this school, she might suffer because of that, despite her current status as a little heroine. I hoped Julie wouldn't go back on seriously considering finding her another school even though it might alienate her from some of her precious lunch friends. She could very well think that because I was gone from the school, Allison would be fine.

Maybe she would be, I thought. What did I really know?

"Well, then," Mr. Martin said. "I'll contact Dr. Marlowe today and get things arranged. They don't have semesters like ordinary schools, so it doesn't really make any difference when you enroll her," he told my father. "I'll call you tomorrow, and most probably you can head up there this weekend. It'll be no problem getting the rest of her academic history to them."

"Very good. Mayfair, any more questions for Mr. Martin?"

I looked at him. He wasn't exactly riding me out of here on a rail, but he wasn't wasting any time, either. "Will you miss me when I'm gone?"

He laughed. "You know I will," he said.

We rose to go. He followed us out to the hallway and extended his hand to me.

"I want to wish you the best of luck, Mayfair. I know that people would say luck hasn't anything to do with it in your case, but I don't see the harm in wishing only the best for you."

"Thank you. I wish you the same, Mr. Martin. You have your challenges, too."

He smiled and watched us walk away.

"Is there anything here you might want, anything in a locker or something?" my father asked me.

"There's nothing here I might want," I said.

"This is for the best," he said.

To me, he sounded more like someone who was trying to convince himself.

I didn't have to be present to see Julie's face when my father told her about the arrangements. I could easily imagine her look of joy, her beaming smile of relief. At dinner, she already showed a renewal of energy. She was back at gossip, opinions on some new vacation places, and thoughts about some home renovation work she was convinced they should now do.

I hated it, but even my father looked happier, like a weight had been lifted from his shoulders. He laughed and smiled at many of the things Julie said. *He really does like her*, I thought. I'd study all sorts of insects and animals in my life, analyze human history from the caveman until now, but I might never come to understand men.

Too bad for me.

After dinner, I started to think about what clothing I wanted to take with me and what else I would bring. When I looked at the clothes Julie had bought me on that shopping spree, I thought about how my improved appearance had attracted male interest. Of course I was curious about what the boys at Spindrift would be like. They'd have to be very intelligent, obviously. Maybe there would be someone who was attracted to me, and I'd be attracted to him, and we'd enjoy challenging each other in many different ways. I decided I would take those outfits after all.

That I was actually leaving didn't hit Allison until

she saw my suitcases being taken out. Julie, trying to look like the good, concerned stepmother, had had my father find out what the school expected me to bring in the way of toiletries and the like. She'd then gone out and bought the items and packed them all for me.

I thought she was like a dog on a leash, panting with excitement. Soon she'd be released and could charge forward.

"Let's have something special for dinner the night before," she suggested to my father.

"Yes," I said, "like a last meal on death row."

She never enjoyed my sense of humor, and she certainly wasn't going to enjoy it now.

Nevertheless, my father had live lobsters delivered. It was one of Allison's favorite meals, not mine. Julie would eat only the tails, because it was simply too messy to get into the rest of it. She had gone ahead and ordered a chocolate cake with "Good Luck at Your New School" written in strawberries on the top.

What hypocrisy, I thought. She hated the idea of spending so much money on this new school, but she couldn't come right out and say that now, especially in front of my father. She didn't want anything to prevent me from leaving. Somehow, even though I was leaving before my senior year had technically begun, she was making it seem as if I were going off to college. That was the way she wanted Allison to see it, but to her credit, Allison did not see it that way.

After everything that had happened, Allison appeared to be the one who was most upset and disturbed by my being sent away, even though both her mother and my father tried their best to explain how much better off I would be and how wonderful this opportunity was for me.

Allison came to my bedroom after dinner. I was sifting through my research papers, deciding what might be of any value at Spindrift, when she knocked and entered. She looked like she might actually begin crying.

"What's wrong?"

"This is all my fault," she said. "It is. I shouldn't have broken my promise and told my mother things."

"It's not your fault. This would have happened eventually anyway, Allison."

I saw that this wasn't making her feel any better.

"Look, Allison, when you first showed me how upset you were after hearing Mr. Taylor talk about his engagement, I really believed he might have taken advantage of you, abused you."

She shrugged. I still didn't want to confess to reading her diary, but I thought she deserved to know more, to know enough to judge me more objectively in the years to come, when she was old enough to look back and understand more fully.

"The reason I would have believed it is that he took advantage of me."

She lifted her head and widened her eyes. "Really?"

"Yes, really, but I blame myself more than I blame him now. I was vulnerable. You know what that means?"

She shook her head.

"I was in a state of mental and emotional turmoil

that made me weak and blind, and he pounced like some fox that had the good fortune to have a plump chicken wander into his den. I didn't watch out for myself. I could have prevented it all from happening, no matter how good-looking and sophisticated he thought he was. Anyway, when I saw the opportunity to hurt him back, I took advantage of it. I took advantage of you, used you. So don't feel so sorry for me."

I looked away and added, "You won't understand how I could say this, but I don't blame him now as much as I did. I'm not saying he was right or anything. I'm just . . . more understanding. When you're older, you might understand what I mean."

I turned back to her. "I didn't do right by you. I'm sorry."

"I thought we were really getting to be like sisters," she said.

"We were. As much as I can be anyone's sister. None of this is your fault. Okay?"

She nodded. "Can I give you a hug?" she asked.

As nice a gesture as that would be, she probably couldn't have said anything that would have made me sadder. I nodded, and she came over and hugged me.

"I hope you'll be happy there, Mayfair," she said. "I won't do as well in math, though."

"You'll do fine," I said. "Really, Allison, you're going to be all right now."

She liked that, and so did I.

Afterward, I didn't read. I didn't go on my computer. I didn't watch television or write anything. I just sat looking out the window at the stars and the occasional clouds that seemed to be tiptoeing across them.

I went to bed thinking of my mother again, picturing her face when she tucked me in or sat reading to me. I knew those images were always trying to come back, fighting to get on the screen of my memory, but I kept them from doing so because I knew what they would bring.

They would bring tears, and I always hated tears.

They reminded me that I was once, for a short while, at least, a little girl, and when I was a little girl, my mother died and left me frightened.

I vowed never to be frightened again.

Right now, try as hard as I could, lie to myself as best I could, put on the best face of bravery I could, I couldn't help but admit that I was afraid of tomorrow.

And so, despite my hard attitude, I was trembling inside on Sunday when we set out for Spindrift. As we drove away, Allison stood at the living room's front window. She waved quickly, as if she was afraid her mother might see her. I waved back, and she and the house disappeared behind a turn.

When the sign indicating that we were finally entering the city of Piñon Pine Grove appeared, Julie exclaimed, "Thank God!"

I couldn't help but laugh.

She turned to defend herself. "Well, it was a difficult drive. Despite the way you explained it, who knew it would be like this on the freeway on a Sunday?"

"Most anyone else who lives in the state of California would know," I said dryly.

"You didn't think it would be this bad, did you, Roger?" she asked my father.

He just looked at her and smiled. She glared at everything out the window.

"It is pretty here," my father said. "Sort of rustic, don't you think, Mayfair?"

"Back to nature," I said. "There's your piñon pine," I pointed out as we approached the hill. This route avoided the actual city of Piñon Pine Grove. "It grows well here because it requires little water. The nuts are edible."

Julie glanced at me with her expression of surprise and amazement. *She's going to miss me, miss learning stuff*, I thought.

The GPS took us to the road that led up to Spindrift. For a while, we could see only the very top of the building. As we drew closer, it seemed to rise out of the ground. The area around it was fenced in, just the way it was shown in the brochure. The long driveway led us to an iron gate at least ten feet high. Beside it was a security booth, and when we approached, a tall, stout man in a gray uniform stepped out, a clipboard in his hand. My father pulled to a stop and lowered his window.

"Mr. and Mrs. Cummings and Mayfair," he told the security guard.

The guard's top jacket pocket had a name tag that read "Edwards." He nodded and tried to smile, but he had one of those sun-worn faces that looked leathery, with deep wrinkles, and eyes that suggested that he was much younger than he appeared. "May I see your license, please?"

"He's kidding," I muttered, but my father took it out to show him.

"Welcome," he said after copying down my father's license number. "You can park right up close to the entrance."

He handed my father a blue plastic card with a black strip across the top.

"This is coded. Just insert it in the front door, and she'll unlock for you. Give the card to Dr. Marlowe after you're finished bringing in your luggage and things."

"Thank you," my father said.

Edwards returned to his booth and pressed a button that opened the gate.

"You have to prove who you are? Gates, special key cards. This isn't what I call protected. It's what I call locked away," I muttered.

"Safety's important in today's world," my father said. "Like Mr. Martin told us, there's a lot of valuable property here, and I don't mean just the equipment, books, and furniture."

He drove us through and up to the building.

"What an interesting house," Julie said. "I'm sure you can tell us about it."

"It's a Queen Anne, an architectural style popular in the 1880s and '90s. Victorian. They're not usually this big. It looks like a lot's been added to it over the years, maybe recently, but it has the typical bay windows, balconies, stained glass, that turret, and the porch."

"Maybe you should become a detective," Julie

said, smiling. She was so happy now she could burst, and she didn't mind lavishing compliments on me.

"Any good student is a detective," I said.

My father turned off the engine. He glanced at me and got out. I followed him around to the trunk to get some of my luggage. Julie even hurried to take a bag. She was that enthusiastic about getting me settled in and gone.

Perhaps I shouldn't hate her so much after all, I thought. Maybe she and my father needed their space. She suddenly seemed more desperate and pathetic to me. I looked at both of them in a new way as I headed with them to my new home, my new world. My father had lost the love of his life and did struggle to keep us both afloat. Julie, for whatever reason, had a miserable start in her life, too.

*Leave them be*, I thought. *Get on with your own life*. Whatever that was.

My father inserted the key card in the front door, and we heard a click. He turned the handle and opened the door. The outside of Spindrift looked like an authentic old Victorian house, but inside we found an entrance lobby with very modern decor, beautifully laid cocoa-shaded tile floors, rich wood walls, and leather chairs and sofas.

A door was opened toward the rear, and an elegant-looking woman, with graying dark brown hair styled neatly around her face with well-trimmed bangs, entered the lobby. She looked about fifty, I thought, had a very nice figure, and, surprisingly, was dressed in a pair of jeans, a dark blue blouse, and a pair of sandals.

"Mr. and Mrs. Cummings," she said. "I'm Dr. Marlowe. Welcome."

"Thank you," my father said, taking her hand. "My wife, Julie, and my daughter, Mayfair."

Dr. Marlowe nodded at Julie and then turned quickly to me. She had intelligent blue-green eyes, and although she didn't wear any makeup, not even lipstick, she was attractive. I sensed a quiet contentment about her, none of the tension, defensiveness, or caution that was common in the school administrators I knew.

"Hello, Mayfair. I'm sure you'll have a million questions, so let's get you settled in. While you're unpacking your things, I'll meet with your father and mother and get our paperwork completed. I'll give your parents a tour of the school, too."

I looked at Julie. She could finally be known as my mother if she wanted.

"Do you need help with Mayfair's things, Mr. Cummings?"

"No, I think we can manage."

"We're going up a flight," she warned. "I can call for help. I have two maintenance personnel."

"I think we can do it," he said, looking at Julie. She nodded.

"Okay. Follow me, then."

"Oh, here's that coded card," he told her.

"Yes. We record all comings and goings."

"No one escapes?" I said.

"No one wants to," she countered with a smile. "So, trip from Los Angeles okay?"

"Longer than I expected," Julie said.

Dr. Marlowe smiled at her. "Well, the good thing about being here is that once you're here, there isn't much traffic with which to contend."

The stairway with its mahogany banister had obviously been rebuilt. It felt solid beneath us.

At the top, we paused.

"I have you in that section that faces the lake behind us," Dr. Marlowe explained to me. "The rooms are small, actually not much different from the way they were when the house was first built. There are two other girls in your section. They both arrived this year, too." She turned to my father. "We had three openings occur."

"Why?" Julie asked. "It's not graduation time, is it?"

"Our students have a different school year," Dr. Marlowe said, looking at me with a twinkle in her eyes. "It's built-in."

"Built into what?" Julie asked.

"Whoever they are," Dr. Marlowe said, smiling.

"What?"

I laughed. Maybe I would like it here, I thought.

My room was spartan. It had a double bed with a small side table, a dresser, a desk, a mirror on the closet door, and a closet half the size of one of our hall closets at home. I was glad I didn't bring all that much.

Julie, despite trying desperately not to say anything negative that might turn me around, couldn't contain herself. "Oh, how small."

"Our students don't spend very much time in their rooms," Dr. Marlowe said. She looked at me.

"It's more than enough," I said, and she smiled.

My father put my suitcases down. "You want any help unpacking?"

"No. Why don't you do the paperwork and take your tour? I'll be fine," I told him.

We heard someone laugh in the hallway. Dr. Marlowe looked out and said, "Oh, great, Corliss and Donna, your neighbors. Hi, girls. Mayfair Cummings has arrived."

The two came to my doorway.

"This is Corliss Simon," Dr. Marlowe said, putting her hand on the shoulder of an African American girl with a slim figure. Her hair was cut rather short. She had almond-shaped ebony eyes and an arrogant tightness in her mouth.

"And this is Donna Ramanez," Dr. Marlowe said as she turned to the light-brown-haired shorter girl beside her.

They both wore gray sweatshirts and jeans. Neither spoke. They stood in the doorway, looking in at us. We looked at each other like gunslingers sizing up the competition.

"Why don't we go to my office and let them get to know each other?" Dr. Marlowe told my father and Julie.

"Very good," he said, and they followed her out.

I turned to my suitcases.

"Need any help?" Corliss asked.

"Offering?"

"She wouldn't have asked otherwise, genius," Donna said.

I turned back to them and smiled. "What are you wearing, the school uniform?"

They looked at each other as if they had just realized they were wearing the same thing. Then they both laughed.

"Where are you from?" I asked Corliss.

"Nigeria. Originally," she added. "West LA. You?"

"Garden of Eden originally. Beverly Hills."

She laughed. I looked at Donna.

"My mother is from Ireland, and my father is from Costa Rica, but I was born in Arizona."

"What are the others here like?" I asked.

"You have a good imagination?" Corliss asked.

"Yes, why?"

"After you meet them, you'll need it," Donna said.

"Great," I said, and began to unpack.

They started to help. We worked quietly. Neither of them commented on anything I had brought. I watched them out of the corner of my eye and then stopped and turned to them.

They paused, too.

"What?" Donna asked.

"Neither of you especially wanted to be here, either?"

"I won the scholarship," Corliss said, "but it wasn't what I set out to do. It's supposed to save my life."

"My choice was either to come here or go to Alcatraz," Donna said.

"Alcatraz was closed a long time ago," I said.

"So I had no choice," she replied.

I laughed and then looked at them more intently.
"What?" Corliss asked.

"I was just thinking. You're the welcoming committee. This didn't all just happen."

They smiled.

"Nothing here just happens," Donna said. "If you belong, you'll know that, and you'll like it."

I nodded.

It didn't take long to size me up.

Maybe, just maybe, I had found a new home.

# Epilogue

I stood outside with my father and Julie after they had returned from their tour of Spindrift and it was time for them to leave.

Since my mother's death, my father and I really had only been separated a few times, including for a little more than a week during his honeymoon with Julie. Most of the other times, his business trips took two or maybe three days.

I could see that this fact was occurring to him, too, as he stood looking out at the beautiful grounds and the fence that surrounded Spindrift.

"This is quite an educational institution," he said, still not looking at me. "We met all of the teachers you'll have, and they are all very impressive. I think you'll finally feel challenged. One thing's for sure," he added, turning to me and smiling, "you won't be bored."

"I saw a couple of very good-looking boys, too," Julie added.

"Don't worry. It's all right," I said.

"What's all right?" Julie asked.

"Your leaving me here. It's all right. Don't worry about it. You don't have to say anything more."

"Well, I didn't mean . . . I mean . . ."

"You can get into the car, Julie," my father said, surprisingly firmly. "I'll just take a few minutes with Mayfair, and we'll be off."

"Okay. Good luck, Mayfair," she said, and went to the car. She knew that if she hugged me or kissed me good-bye, it would feel like she had hugged or kissed a tree.

"Let's take a little walk," my father said.

We stepped down and went to the right, where there was a small pond. We stood next to it, looking into the water and at the colorful rocks.

"I know you need this place or something like it," he began, "but I hope you don't believe I failed you, Mayfair, even though I believe that."

"We failed each other, Daddy. I'm not as smart as you think, and anyway, Julie's right. Brains aren't everything. I don't want to be just a brilliant student. I want to be a brilliant person, too. I have a ways to go. Maybe I'll find my way here."

"I bet you will," he said, smiling. He put his arm around me. "I love you, May. I'll never stop loving you."

"I know, Daddy."

"I have something more to leave with you," he said, taking my hand.

We walked back to the car, and he opened the trunk to give me a package tied with a cord.

"I'm not good at making it look fancy."

I started to open it, and he stopped me.

"No," he said. "Open it when we leave." He kissed me again and opened his car door. "I'll call, or you call us whenever you need anything or just want to talk, okay?"

"Okay, Daddy."

"See you soon," he said. "Show them what a real genius can do, will you?"

"I will."

He smiled his winning smile and got into the car. I stood and watched them drive down to the gate. It opened, they drove out, and the gate closed.

I was about to feel very bad, but then I began to open the package.

I didn't have to open it all the way to know what it was.

He had brought me something I had forgotten, my special teddy bear, the first gift he and my mother had ever given me.